Cover design created by Ron Bell of AdVision Design Group
(www.advisiondesigngroup.com)

ISBN 978-0-9766083-2-5

Printed in the United States of America

White Feather Press

Reaffirming Faith in God, Family, and Country!

We Hold These Truths

Skip Coryell

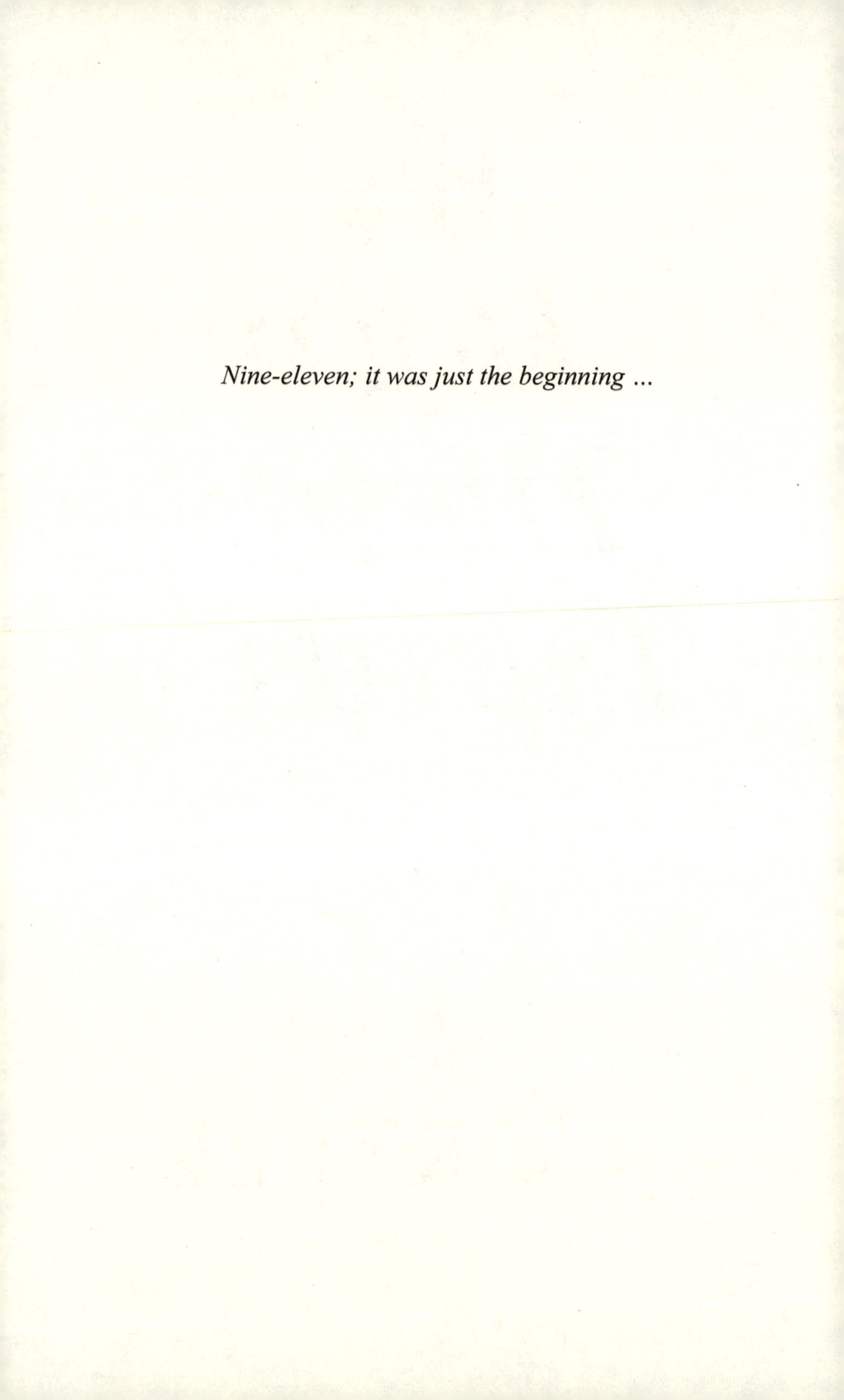

Nine-eleven; it was just the beginning ...

Chapter 1

"I think we ought to nuke 'em, that's what I think!"

Pastor Josh McCullen interrupted him with a half-hearted rebuke. He wanted to nuke them too, but his Christian faith commanded restraint.

"Oh just calm down now Luke! We don't even know all the facts yet. Let's not rush to judgment!"

A small group of four men were huddled at a corner table in the Mudhen Grille, staring up at the television screen, watching the news reporter as he stood in front of the twin towers of the World Trade Center in New York City. Black smoke was billowing from both buildings as firemen rushed into the blaze and police officers tried to calm the people coming out.

Jack Sanders, the local garage mechanic silenced them with a tense sneer.

"Just shut up, both of you! I'm trying to hear!"

A fourth man, Henry Bolthouse, turned up the volume and they all sat grim-faced, as they listened to the sounds of mayhem and destruction.

"All we know Brian, is that at approximately 8:50AM this morning, the first of the two airliners crashed into the north tower of the World Trade Center, leaving it smoking and engulfing the top part of it in flames. We assume that all the passengers aboard were killed instantly. Then, at approximately 9 AM, the second airliner crashed into the south tower near the 80th floor. Both towers are blazing and smoking now, . . . "

The announcer hesitated, then yelled out.

"Oh my God! Did you see that! A man just jumped through a window, Brian! I saw a man jump out and land onto a car from about 50 floors up! Oh my God! Look, there's more jumping!"

The camera moved off the announcer and onto the smoking building. Tiny specks, like human bugs were clinging tenaciously to the outer wall of the building, then, one by one, they separated themselves from the burning tower and plummeted through the air to their deaths. The cameraman tried to zoom in but couldn't do it. Brian Becker then interrupted him.

"Neil, you need to get out of there. Fall back to a safer position and report from further out."

There was no answer.

"Neil, are you there?"

The camera moved back down to view Neil Champion, veteran newscaster, bent at the waist, and hugging his arms around his torso. There were tears streaming down his face and falling to the dirty pavement.

"Neil, can you talk to us?"

Neil took a deep breath, and then stood up, wiped his eyes and began to talk again.

"Everything seems out of control here and the firefighters are concentrating on getting as many people out of the buildings as they can." He hesitated. "I'm sorry. I just never seen anyone die before. I . . . I, just don't . . . don't know what to say."

Brian Becker interrupted him, his voice sympathetic and soft.

"It's okay Neil, just tell us all what you see."

The announcer turned around and pointed to the buildings and the camera zoomed in on the top half of both towers.

"As you can see, Brian, the black smoke is getting thicker, and. . . Oh my God!"

The four men huddled at the table jumped to their feet, aghast at the sight before them.

"Oh my God! Oh my God! Brian one of the towers is coming down! Oh my God!"

"Neil, get out of there!"

A wall of dust and smoke and debris came pushing toward the camera like an unstoppable tidal wave.

"They're all dead! All those people are dead! The tower just collapsed on top of itself and a cloud of dust and smoke is coming towards us. All those people are dead!"

The men in the Mudhen Grille watched as the smoke and dust and debris spread out across the city and eventually engulfed the news reporter in blackness. The camera jumped back and forth and the picture suddenly went black.

Pastor McCullen, blurted out in shock.

"Oh my God! They just toppled the Twin Towers! Oh God help us! All those people are dead!"

He dropped to his knees and began to pray.

Luke, the owner of the Mudhen Grille jumped up and ran over to the phone.

"My daughter works near one of those buildings! I have to make sure she's safe!"

Henry fell silent as they watched the empty screen and listened from a distance as Luke tried in vain to call his daughter in New York City.

A few seconds later a different newscaster came on the screen, filling the void.

"Ladies and gentlemen, this is Brian Becker of TV 8 news in New York City. It would appear that we have lost contact with Neil Champion who was covering the attack on the twin towers. We have no word yet as to his condition, but we can only hope and pray that he is okay and especially that most of the people inside the building were able to get out in time."

The announcer hesitated, waiting for information coming in through his earphone.

"Our sources now tell us that both World Trade Center buildings at this time of day contain approximately 10,000 people either working or visiting to do business. But of course, we have no way of knowing how many have just been killed or injured. I don't see how anyone could have survived the collapse. I just don't see it. Tears welled up in Brian Becker's eyes and the camera zoomed in on him.

"How could anyone do such a heinous thing to so many innocent people? I don't understand. I just don't understand!"

He listened to his earpiece again and hesitated once more, then continued in a more animated voice.

"Ladies and gentlemen, we take you now to Arlington, Virginia, for a live eyewitness report, where a third airliner has crashed into the Pentagon."

Both men at the table walked around their chairs and stood transfixed in front of the television screen, their mouths dropped open gaping dumbly like big, black holes.

"I don't believe it Henry! I just don't believe it!"

Henry, a large-bodied farmer in bib overalls, about 70 years old, closed his mouth and stood resolutely in place.

"It don't surprise me none Jack. It's been a comin' for a long time."

"What do you mean?"

"You know darn well what I mean. We let ourselves get weak and it's happened again. Pearl Harbor all over again. Why don't people ever learn?"

Jack looked up at the Pentagon's broken rim, the symbol of our nation's might, burning in flames.

"My God! What's gonna happen now?"

Luke hung up the phone and walked back over.

"Can't get my daughter."

He bowed his head solemnly, the look of hope, slowly fading from his face, gradually being replaced with anger and rage. When he looked up again, his lips pursed tightly together and then he spoke with a resolute sneer.

"I'll tell you what we do - only one thing to do. We find 'em, and we nuke 'em! We're obliged to."

Henry and Jack nodded their heads in unison.

"Yep. I guess we have to. We're obliged."

Josh McCullen stopped praying long enough to look up at the smoke and the flames. He wanted to agree with them, but, instead, he forced his head back down and continued to pray quietly into his open hands.

"Dear Father in heaven – What has been done?"

§ § §

Angela had just sat down at her desk to begin a new day when she felt the first airliner slam into the World Trade Center. The sound of the explosion was deafening and the force of the blast knocked her to the carpet, altering her life forever.

Immediately, terror filled her heart, a physical, spirit-wrenching terror that sucked the courage from her bones and left her muscles weak and unable to function. People were screaming outside her office. She opened her mouth too, but no sound came out. Then, along with the sound of the explosion, she heard the roar of a locomotive, like she was lying on the tracks as a train ran over her. Dirty, orange flames rushed up passed her window outside and continued on up several stories. She watched in awe at the heat and power as the flames frosted and charred the window of her once-plush office view. Angela buried her face into the carpet and felt the titanic vibration and shaking of the floor beneath her.

She wasn't sure how long she lay there, probably only seconds, but it felt like hours, and then the acrid smell of smoke passed into her lungs. It was like a million smells all fused into one: plastic, rubber, metal, carpet, wood and paper, human flesh, all burning, and all reaching deep down inside her body and violating her in ways that should not be. In desperation she wanted to cry out to God, but she couldn't, because she had never believed in God, so she choked the words back and swallowed them with the soot and the smoke.

And then she realized that if she was going to survive, she had to get out of the building. She had to move. Angela began to crawl toward the office door, but bumped into something she couldn't see. The rising smoke had blotted out the sun and left it dark and shadowed inside the office. Then she smelled a new odor, and reached out to move the obstruction. It was Marge, her secretary of 3 years. In the dim light, she saw the thing she smelled; it was a mass of blood, flowing from a gash in Marge's throat, and soaking, wet and sticky into the carpet. A large shard of glass was still protruding from Marge's throat, and the smile-shaped gash seemed to be quietly laughing at the shocked look on Angela's face.

Angela screamed, but the sound of licking flames and her pounding heart was all she heard. And then, the carpet beneath her quickly warmed. She grabbed onto the shag and held on for dear life, but the heat from below turned up as the carpet melted between the squeezing flesh and bones of her fingers.

It seemed odd to her, thinking the last thoughts of her life, feeling the last feelings, smelling the last smells, and, all the while, knowing that soon she would be dead, would cease to exist, and be snuffed out for all of eternity with the stark realization that she had wasted her life.

So Angela took one last deep breath, held it as long as she could, and then passed out of conscious being.

§ § §

As the second of the twin towers fell, a chorus of Arabic cheers rose up from the four men huddled close to the television set. Another man sat off to the side, not cheering, not smiling, just sitting and watching the smoke and debris as it billowed upward against the New York City skyline on the little 13-inch television set.

His comrades were on their feet now, dancing arm in arm in a circle, using every inch of the small living room inside his rundown, 3-room apartment. The lady who lived down below, thumped her ceiling with a broom handle, yelling in English for them to knock it off. He hated that woman. Someday he would enjoy her death. Someday he would kill them all - all the infidels, all the arrogant Americans – and great would be his reward.

Momin had mixed feelings about the success of the twin towers; it had been a great battle, a mighty victory for Islam, but it was still too small. America was too big to destroy a few thousand at a time. He knew that, but others didn't share his view. They wanted to take the United States one piece at a time. They were just small thinkers, and Momin tolerated them only because he wasn't done using them yet. He had bigger plans, plans that would make the twin towers seem like tiny ant hills under the boot of Mohammed. His brother warriors had slain their thousands, but Momin would slay his ten thousands, and hopefully even more. He just needed a little more time, and a little more training.

Yes, the infidels would die, and he would enter into his reward in the afterlife. He would be the great hero of Islam, and Mohammed himself would greet him.

Momin left the others and went into the bedroom and closed the door. The woman was still naked on the bed where he had left her 4 hours ago. She still whimpered, but could make very little noise with the gag in her mouth and her arms and legs tied to the bed posts.

In the corner, his prayer mat was all rolled up and leaning against the wall. Beside it, was a small lampstand with a bowl of water resting on top. He ignored the woman and went to it now. Momin placed his hands in the water and left them there for a moment, then he washed his hands, head and feet using the washcloth inside the bowl, before drying them on a clean towel beside the bed. Momin unrolled the prayer mat and then kneeled down on top of it, being careful to face east. He always liked to pray on thick carpet; it was much softer on his knees. Momin prayed mechanically for several minutes, like a robot, like someone reciting a poem he'd learned as a child. After he finished, he kissed the ground and rolled up his mat, placing it back in the corner.

He turned back to the woman on the bed now, and a transformation seemed to move over him, like mud rolling slowly downhill. Women were so weak and undeserving. He knew that, but he would allow her to pleasure him, and, in so doing, she too might gain access to paradise. Momin smiled as he let his pants fall to the musty carpet floor. Now, to celebrate their victory, he would give her something to cry about.

§ § §

Angela didn't feel the large, powerful arms reach down to embrace her. She didn't feel herself being lifted from the burning carpet and pulled close to his bosom like a small child in need of comfort. She was oblivious to it all as the man stepped over the burning bodies of those already dead. He walked with all the surefootedness of a mountain goat and all the grace and quickness of a lion.

The stairway was still intact, but engulfed in smoke and flames. It too, was littered with the bodies of the dead and dying, but with a singleness of stride and purpose, he stepped over and around them, making his way down many flights of stairs. Eventually, the smoke and flames cleared and he lay her down on the landing. But her body did not move. Urgent voices from far below reached up the stairwell, coming closer, and soon the sound of hurried footsteps was audible.

The tall man, shining bright, in the dimness of the emergency lighting, knelt down beside the childlike form. He turned her face to his and smiled. Then, with the gentle power of all the ages, he blew onto her face and she began to stir.

"Take care my little one."

He nodded in satisfaction, and then stood back up to his full height.

And when the firemen arrived, he was gone.

Chapter 2

Hank and his four kids sat quietly in the third pew back. They hadn't gone to church since they'd moved to Freidham Ridge over a year ago. But after nine-eleven, everyone seemed to have a renewed interest in God and all things greater than themselves. So they came now from all over the county, over a hundred of them, more than Freidham Ridge Community Church had ever seen.

"I see a lot of new faces here today. And that makes me happy."

Pastor McCullen paused before going on, as if searching for the right words.

"However, I know why you're all here, and it grieves me to have to talk about the death of over 3,000 of our fellow Americans."

Hank put his arm around the shoulder of his oldest daughter, Susan, and gave it a little squeeze. She smiled bravely up at him. Phillip looked over and Hank nodded his head in reassurance to his oldest son. Hank hadn't been to church in years, but he had always believed in God and prayed. Sometimes he even read his Bible. Then after nine-eleven, he had felt an unrestrainable urge and need to get closer to God, as if closeness to God would somehow ward off the evil, would protect him and his family. But, most of all, he just wanted to feel God's closeness again, to know that someone greater than himself was in charge, the way he had felt as a child.

Deep down, he knew that people weren't qualified to run the world, so it reassured him to know that God was the boss. He trusted God, the same way he had trusted his own father. It seemed odd to him, but suddenly at 42 years of age, he needed his father's hugs more than at any other time in his life. He turned his attention back to the pastor. His father would never hug him again, at least not in this world.

"I don't feel capable or worthy to speak on the subject, but I know that I must, and that it is what God would have me do today. So I've been struggling to figure out what to say."

He threw up his hands in a useless gesture, looked down, and then quickly back up again.

"What can I possibly say to ease your pain? Can I reassure you that our fallen countrymen are with God and that they are better off? No. I don't even know if that's true. Or should I quote you scripture like Romans 8:28, 'For we know that all things work together for good to them who love God, to them who are the called according to His purpose.' No. That would seem trite in a time like this."

He bowed his head as he spoke. Hank listened intently, as did his children and everyone else in the sanctuary.

"I don't have the answers you're looking for. I can't just kiss the hurt and make you feel all better. I can't make the pain go away! I wish I could, but I just can't! That would be like putting a band-aid on a sucking chest wound."

Pastor McCullen looked up again and seemed to meet the gaze of every person in the room simultaneously. His voice was strained and filled with tension.

"All of life is filled with suffering. There's no denying it or getting around it. But the suffering is just one side of the coin. There is also joy and happiness. But that fact is of little consequence today. We are all so steeped in the moment, our moment of pain and sorrow and of suffering, that we feel like we want to die, like we just can't go on anymore. This is our nation's dark night of the soul."

Several people moved uncomfortably in their pews.

"But we must go on. We must! It's what God wants us to do. It's what he demands of us, what He has always demanded of his servants since the creation of time. And He just wants us to trust His judgment, have faith that a new day will dawn, and He never ever, ever, wants us to give up the fight. Because my friends, it is a battle of the spirit. It's black and white. It's good and evil - right and wrong - us against them. But this one event is just a small part of all that is pure terror and unholy evil. There's no other explanation for it. We are at war my people, at war with Satan and all his fallen ones, and none of us will rest until Jesus Christ has returned and defeated him in that one, final and decisive battle."

Hank looked around and could tell no one was being comforted by the Pastor's words. He was still withholding judgment, for now.

"As the good book says, 'For we wrestle not against flesh and blood, but against principalities, against powers, against the rulers of the darkness of this world, against spiritual wickedness in high places.' So, with that in mind, let us examine what exactly happened on nine-eleven."

He paused, placed his hands on the oak face of the pulpit as if gathering strength to continue.

"I'll tell you what is was. It was an incarnation of evil and hatred and malice the likes of which this present generation has never seen. It was Hitler and Stalin and Genghis Khan all rolled into one. And it's not over yet. I believe it's just the beginning. I believe it's been going on for centuries and is just now intensifying. I believe that this present battle we fight is simply a delaying action, one that we must fight until Jesus returns to us on that glorious day of his reappearance. On that day, that pre-appointed day, he'll kick Satan's mangy rear end clear on down into the bowels of hell!"

Hank cocked his head to one side and furrowed his brow. Did the pastor just say "Kick Satan's rear end?" He looked around, but no one else seemed to notice the oddity.

"But until then, He has given us dominion, and with dominion comes the responsibility of defending ourselves. When God created the animals, He also instilled in them the instinct of self-preservation. And they defend themselves by either fight or flight. And when He created mankind, He also gave us the ability and the obligation to defend our lives and our families from all harm, whether evil or benign."

Hank looked over and saw Lance Stuart two rows ahead of him. He was the only famous person that Hank had ever seen in Freidham Ridge.

"So for now, we'll continue to grieve, and weep, and mourn for our dead. But, when that is done, we will defend ourselves. And like the President said, they can run, but they cannot hide. We will hunt them down and bring them to justice. In the name of good; in the name of decency; in the name of God our Holy Father, we will hunt them down, and we will defend ourselves, our families, and our country."

A chorus of amens reverberated around the big room, and Hank found himself nodding his head in agreement without even realizing it. He was surprised to hear people begin to clap, a few at first, then more and more, until, finally, the entire church was standing and applauding.

Pastor McCullen waited in silence for several moments, then motioned for all to sit back down. He hesitated before continuing.

"But that's just part of the story: the easy part. The difficult part is this. Jesus loves those terrorists. He loved them when they slit the throats of unarmed passengers, and He even loved them when they flew those planes into balls of fire causing thousands of His children to die in flames and blood and agony. And He continues to love them still as they roast in eternal hell and damnation."

Hank looked around the room again, trying to gauge the reaction of others. It was a reporter's habit that he'd developed over the years, and couldn't suppress no matter how hard he tried. The people had a myriad of perplexed looks which were not readily understandable.

"The trick is this my friends. We must kill and love at the same time. We must hunt them down, kill them if they resist, but love them even as they lay dying. Be angry. Be indignant. Hate the sin, but love the sinner. We must pray for our enemies as well as our friends and the ones we love. Because if we pray for them, they may repent, seek God's face and turn from their wicked ways. And, if they repent, then we no longer have to kill them. And that's the awesome goal my friends. We must love them and survive. Kill them and survive. Pray for them and survive. It seems an awful, irreconcilable paradox – and it is. But so much of what Jesus taught was a paradox. The first will be last, the last will be first. If you want to live you must first die to sin. If you want to be great, then you must first be the servant of all. And the paradoxes go on and on and on."

Pastor McCullen placed his hands back on the pulpit and leaned on them hard, causing his knuckles to turn white.

"But all of that is for tomorrow. For today we rest. Today we pray. Today we mourn. Today we cry. And then – we defend – with conviction, with a holy, mighty, righteous conviction!"

He bowed his head and the rest of the room followed.

"Dear Father, deliver us from evil. Deliver us from hatred. Heal our wounds, heal our souls. Give us inner peace in a world of dead and dying. Help us to love, even as they lay dying. Amen."

Chapter 3

Angela Benning knelt alone at the altar inside the hospital chapel. She could no longer say she was an atheist, because it was impossible to think and feel so profoundly about someone who didn't exist. She had come here because she wanted to be alone with God, she wanted to yell at Him, scream at Him, love Him and thank Him all in the same breath. But if she could make all the ambivalence and confusion go away, she would. She would shake her fist at the sky and curse God once more into nonexistence, thereby changing everything back to a simpler time when God no longer complicated her life. But she couldn't do that. God had saved her life, therefore, He must exist. It was logical, and she prided herself in her rational thought and intellect. She would have to adapt to a world with a living God, and that realization brought a sudden and irrefutable accountability to the world and terrified her to the core of her being.

The last thing she could remember was lying with her face in the carpet, feeling the heat and smelling the acrid smoke, clawing its way up into her nostrils. And then, nothing, until she'd woken up inside the ambulance with an oxygen mask over her face. But even after a week of recuperation in the hospital it was still all so confusing to her, and the difficult questions continued to nag at her brain. What had really happened? Why was she alive when so many other good people were dead? Why had

God saved her? Why?

She pressed her forehead against the padded altar and bit her lower lip in frustration. Oddly enough, she felt guilty about being alive, felt as if she should have died with the others. Especially after she'd seen the reports on television of men and women throwing themselves off the building and plummeting to their deaths. The sheer numbers were staggering. Over 3,000 people had died - some of them co-workers, some of them friends, some of them her own employees - people she was responsible for, people she saw and talked to every single day for the past 3 years, or, at least "had" talked to, because she would never see them again, never talk to them again. They were all dead and gone, but she was still here, still alive, sucking up air and pumping red blood – still alive, still here, not dead, so not dead, so very not dead. And the guilt, it ate away at her like acid on rock.

A lone, salty tear trickled down her cheek and then broke free; it hit the leather padding with a crash heard only by her heart, and splashed out and down into a host of tiny droplets – 3,000 tiny, screaming, drops that fell to the earth in one final, deafening voice.

Angela was so engrossed in her own personal agony, that she hadn't heard the man in the wheelchair roll quietly up to the altar and stop beside her. He watched her a moment before speaking, wondering if he should say something or just wheel himself back out and give her the privacy she needed. But something, something unseen and incapable of understanding, beckoned him to stay and to speak.

"Hello little lady. Why so glum?"

His voice was old and frail, ancient in fact, a voice so old and experienced that it seemed to have texture and a physical feel. Angela was startled and jerked her head up quickly to see the white-haired old man in a wheelchair offering her a tissue.

She met his gaze for a moment, but couldn't hold it. His bright, blue eyes seemed much too young for their sockets and the wrinkled, dry skin surrounding them. They were smiling, softly smiling, compassionately and intelligently smiling at her, so she turned away and grasped the tissue without looking. The old man spoke softly at first, slowly, then accelerated as if the kinetic energy of his voice was feeding upon itself.

"Whatever is wrong, then I'm sorry and I wish I could change it for you. I wish I could kiss your forehead and make it all better. But . . ." He threw up his frail old hands in an impotent gesture. "I can't. Not God. Just some old man who wants to help but can't." He pointed up at the ceiling. "He's God – I'm not."

Angela turned back to him. The wetness on her cheek was still there, and she made no effort to remove it. She moved back a little when the old man's left hand reached over and touched her right cheek. She expected his finger to be rough and cold to the touch, but it was not. It was warm and soft. He brushed his finger across her young skin and smiled.

"It's going to be okay, child. You're going to make it. God does everything for a reason, leaves nothing to chance, does it all, plans it all, all with purpose, all with meaning, all with love, all with care, all with . . . " The old man hesitated a moment and his smile broadened. "And if there's one thing I've learned in my 93 years on this little clump of dirt, God does it with wonderful style and timing. In His way and in His time."

Angela wasn't sure why she found the old man's words so soothing. Perhaps it was his disarming appearance, his kindness, his gentleness, or maybe it was just that she couldn't remember a man ever speaking to her like this.

The old man's voice reminded her of Aunt Millie, the woman who had raised her after her parents had died when she was only 1 year old. To this day she suffered no remembrance either of her father or her mother. Maybe it was just that this man felt like the father she would have wished for. She wanted a father so much. A father to hold her, to speak softly and gently to her, a man who would encourage her and feel proud of her for who she really was.

For many years she had tried to find all those qualities in a potential husband, but had finally admitted that men like that just didn't exist. As an added obstacle, all the quality men seemed afraid of her. They found women managers to be too strong and intimidating, and no one of quality had ever wanted to date her. Secretly, she found herself wishing that this old man was her age. When she finally spoke, her voice shook, lacking confidence and conviction.

"I've never believed in God. Never in my whole life."

The old man smiled again and nodded his head knowingly.

"Then why are you here? Who are you talking to?"

Angela was troubled by the question. It required too much thought and surety that she was just not able to provide at the moment. She shrugged her shoulders and decided to tell him the truth. He was a good man. He deserved it.

"I have no idea what I'm doing. I feel like I'm just kind of hanging on right now. I feel like a kid out of control and incredibly inept."

The man nodded again.

"Yes, you feel like there's no holes in your bowling ball. It feels big and clumsy and awkward and you can't get a good grip on it. You can't control it."

He hesitated as if deciding what to say next. Then he looked Angela straight in the eyes, probing, searching, laying her soul bare and naked. She squirmed uncomfortably on her knees.

"God doesn't come with handles, little one. He doesn't want to be controlled and thrown down the alley every time for a perfect strike. Life's not like that and neither is God. You will never totally understand God, and He will never spoon feed you with all the answers about life. Some things you just have to figure out for yourself, others, He will show you in due time. In His way and in His time."

This answer was unexpected, and a surge of anger flared up inside Angela's heart.

"Then why did He save me? There were 3,000 of us and he saved only me? Why! I want to know why!"

The old man's face turned sympathetic, and Angela got the impression he'd answered questions like this many times before in his long life.

"I don't know Angela. I don't have that answer. Only God does."

His voice seemed to take on a more relaxed tone.

"But this one thing I do know. God is your father. And if you want to understand God, then you first must understand fatherhood. That is why it's so difficult for some people to comprehend. It's outside their realm of experience. Children without fathers have little concept of God, and children with bad fathers have a bad concept of God. So, many children confuse God, their heavenly father, with their earthly father. While that is understandable, it is also very sad and unfortunate. Angela, you will never understand God, until you understand firsthand, what it is to know a kind, loving, strong, father."

Angela looked down at the floor in shame.

"Then if fatherhood is the answer to knowing God, then I am doomed before I start."

She buried her face in her hands and pressed them harder against the leather padding of the altar.

"I have no father. I know no father. I am an orphan."

She cried openly, without reservation, and the old man reached over and placed his hand reassuringly on her shoulder.

"God knows that, and He will provide you with what you need. He is your heavenly Father – you are his child – therefore, you are no orphan. God is the provider, He has already anticipated your need and made provisions. You will be given an opportunity to understand fatherhood. And then, your relationship with Him can be restored. In the meantime, go on faith. Remember my words. For the time being, give God the benefit of your doubt. When you lack requisite experience, then only faith can carry you through. Have faith. Believe. Just believe!"

Angela turned her head away and rested the right side of her tear-stained cheek on the wet leather. She cried a moment, allowing herself this one episode of weakness.

"I don't know if I can. I have never believed in anything beyond myself. Believe? I don't know if I can do it. Faith has never been my strong point."

A sudden realization swept over her, and she felt a wave of adrenaline in the pit of her stomach.

"How did you know my name?"

Then she felt that something had changed, and she looked up suddenly as if surprised. The old man and his wheelchair were gone. But she heard his lingering answer deep inside her head, not an audible voice, but just a whispering echo inside her heart.

"A father knows his children, and he knows them all by name."

With a desperate cry, she rose to her feet and ran out into the hall. But it was too late. The man was gone, nowhere to be found.

Chapter 4

"Today, the United States Army dispatched 1,000 soldiers to the former Soviet Republic of Uzbekistan. Uzbekistan is on the border of Afghanistan, and many officials speculate that this could be the precursor to a military operation against the Taliban."

Hank turned up the volume on his radio and listened more closely.

"In other news, Bob Stevens, who was hospitalized in Florida with anthrax has just succumbed to the disease. Mr. Stevens is the first anthrax death to occur in the United States in 25 years."

Freida walked over to Hank's desk so she could hear the newscast better.

"Wow, did you hear that Hank? We're under attack again!"

Hank waved her to be quiet and put his head closer to the speaker.

"In an interview earlier today, Secretary of Health and Human Services, Tommy Thompson, said that it appears to be an isolated case, and that sporadic cases of anthrax do occur in nature, that it is not contagious, and that this case is in no way related to a terrorist attack."

Hank turned off the radio and leaned back in his chair before speaking.

"Why are you always jumping to conclusions Freida? There's no anthrax attack. It's just a freak of nature. Didn't you hear that?"

Freida walked back to her desk.

"Yeah right. If you believe that, then I've got some swampland to sell. You know as well as I do that the whole world is falling apart. Things just aren't like the way they used to be. You can't deny that."

Hank thought for a moment before answering. On the one hand, he couldn't deny that the world was getting crazier by the minute, but on the other, well, he couldn't think of the other. He just didn't want to concede the point to Frieda or to even believe that the world was falling apart, as it seemed it was.

"Look what I bought at the army surplus store last night, Hank. Isn't it cool!"

Freida pulled an olive drab colored military style gas mask out of her desk drawer and began to put it on. Hank slammed his open palm firmly on the desk.

"That does it Freida! You have been working way too much overtime. I've been thinking about hiring someone to help you out around here, and this clinches it. Have you gone as crazy as the rest of the world?"

"Maybe the rest of the world makes more sense than you think, Hank." Her voice was muted from inside the mask. "Besides, why should I take any chances? I can carry this thing around and be safe from anthrax, saran gas, blood agents, everything short of a nuclear explosion. And if that happens we can all kiss our lives good bye anyway."

Hank shook his head from side to side. They'd been so busy since nine-eleven, and now it was finally taking it's toll on his secretary.

"I can't believe I'm hearing this from you. No one's going to attack us here in America."

"Hey! Wake up and smell the coffee and donuts Hank! We've already been attacked! Three thousand people are dead! Do you need me to draw you a picture? I heard last night that another major attack is imminent, and that only those who are prepared for it will survive."

She lifted up the bottom of the mask long enough to shove the last of a raspberry jelly roll into her mouth. Hank stood up and put his hands on his hips.

"And just where did you get your information? From a reliable source?"

"You bet it was reliable. It was from 44magnum."

Hank's mouth dropped open in disbelief.

"I can't believe it! Are you still spending time in those right-wing chat rooms? Only kooks and lunatics log on to that. 44magnum's probably a mass murderer and he's logged on in some prison library somewhere. You'd better be more careful Freida. You are way too trusting of these loonies."

She shook her head back and forth in disgust. Hank thought she looked ridiculous in a pink flowered dress and an olive drab gas mask.

"You're just not trusting enough Hank. That's your problem. 44magnum probably works for the U.S. Government, maybe even the CIA. That's how he knows so much. Last night he told me to stock up on canned goods, bottled water, ammunition, and to go out and buy a gun!"

Freida bent down and picked up her large handbag off the floor. She opened the purse and pulled something out. Hank moved closer to see what it was.

"Freida is that a pistol?"

She held it up and waved it back and forth so Hank could get a good look at it. Hank jumped back behind his desk and started yelling at the top of his lungs.

"Frieda! Put that gun down! Put it away right now! I won't have guns in my business. You're going to shoot someone, probably me!"

"It's a 10 millimeter Glock semi-automatic pistol with a 15-round high-capacity magazine. I got enough firepower here to blow away any terrorist in the county."

Hank peeked out from behind the desk.

"Freida, we're in Northern Michigan, Iroquois county, Freidham Ridge, population 562. This isn't exactly the kind of place terrorists target now is it?"

"Ya never know. These people are crazy. Total lunatics. It can't hurt to be prepared. My dad was a scoutmaster you know. I always like to be prepared."

Just then the front door swung inward, ringing the bell over the top of the entrance. Pastor McCullen walked in and leaned his forearms up on the counter.

"Nice gun Freida. Is that a Glock?"

The gas mask bobbed up and down as she nodded her head enthusiastically. The pastor saw Hank hiding behind the desk and smiled calmly.

"There are better ways to get a promotion Freida. Maybe you should put the gun back in your purse. At least take your finger off the trigger. I'd certainly feel better about it if you did."

Freida put the pistol back in her purse and removed the gas mask. She threw it down on the desk in front of her.

"Man that thing gets hot inside! How do people wear those things? Don't worry, Pastor. It's not loaded anyways."

Hank stood up, his eyes still locked onto Freida. He walked over to the counter, trying desperately to retain his dignity and composure.

"What can I do for you Pastor?"

Pastor McCullen ignored Hank's question, and continued speaking to Freida.

"Well, before you put any bullets in it, why don't you come on out to my house and I'll show you how to use it safely and effectively. I teach firearm safety classes, and if you're going to be packing heat, I'd just as soon you did it right. We'll get you all fixed up with a certificate, and then you can apply for a permit."

Freida's face beamed with excitement.

"Really? I could be like James Bond – licensed to kill!"

The pastor's smile became a little uneasy.

"We'll talk about that too, Freida. Just come on out this Saturday. But until then, why don't you put that gun out in the trunk of your car. That way you're legal and Constable Fitzu won't get so nervous. You know how high strung he can get."

When he finished talking, the pastor smiled and gave her a friendly nod. Freida smiled back and walked out past him with her purse. The door closed behind her and Hank buried his face into his folded hands in exasperation.

"Pastor, she's going to kill us all. Why are you encouraging her to carry a gun?"

Pastor McCullen's laugh was full and robust as it echoed off the walls and came back towards him.

"Now Hank, let's not get too eager to judge. Besides, she's already carrying a gun, and if she's going to do that, then she needs to know how to use it safely. Doesn't she watch your kids sometimes?"

A concerned, parental look came over Hank's face and he nodded.

"Well don't worry about it. Freida may be a little gullible, but she's not stupid and without all common sense. I'll teach her how to safely store it and how to keep it out of unauthorized hands. I'll give her the full 12-hour course and she'll be good to go."

Hank relaxed a little.

"I don't know Pastor. I just don't like guns. They scare me. And people who carry guns scare me even more. I can't believe you're a firearms instructor. You're a Pastor. I thought you didn't believe in killing?"

The pastor's smile faded and he grew suddenly serious.

"Of course I believe in killing. It's basic to the human race, basic to all living things. Killing is a very necessary element of life. It's murder that I have a problem with. But killing in defense of yourself and your family. I got no problem with that."

Hank looked on in disbelief.

"I can't believe you just said that. You're a man of God and you advocate killing another human being! How can you justify that?"

A cloud passed over the other man's countenance, and suddenly he took on a stormy look.

"Aren't you being just a little self righteous there Hank? Let me tell you how I look at it. If I'm over at the Mudhen and my wife and I are eating a burger and in walks a man with a ball bat and he starts to crack skulls, what do you think I'm going to do when he comes towards my wife with that bat? Do you think I'm going to get on my knees and pray for him? Do you think I'm going to let someone kill my own wife, the woman I love? Would you let someone kill your children just so you wouldn't have to get your hands and your conscience dirty? Sometimes killing is necessary, Hank. Didn't you hear my sermon a few weeks ago? Being defenseless is irresponsible behavior. And that's behavior that a father with small children like yourself simply can't afford to display."

Hank didn't answer for a moment. He hadn't expected an answer like that from a man of God.

"But wouldn't you feel bad if you killed someone?"

Pastor McCullen slowly nodded, and the muscles in his jaws relaxed a little.

"Yes, of course. But look at it this way. If I have to kill a guilty man to save an innocent life, then it's worth any amount of mental anguish that I may have to suffer. Yes, I would feel bad. But I would eventually get over it. But how would I feel if I stood idly by and watched that same man kill my wife or someone's child? I couldn't live with that Hank. I don't think any decent man worth his salt could. To be defenseless is irresponsible. And to fail to defend the innocent and the helpless against evil attack is more than irresponsible, it's criminal and downright immoral."

Hank lowered his head. He hadn't really thought about it that way. He'd certainly never heard it described like that before. The door opened up and Freida walked back in and sat back down at her desk.

"Ya want a doughnut Pastor? They're fresh day olds from the gas station."

Pastor laughed and nodded appreciatively.

"You bet Freida. Got one of those white powdered ones? I just love those things. They just melt in my mouth."

Hank turned and walked back toward his desk.

"Hey Hank!"

He stopped and pivoted back around.

"Yes Pastor. You're not going to preach again are you?"

A light, sympathetic smile touched the pastor's lips.

"Of course not Hank. Only on Sundays. But I wanted to let you know that the church is sponsoring a freedom rally next week, and I was hoping you'd give us a free public service announcement and then maybe show up and write a story about it. The congregation will be saying good bye to several boys who just enlisted in the military. I thought it might be newsworthy."

Hank nodded in agreement.

"Yeah, sure. I'll tie it in with the war on terror. Just give all the info to Freida, and I'll make sure it gets in next issue."

He sat back down at his desk and turned on the radio. That Lee Greenwood song was playing again.

"And I'm proud to be an American, where at least I know I'm free. And I won't forget the men who died, and gave that right to me. So I proudly stand up . . . next to you and defend her still today. Cuz there ain't no doubt I love this land. God bless the USA!"

Hank glanced over and saw Josh looking at him. He held his gaze long enough to see the pastor wink playfully with his left eye.

Hank shook his head and looked back down at the blank paper in front of him. He'd spent his whole life in the city, and it just hadn't prepared him for living in Freidham Ridge. Suddenly, he was reminded of something he'd heard on an old movie. "Ya'll ain't from around these here parts are ya!"

In the big city, he was the norm, but out here in the great American heartland, he might as well be an alien from outer space. Hank Simmons just didn't make a very good redneck.

Freedom, liberty; they had always been just words to him before. But, perhaps, maybe, they were something more, something he didn't yet fully understand.

The last chorus crescendoed and then slowly faded out. Hank found himself singing along softly. He tried to stop but couldn't. The words and the music carried him on, owning him for the moment.

"And I'm proud to be an American, where at least I know I'm free. And I won't forget the men who died, and gave that right to me. So I proudly stand up . . . next to you and defend her still today. Cuz there ain't no doubt I love this land. God bless the USA!"

Chapter 5

Special Agent Richard Resnik sat at the table of the café, pretending to read the local Arabic newspaper. It had been almost a month since nine-eleven, but still, the war against terror was just now getting started. It was a war like no other, one without national boundaries, without uniformed armies, but, nonetheless, bristling with hatred, malice, and treachery. Out of the corner of his eye, he watched the five suspects as they laughed and bantered back and forth. They were speaking in Arabic, but he understood every word they said, despite his Jewish heritage and upbringing.

Richard had been raised in Israel, and his parents had immigrated to New York City when he was 10 years old. That had been over 25 years ago, but he still remembered everything about the customs and culture of the Mid-East, as if it had been only yesterday. That was one of the advantages, or some might say disadvantages, of being raised in a traditional Jewish family. Your heritage and upbringing just never quite left you; it followed you through time, shaping you, defining you, guiding your destiny for the rest of your life.

Once, many years ago, he had considered a name change, but, in the end, had decided against it. A move like that would have destroyed his parents, perhaps even his entire family. They had never understood his final rejection of the Jewish faith, and he wasn't so sure he understood it himself, or, that it was indeed, final.

He studied Mominul Islam, the suspected leader, the dark-skinned man sitting in the center, from over the top of his newspaper. That was an interesting name by American standards; it meant 'pure submission'. His comrades appeared to call him Momin for short. Richard had become very adept over the years at watching people without their knowledge. He had been following these five men for over two weeks now. They were suspected to be part of a terrorist cell, and his job was to obtain the proof. So far, he'd made very little headway.

Part of the problem was the close-knit social fabric of the Moslem community in the city of Dearborn, Michigan. Not just anyone could waltz in and go unnoticed. You had to know the customs and the language. Special Agent Resnik knew 6 languages, and was an expert in Mid-Eastern culture and mentality. More than most in the bureau, he knew how they thought, and how they were likely to act in any given situation. That's why he'd been chosen for this surveillance. All of a sudden, since nine-eleven, his superiors, who had once viewed him as a maverick and a nuisance, suddenly had gained a new appreciation for his rare skills and talents. For years they'd had him shoved away in a basement room in DC translating reams and reams of radio messages and written correspondence, but now, finally, he was out on the street. And he was enjoying it.

Even though he was a Jew, he had no special feelings against Moslems in general. He just wasn't that religious. However, he was an American patriot. He loved America, and he wanted desperately to protect and defend her from anyone who would do his country harm. Right now, tracking down terrorist cells was the best way he could help his country. He took a sip of his coffee and set it back down.

His suspects were talking about the soccer playoffs and who was likely to progress to the next round. The subject bored him, but he forced himself to listen anyways.

After another 5 minutes, the man in the center got up to leave, and the others followed suit. He waved them off. “No, you stay. I’ll meet you back at the apartment. I have to do something alone.” The others sneered like hungry wolves and laughed knowingly. He swore at them in Bengali and walked out the door.

His research on this man showed that had he had been born and raised near Chittagong in southern Bangladesh. His parents were wealthy, and this had enabled him to travel to Mecca at age 20 on a pilgrimage. While there, Momin had been recruited into Al-Qaida. That had been 10 years ago, and Momin had never looked back. Because of his fanatical dedication to the cause and his own insatiable penchant for violence, he had quickly risen through the ranks of Al-Qaeda, eventually surpassing even many native Arabs. This had been unusual, since Muslims from third-world countries, though they comprised the majority of the Moslem population, were considered to be of a lower class than Moslems of Middle-Eastern descent.

Richard had to decide what to do: follow Momin, or stay with the others. He stayed. It was less risky. Perhaps the underlings would loosen their lips when the boss was not around. He felt his stomach growling, so he waved the waitress over, and ordered some toast and cottage cheese. Might as well dig in for the long haul. This could be another marathon night.

He looked out the window and watched Momin’s dark figure disappear into the sparse neon light of the city. Then he turned back to his newspaper. Maybe he should have followed him. Who knows. This job was a crapshoot, and to be successful, you needed patience, perseverance, and luck - plenty of luck. Oh well. Luck never had been his strong suit. But, then again, neither was love. He shook his head in disgust. Life was so unfair. What was a poor FBI Special Agent Jew to do while living among Islamic terrorists? It was a question for the ages. He sipped his coffee and stared out into the neon night, all the while listening to the Arabic small talk from across the room.

And, suddenly, he longed for simpler times, times of long ago, times as a child when all was black and white and life was safe with mom and dad. He sighed. The times, they are a changing. Then he smiled, and chewed his toast in resolute silence.

Chapter 6

Angela hovered over her cell phone a moment longer, then she made her decision and picked up the tiny phone. She punched in the numbers and waited.

"Hi Aunt Millie. It's me, Angela."

She nodded her head in answer to the unseen voice and then began to pace nervously back and forth in her apartment.

"Yes, I know. It's been almost a month. I know I should have returned your calls. I'm sorry."

She stopped in front of the window and looked out at the light wisp of smoke still rising from ground zero. It was always there – a constant reminder - nagging at her, bringing back all the painful memories of that day and all the ones who had died. But she had lived, and Angela still wondered why.

"I know Millie. You know I love you. Of course I do."

A tear welled up in the corner of her left eye and she looked down at the plush carpet. Aunt Millie had raised her after her parents had died. She was the most unselfish person that Angela had ever known, and she felt ashamed for not returning her calls. But, she just hadn't been able to bring herself to do it. And she knew why.

"Yes, I was thinking about it. I just feel like I need family right now, and you're the only family I have. All I have is you, Millie."

She broke down and cried now, without shame, and without inhibition. She wanted to escape the ghosts. New York City, once so vibrant, so exciting, and full of life, now felt like a tomb to her. When she'd left Freidham Ridge to go away to college, she'd vowed that she would never return to that boring little cul de sac town. When she thought of Freidham Ridge, she was reminded of George Bailey, played by Jimmy Stuart, in the Christmas movie "It's a Wonderful Life". His words had become her own personal mantra for many years. "I'm gonna shake off the dust of this crummy little town and I'm gonna see the world!" But now, things were different, and she had seen the world – more than she'd bargained for - and now all she wanted was to go back home to that crummy little town and recuperate. She was reminded of that song from an old sitcom that she used to watch as a kid. "Sometimes you wanna go where everybody knows your name. And they're always glad you came. You wanna go where people know, your troubles are all the same. You wanna go where everybody knows your name."

"I will Aunt Millie. I'll call you soon as I know when I'm getting there. I don't want to fly though. It scares me now. I'll drive my car."

Driving would take so much longer, but it would give her time to think outside of New York. She felt like she needed the transition time. So much had happened. So much had changed, and Freidham Ridge, though familiar, seemed a whole new world to her now. She wasn't even sure she could adapt to it again. But, it couldn't hurt to just go there for a few weeks while her company finished relocating.

"I love you too Aunt Millie. Bye."

She just wanted to go where everybody knew her name. She wanted to be held, to be loved; and Millie was always glad she came. Yes, Aunt Millie knew her name better than anyone.

Angela hung up the phone and then sat down on the couch. Things were different here, but not in Freidham Ridge. They would be the same. Freidham Ridge never changed, and she needed that stability, that immutable law that seemed intrinsic to small-town middle America.

"You wanna go where people know, your troubles are all the same. You wanna go where everybody knows your name."

The little tune was stuck in her head now, and she couldn't get it out. Angela closed her eyes and imagined the big hug she would get from her Aunt Millie. "You wanna go where everybody knows your name."

She closed her eyes and smiled nervously.

Chapter 7

"We hold these truths to be self-evident, that all men are created equal, that they are endowed by their creator with certain inalienable Rights, that among these are Life, Liberty, and the pursuit of Happiness."

Retired Professor Lance Stuart's body was old and bending, but his voice belied his age as it bore down now with all the conviction and power of a Marine Corps Drill Instructor. Although his hair, white and frayed, stuck up at odd angles here and there all around the perimeter of his balding head, like skinny little parapets of medieval foreboding, there was an electricity in his voice that seemed to radiate strength out into the crowded auditorium of Freidham Ridge Community Church. He had been invited to speak on the topic of freedom and liberty, in which everyone seemed suddenly interested during the aftermath of nine-eleven. All of a sudden, people no longer took their rights for granted. Perhaps this was one of the silver linings to surface from the war on terror. That, and everyone's renewed interest in community and faith.

"I often wonder what Thomas Jefferson would say about the present course of human events if he were alive today. Would he be alarmed at the present trend towards liberalism and big-government control? Would Thomas Jefferson subscribe to the popular doctrine of political correctness, or would he rail against it? I think Thomas Jefferson would tilt his head to one side and ask, 'What part of self-evident didn't you understand?'"

The crowd of farmers, factory workers, and housewives looked on, transfixed on every word, and Lance couldn't help but wonder why it was the least educated, the ones lacking his own Ivy League sophistication and background, who understood his message best. It seemed second nature to them, intuitively obvious to those his colleagues would call the riff-raff and rabble of the nation, but these common folk knew what was in their hearts; they felt the freedom inside them that modern-day education had stifled and killed in so many others. They were close to their roots, and Lance bore down on them now, unwilling to let them rest.

"The Declaration of Independence was based primarily on the Laws of Nature and of Nature's God. Laws of Nature, are intrinsically Laws of God, our Creator, higher laws, laws which when broken set off a chain of natural events and consequences which cannot be halted or harnessed regardless of what artificial law a man-made legislature may institute via a temporary government."

"The Declaration of Independence, indeed our entire American revolution, was a natural consequence of a government repeatedly breaking the laws of God and Nature. Many people today do not understand that the sole purpose of government is to protect these higher laws, and when government serves no longer as our protector, then they have become our oppressor and thereby a threat to our families and the liberty on which this great nation was founded."

Hank Simmons, owner of the Iroquois County Gazette, scribbled desperately on his notepad, cursing under his breath for not bringing his micro-recorder. He wasn't sure he subscribed to Lance's views, but he sure enjoyed listening to the old man talk. And from the size of the crowd tonight, so did others. Lance Stuart had a way with words, a connection with the people, a way of reaching out and latching onto the human soul and milking it of every will and ambition, and as a writer, Hank envied that talent.

"'We hold these truths to be self-evident' Where did we lose our way America? What part of self-evident don't we understand? How did the moral compass of our great nation become so skewed? We are indeed backwards: North has become South, and South has become North. The Bill of Rights was not written to protect government from the people, but rather, to protect the people from government, from the natural consequences of a corrupt government, wielding entirely too much power, in a way which perpetuates their downward spiral into graft and corruption."

Lance paused only long enough to catch his breath, then he looked out onto the crowd like a shepherd concerned for the well-being of his flock.

"There is a verse in the Bible which reads: 'Woe to those who call evil good and good evil, who put darkness for light and light for darkness, who put bitter for sweet and sweet for bitter'. How did we get here America? When did we turn our backs on the precepts and common sense on which this country was founded? As a country, we have collectively lost our way, and nothing short of a total about face can save us!"

Several in the audience nodded their heads, while a bolder man shouted out 'Amen!'. This encouraged Lance and his voice crescendoed higher and louder when he continued.

"Our founding fathers recognized self-evident truth for what it was, and because of this, they pledged their lives, their fortunes, and their sacred honor. But with great Truth comes great responsibility, and our founding fathers were willing to die to preserve the natural laws of God and Nature. Indeed many of them made the supreme sacrifice for each and every one of us, and their blood cries out to us now from the ground they fought to free! Their blood cries out to every politically correct, brain-dead American who takes his freedom for granted, and who passively accepts without question the anti-American sentiment so prevalent in our society. Their blood cries out to us in outrage! 'Did I die in vain! I gave my life, my fortune, my sacred honor so that you and your family could be free!'"

Lance paused slightly for effect. Then he pressed on.

"Whenever any form of government becomes destructive of these ends, it is the right of the people to alter or to abolish it!"

The old man paused long enough to slam his fist into his palm, causing every purple vein on his receding forehead to stand up and pump blood with the ferocity of a half-starved mountain lion.

"What part of this do we not understand? Our duty is clear. Parts of our government have become greedy, corrupt and repressive. 'Destructive of these ends, ...' Our duty is clear! We must alter our government - now, while we still have the liberty to do so. We must get out and campaign and vote. We must write and talk and speak our minds! We must unite as Americans who love our country and are willing to work and live and die as did our forefathers. Now is the time to act! Do not be afraid of what people may think about you. Ours is not a spirit of fear, but a spirit of power! I implore you; I exhort you to press onward; to seize the day and all it holds while you still can!"

Lance lowered his head and paused long enough to catch his breath. Then he surged forward once again like a soldier, charging the front lines in a battle that must be won.

"Presently, there are those in our government who seek to strip away our rights and subjugate us one tiny piece at a time. But there is one right that we must not lose, because it is the gatekeeper of liberty. It is nothing more than the right to self defense; the right to hold our government accountable; a self-evident right, given to us by God. In short, the one right that protects all others. It is of course, the Second Amendment to the Constitution of the United States: the right to keep and bear arms. Our liberties, acknowledged by the Bill of Rights, stand side by side, lined up like dominoes, and when one falls, so do they all. Then we are enslaved!"

The crowd grew deathly quiet as Lance grew silent, paced back and forth, then looked out with pleading brown eyes.

"I urge you now, as we stand in the shadowy dusk of our independence, to remember and ponder the blood of our ancestors, the blood of those who fought and died so that we might live free. Do not cheapen its memory with apathy. Do not devalue its worth with passivity. Our founding fathers may have lived long ago, but there are natural powers which bind us together even beyond death, powers which transcend space and time, spiritual powers of the heart and soul of humanity. This bond cannot be denied or stripped from us. It is the irrevocable law of God and Nature. It is not a physical bond. It is a spiritual bond. A bond of the deepest, strongest kind - a bond of unseen blood!"

For a moment there was silence, then one farmer in the front row stood up in his dirty bib overalls and began to clap his thick, callused hands together. One by one, his neighbors stood to their feet until the audience was roaring with applause. Lance stood awkwardly in front of them, humbled at their response.

But in the back of the room, Andy Fitzu was not amused. He scribbled furiously on his notepad while everyone else clapped and cheered. To Andy, this man was a subversive, and he had been watching him for a long time. Someday, Lance Stuart would get what he deserved! Andy would see to that! It was . . . his duty.

Chapter 8

To say that Hank's marriage had a been a failure, was tantamount to saying that the HMS Titanic was running slightly behind schedule. So, finally, after 12 years of complete and utter misery, he had concluded that some ships never come in, and that to continue waiting alone on the docks was crazy. On this particular day he felt like a total failure - a real loser.

Okay, so you could argue that his entire life wasn't a failure. He had four wonderful kids; he managed to put food on the table every week, and he had a respectable, low-paying job. Then again, if you had to work at convincing yourself of your own success, then just maybe . . . . Hank let that one slip on by where it belonged. No sense picking at the scab. It was best just to let it heal; to get some time between himself and the wounding.

In a divorce, usually the mother gets the children, but Hank's ex-wife had never been much of a mother, though he was sure she'd done her best, in her own sick and twisted way. He could still remember the innocent, self-righteous look on her face the day she'd beaten their four-year-old son's yellow kitten to death for peeing on the kitchen floor. At first he'd deplored her brutality, but as time passed, episodes like that began to feel more and more normal, as if he was becoming numb to reality and the lines of right and wrong were blurred. The desensitization had scared him perhaps more than anything else.

Eventually, he'd come to realize that despite her alcohol and drug addiction, her kleptomania, her violent fits of rage, and her bulimia, Caroline wasn't really a bad person. She was just plain crazy. And through those twelve years of pain and suffering, Hank had come to believe that while some people spend a lifetime acquiring insanity, Caroline had come upon it honestly, had, indeed, aspired to attain it. It is said that God loves wondrous variety, and if this were true, then God loved Hank's ex-wife more than anyone, because she was seldom the same person two days in a row.

Nonetheless, everyone has their limits, and Hank was no exception. During the last year of the marriage, Hank's ex-wife had been caught shoplifting three times, drunk driving twice, had overdosed on Nyquil, had an affair with his boss, and had poisoned his dog. And that, of course, had been the last straw. Because . . . Hank loved dogs.

He stared semi-catatonically at the clean, white, but regrettably blank sheet of paper nestled against the platen of his typewriter. Even here in the small town of Freidham Ridge, deep in the heart of Iroquois county, computers were everywhere, but Hank despised them. They were icons of overwork, frustration, and time compressed into unmanageable Herculean blocks of effort. He always typed his newspaper articles out on the typewriter, then let his secretary scan them into the computer. But then he could do that. He was the owner/editor/publisher/reporter for the county's only weekly newspaper. After the divorce, he had left the big city and bought this tiny, little, one-horse publication, with which he had two things in common: it was failing, and it had no future. Nonetheless, he was satisfied.

Freida, who constituted the remainder of the payroll of the Iroquois County Gazette, was a very patient and cooperative woman. She answered the phone, made the coffee, bought the donuts, and at times even picked up his kids from school. In short, Freida was an indispensable commodity to a single, working father, indeed, the glue that held his life together. She was worth her weight in technology, and that was no small statement since Freida ate most of the donuts herself.

Hank had been grappling with this article on the freedom rally ever since last Friday, but now he'd run out of time. He just couldn't seem to give Lance's speech justice, and the words just wouldn't come to life for him the way they had for Lance. Perhaps because he didn't understand what Lance had been talking about? Every sentence Hank wrote seemed to ring hollow and empty. They were just words, empty, hollow, echoing, reverberating, bouncing off the wrinkled walls of his brain and falling helplessly to the ground, like tiny BBs off a battleship.

He had to do something soon. He yelled out of his office to Freida.

"Hey, Freida! Can you get Lance Stuart on the phone for me?"

Frumpy looking Freida, overweight and unkempt, looked up from her powdered sugar donut out past the thick lenses of her glasses. Crumbs fell onto her lap when she spoke.

"Sure thing boss!"

Then she whispered under her breath.

"It's about time. The article's due day after tomorrow and I still have to type it into the computer for you."

"What's that Freida?"

"I said I'm getting him now, Hank."

She shook her head from side to side, pretending to be irritated, but deep down inside, the discombobulation of Hank's life helped to lend meaning to the boredom and predictability of her own. She punched a few buttons on the phone.

"He's on line one, Hank."

She laughed under her breath. They only had one line, but Hank insisted that she say it that way, especially when other people were in the office. He said it sounded more professional. Freida considered him a ridiculous, absurd man, but he had a knack for making her feel needed and indispensable, and for that, she was willing to tolerate a multitude of absurdities.

"I'm going home for lunch now. Be back at 1."

Hank shot back a retort.

"Yeah, well, just be back by 1. I'm expecting an important call from the Mayor of East Cupcake. And you know how he hates to leave messages."

Freida tried to hide a smile, but failed.

"Yes, I remember. Last time he was really frosted!"

But Hank was already talking to Lance and just waved her off. Freida shook her head, picked up her purse and walked toward the door. Yeah, she liked Hank Simmons, eccentric as he was. He was a real nice guy.

Chapter 9

Lance Stuart hung up the phone and went back to rocking, listening to the old pine boards creaking beneath him, lending rhythm to his life, and recalibrating the center inside him. He wasn't surprised that Hank Simmons didn't understand his speech. It wasn't that he lacked the talent or the intelligence, because Lance had long admired Hank's writing skills and wondered what he was doing in this one-horse hick town. He could obviously do much better for himself in the big city. So Lance suspected something deeper, a matter of the soul, and the telephone call confirmed his suspicions.

Ten minutes later, Lance watched the dust kick up behind Hank's old beat-up station wagon, then drift lazily off behind him, before settling lightly on the dried grass of mid October. The newspaperman hopped out of his car and walked toward the old man, a smile on his face that rivaled the sunlight.

"Hey, Mr. Stuart. Thanks for letting me drop by on short notice like this."

Lance stayed seated and motioned with a nod of his head toward the rocking chair beside him. It was a solid oak rocker, with a cloth pad on the back, a gift from him to his wife Irene many, many years ago. This chair had been sadly empty for a long time.

"What can I do for you Mr. Simmons?"

Hank, dressed in a sweatshirt and jeans, lowered his head and fidgeted with his hands. He hadn't been this nervous in a long time. This always happened to him when he interviewed famous celebrities. Now, if he could just keep from saying stupid things, he'd be alright.

"Well, I'm glad you asked. Are you rich? Can I have some money? How about this house? I'll give you 10 bucks for it!"

Hank winced inside. Why did he always do that? It's like he couldn't stop. Lance forced himself to keep a straight face. A sense of humor – of sorts. He liked that. Most people around these parts treated him like a celebrity, and here was someone different at last. He decided to play along.

"I'm sorry Mr. Simmons. The house is for sale, but I'm afraid 15 dollars is the lowest I can go. However, this is a nice shirt I'm wearing. Would you like it?"

Hank laughed nervously.

"Oh no, no. I appreciate the offer, but a nice flannel shirt like that must have cost you pennies. Besides, it looks much too manly for me. I could never pull off that Midwestern, rural, redneck motif."

Lance finally gave in and smiled.

"Alright then, Mr. Simmons, suit yourself, no pun intended. Would you settle for some ice-cold lemonade?"

Hank was slowly gaining control over his nervousness – just a few more stupid comments and he'd feel right at home.

"Well, usually I don't drink on the job, but this being a weekday and all, I suppose one couldn't hurt."

The old man glanced down to Hank's feet and pointed with his eyes. Hank followed Lance's gaze and saw the glass of liquid waiting at the base of the chair, condensation beading up, forming tiny rivulets before running down to soak into the dry, weathered boards of the front porch. It was dramatically warm for October, almost 70 degrees, so he was grateful for the cool refreshment.

"Hey, neat trick! How'd you do that?" Hank closed his eyes and raised his head to the heavens as he spoke. "For my next wish I'd like a stretched limo and a million dollars!"

The old man quietly smiled and looked out across his weeded lawn to the dying cornfield beyond the gravel road. Hank took a moment to study this man before him, an enigma, a mystery to all of Iroquois county. Hank was very nervous, and trying to hide it with off-the-wall humor didn't seem to be working. He'd heard the townsfolk talk about Lance many times in hushed tones over beer at the Mudhen Grille near the edge of town. No one out here understood a man who'd earned five post-graduate degrees, taught at Harvard, and then won the Pulitzer prize for his first and only novel. Now all he did was teach a few classes at the local junior college and the high school. Then Hank took a drink and without hesitating spoke his mind.

"What are you doing here, Professor Stuart?"

Lance turned back to Hank and stared blankly at him with one raised eyebrow. At that moment, he reminded Hank of First Officer Spock on Star Trek.

"Oh, I'm sorry. Did I say that out loud?"

Hank wasn't sure, but he thought he saw the beginning of a playful look come into the Professor's eyes. When Lance finally spoke, it was with a formal diction and perfect elocution.

"If you want a precise answer to that question, then I require a higher level of specificity."

The serious look on Hank's face disappeared and he began to laugh out loud.

"Specificity? Do they even make that anymore? I think I saw some on sale at K-mart's just last week."

He laughed again. But the old man's playful look went away. Fearing he was losing him, Hank became serious too.

"I'm sorry Mr. Stuart. I don't usually come on like a game show host, but I'm just kind of nervous right now. I've heard a lot about you, and you are famous you know."

Lance nodded his head.

"Yes, I've heard that. Success at an early age will do that to a man."

Hank thought he sensed a bit of sadness in the old man's tone, and his reporter's instinct took over. As he probed further, his nervousness began to melt away.

"Are you saying you regret your success?"

Lance smiled softly and shifted in his rocking chair.

"You're perceptive. That's good."

He looked out into the sleeping field of corn across the road, but Hank got the impression he was not looking through space but through time.

"I can't say as I regret my success. However, there is a downside to peaking at age 31."

Hank didn't say anything.

"And when Alexander looked out over the expanse of his domain, he wept, because there were no more kingdoms to conquer."

Hank felt the need to sit down. He wanted to find out more.

"I read your novel when I was in college. It was incredible. Your use of imagery and the characters you created were amazing. You inspired me for a long time."

Lance looked away from the field and deep into Hank's eyes, making him feel intellectually naked, his soul laid bare.

"I remember when I was 22. I wanted nothing more than fame and fortune. I wanted the Pulitzer Prize most of all I suppose. So I set myself to the task. I was like that man in the Bible parable who found the pearl of great price. When he found it, he went out and sold all he owned to buy that field so that he could possess the pearl. It was an obsession for me.

But with success comes great sacrifice. I gave up everything for that pearl, and I've lived to regret it."

He looked away from Hank again, out into the bare, dirt field just to the right of the corn.

"It wasn't until after I'd achieved all my dreams that I realized that I was unhappy and alone. Life is confusing sometimes."

Hank was surprised, and his voice betrayed that.

"But most people would kill to be in your shoes. I would kill to be in your shoes! You have everything. Money! Fame! Prestige! The world is your oyster!"

Lance gave him the Spock look again.

"Do you always speak in clichés, Mr. Simmons?"

Hank smiled again.

"Well, you know what they say, No good cliché ever went unpunished."

Lance sipped a bit of his lemonade and Hank followed suit.

"People actually say that? Where?"

"Over in Catville. They say it there."

"Catville?"

"Yeah it's a little place just south of Freidham Ridge, west of Podunk Holler."

Lance smiled and looked down a moment.

"I suppose I deserved that. I see you're a pretty straight shooter, Mr. Simmons. I like a man who says what he means and means what he says. I have little patience for pretense."

Hank took a sip of lemonade and nodded.

"Well, thanks. I guess. Blunt and tactless is my trademark. Ask anyone who ever fired me. I never did fit in very well at the big city newspaper with its politics and all its rules. I used to get myself in a lot of trouble, but I always slept well at night."

The old man began to creak his rocker back and forth, remembering all the times he'd argued with his Department Chairman as well as all the times he'd been called in to talk to the Dean. When he spoke again, his melancholy tone was gone.

"Well, Hank, I've never been much for political correctness myself. Yep. As far as I'm concerned, politically correct is just another name for brain dead."

Hank paused in mid sip. Did he just hear Professor Lance Stuart, a Pulitzer prize-winning author say "yep"?

"So why did you move way out here in the boondocks Dr. Stuart?"

"Call me Rock."

"What?"

"My friends all call me Rock."

"Oh, I didn't know that. Well thanks. I appreciate that . . . Doctor Rock."

The old man shook his head and smiled again.

"So you're asking why I moved way out here in the boondocks?"

"Yes sir."

"Rock! Call me Rock!"

"Sure thing Doc Rock. That's what I'm asking. Just my natural reporter's curiosity at work."

Rock crossed his legs and gazed out past the lawn and the road to the newly plowed field, just to the right of the standing corn. This man was starting to get on his nerves.

"Can you smell that black dirt over there Hank?"

Hank tested the wind and nodded as Rock continued on.

"Yeah. Me too. Just plowed it yesterday. You can't smell that in the city. There are roots in that dirt. Roots that run deep and strong. I grew up in the country surrounded by dirt like that, and after I retired, well, it just felt natural to get back out into the real America, back into the heartland where real people live and breathe and can smell the rich, black dirt of the earth."

Hank didn't interrupt. He was already transfixed by the old man's words, and he simply nodded as if in encouragement.

"Take for instance my speech of the other night at the rally. Every last one of those farmers and factory workers understood what I was talking about it. They understood that the Second Amendment is not so much about guns as it is about accountability, and politeness, and the basic freedom of self defense. People who live around dirt are very simple folk and they look at the world through simple eyes, untainted by political correctness or liberal ideology. And because they live around dirt, they remain close to their roots, and the simple things that city people don't understand are just plain common sense to them."

Hank's face tightened in confusion.

"What exactly do you mean by that? I guess I'm one of those dull-witted city folks."

Rock smiled ever so slightly.

"No, not dull-witted, just asleep at the wheel, anesthetized so to speak."

Rock thought about it a moment and then pressed on.

"Let's try a different tack. Do you know old Zeke Tyler who farms over in the south corner of the township?"

Hank nodded.

"You mean the guy who punched out the County Commissioner last year? I wrote an article on that. They tried to make him mow his lawn, because it violated some county beautification ordinance, or something like that. I asked him why he did it and he just grunted and said. 'I was obliged to'. I have no idea what he meant by that so I just quoted him."

The old man smiled softly and nodded his head.

"That's right. He was obliged to. In his simple, down-to-earth way of looking at things, you don't tread on other people's rights. You don't tell people what to do with their own property. And if you do, then you need a good whoopin'!"

Hank busted out laughing.

"I can't believe a Pulitzer Prize winner just said 'whoopin'!"

Rock loosened up and laughed along with him. He was starting to like this man despite his annoying humor and obvious lack of common sense.

"Let me bring it closer to home for you. Suppose that same County Commissioner came to you and told you not to publish this article you're writing about the freedom rally? What would you tell him?"

A sudden and unexpected cloud came over Hank's face.

"Well I'd tell him that he has no right to tell me what I can and cannot publish. I'm protected by the Constitution, and . . . ."

Rock watched as a light went on inside Hank's head.

"Oh-h, I see. So are you saying that the Second Amendment is every bit as important as the first? But a lot of people say it's not an individual right, that it's not even needed anymore. The crime rate is way down you know."

"The Second Amendment will always be needed, if for no other reason than to protect your right to publish free of government censorship. The Second Amendment is the one right that protects all others. It's about accountability. An armed society is all that holds the government accountable to the people who elected them. All people are inherently flawed. We are predisposed toward selfishness and vain ambition."

Hank interrupted him.

"But some people believe humans are inherently good."

Lance smiled patiently.

"How can you even entertain that notion in the world of post nine-eleven? Besides, if that were true, then we wouldn't need laws or rules, because they would be second nature to us and we would be nice to each other without giving it a second thought. But because we are predisposed to selfishness, then we need the rules and their associated accountability or else the rich will steal from the poor, and the strong will enslave the weak. Our founding fathers knew that, because at the time they were being oppressed by King George of England."

Hank stroked his chin and was lost deep in thought.

"So you're saying that the Second Amendment isn't just for hunting or for self defense. It's what protects our freedom?"

"You've got it! Of course self defense is a basic human right bestowed upon us by the creator, not by the government. The government simply either acknowledges that right or infringes upon it. But there are many kinds of self defense. Hunting defends us from hunger; carrying a concealed pistol defends us from crime; an armed civilian population defends us from an out-of-control totalitarian government. There is an innate wisdom in the Bill of Rights which transcends the politics of the moment and makes it relevant and important from one generation and culture to the next."

The reporter looked overwhelmed.

"Wow! That's a lot to think about."

A resolute smile ebbed onto the old man's face.

"Have you ever shot a handgun Mr. Simmons?"

Hank glanced over at Lance with fear growing in his eyes. He remembered the night he'd shot his wife's gun, could still see her naked body bobbing up and down on the waterbed beside his old boss, but the recollection brought him discomfort, so he quickly denied the pain of his past.

"Of course not! Those things are dangerous! I have kids at my house."

"And that's exactly why you should carry a firearm - to protect them. They're depending on you."

Rock stood up and pointed out to a dead stump 20 feet away from the porch.

"See that stump?"

Hank nodded.

"Watch this."

With one fluid motion, Rock reached into the inside of his flannel shirt, and pulled out a .40 caliber pistol. He raised it in both hands and fired 15 shots into the old stump. The sound was deafening, and Hank fell off his chair onto the old creaky floorboards of the porch. Then Lance looked down calmly at the reporter and smiled.

"Guns are supposed to be dangerous Mr. Simmons, as are chain saws and axes and knives. Guns are, quite simply put, the power tools of freedom."

Slowly, and precariously, Hank moved to one knee and then back to the rocking chair where he knelt and gripped the wooden arms until his knuckles turned white. He suddenly felt trapped inside NRA hell, and this man was Satan!

The old man laughed again, this time louder than ever.

"Would you like to try it?"

Hank shook his head from side to side. All he wanted to do right now was get away from this crazy old man with the gun.

"Ah-h-h, perhaps another time. I do have an article to write and press time is creeping up on me fast . . . ."

Rock nodded his head knowingly.

"Well, you know what they say - the pen is mightier than the sword. . . and the pistol I might add. Have a good day Mr. Simmons, and feel free to stop in anytime."

As Hank rose to his feet, the old man pulled out a fresh magazine of 15 rounds, jammed it into place and let the slide rack forward. He put the safety back on and returned the pistol to its holster inside his shirt.

"There, I'm cocked, locked and ready to rock!"

Hank backed away cautiously.

“Thank you for your time Mr. Stuart.”

“It’s Rock. Call me Rock.”

Hank walked slowly off the porch, never taking his eyes off the old man with the gun.

“Yes sir. I will sir.”

Rock sat back down and yelled after his departing guest.

“That’s what I like about you Hank, you’re always so polite. Let me know if you need more help with the article.”

He smiled as Hank turned and hurried over to his car, jumped in and sped away, throwing up another cloud of dust. Rock spoke now only to the dying cornfield across the road.

“Class dismissed.”

Rock’s wife, may she rest in peace, used to get so mad at him for doing off-the-wall things like that, but he just couldn’t resist it sometimes.

After all, people are inherently evil.

Chapter 10

"Good afternoon officer. Is there a problem?"

Township Constable Andy Fitzu glared down at Hank with all the compassion and understanding of a battle-hardened nun.

"I'll say we have a problem all right Mr. Simmons. I got you on radar going 39 in a 35 zone. Are you trying to get someone killed?"

The look on Hank's face began to change.

"Well, no, I just have a deadline to publish my newspaper, and . . . ."

"Well, deadlines are no excuse for breaking the law, not even for fancy, big city newspaper reporters. They may not enforce the law where you come from, but here in Iroquois the law reigns supreme!"

The wheels in Hank's brain began to turn at the speed of light, trying to form a response that would end the officer's lecture and get him back to the office. Finally, he opted to take the humility route.

"You're absolutely right sir. I really should slow down. After all, the law is the law, and I respect that. I want nothing more than to cooperate sir."

The face of Constable Fitzu turned beet red.

"Don't patronize me! You were 4 miles over the speed limit, and no one, not even the press, is above the law!"

"Of course not, that's not what I meant . . . ."

"Driver's license, vehicle registration, and proof of insurance please!"

Hank handed over the documents, and sat slumped over the wheel as the officer went back to call it in. Was this what Lance Stuart had meant by an out-of-control government? No, this was just one out-of-control idiot who happened to be in a position of power within the government.

Five minutes later, Fitzu came back and handed him a ticket for speeding.

"Where are you coming from so fast, Mr. Simmons?"

"Oh, I was just over at Lance Stuart's place."

A look of suspicion came over the policeman's face.

"Really, and what were you doing over there?"

Hank hesitated. This whole scene was beginning to remind him of an old World War II movie where the Nazi Storm trooper demanded to see his papers.

"Well, I was just interviewing him for an article I'm writing on his speech he gave at the freedom rally a few days ago."

"Really. Well, you need to be careful of those Second Amendment types. A lot of those people are gun-toting maniacs. They just want to walk around with guns scaring innocent civilians. Who do they want to shoot so bad anyhow? I don't trust them. Not any of them. You'd do well to stay away from those types and just leave these matters to the police."

Hank nodded his head.

"I was just writing a story, not starting a revolution or anything like that. I assure you that I'm about as law-abiding as they come."

Fitzu grunted his disapproval and then wiped his nose with his left hand as he turned away.

"Yeah, well, that didn't stop you from recklessly endangering the lives of innocent civilians now did it! From now on slow down, because I'm watching you Simmons. I've got my eye on you!"

With that, Constable Fitzu turned and began the long, slow swagger back to his patrol car. Hank just sat there with his mouth open, wondering what part of this was dream and what part was reality, and suddenly, without warning, the once-vague words of Lance Stuart suddenly took on new meaning, and his writer's block faded away.

Chapter 11

Spunky Cannon had been accused of many things in his 40 years here on earth, and, for the most part, they were all true, but one thing he would zealously deny until his last breath, was that he was a worthless, no-good-for-nothing drunk. Why the unmitigated, self-righteous gall of anyone who called a drunk worthless. It was a not well-known fact that the production and consumption of alcohol had long been regarded as an important stimulant for the economy. Why Spunky could remember several times in particular where he had single-handedly caused the New York Stock Exchange to rise several hundred points in a single day!

Cursing under his breath, with a wrench in one hand and a bottle of Jack Daniels in the other, Spunky sat down on the tire of his old biplane to contemplate why the engine wasn't getting any spark. He put down the wrench and held the bottle with both hands. The morning frost had burned off hours ago, and the afternoon sun beat down on him now, making him thirsty.

"I'd better drink about this for a while."

His voice was deep and gravelly, and when he talked it sounded more like the results of sandpaper on a bear's behind than the voice of a man.

"Besides, I only drink during the day. Course at night when I'm sleeping I just dream about drinking. But everybody does that, so it don't count."

The weed field he'd landed in was thick and bushy beneath his feet, contrasting sharply to the black of his boots as he drank deeply over and over again.

"Everybody drinks a little bit. Even people who say they don't really do."

In Spunky's mind, drinking was like sex, either you did it, or you were lying about doing it. Either way, he felt it was just best to go ahead and do it and get it out of your system. It seemed more honest that way. Spunky thought for a while, then he let his cover-alled back slide down the rubber tire onto the dead, yellow grass.

His third wife had asked him once why he drank so much, and he'd looked at her as if she was crazy, as if he couldn't believe she'd pry that far into a man's personal life. She may as well ask him about his bowel movements as drinking. They were both private. He'd just looked at her and said, "Why do I drink so much? I don't know. Why do you talk so much?" She'd filed for divorce shortly after that. So much the better. Good riddance to bad rubbish as far as he was concerned.

He began talking now as if she were still there beside him, like he was arguing with her ghost.

"Hey, you knew I was drinker when I married you. What'd you expect me to do, quit or somethin'. Not likely woman! How many times do I have to tell you? Don't marry a man expecting him to change! You women are so funny that way. Stupid too."

He looked over at the plane as if listening, and then replied to the unheard voice.

"Of course I cheated on you! I cheated on almost all my wives! I cheated on my second wife with you. Did you think you were so good in the sack that I'd never cheat again. Not likely!"

The bleary-eyed man took another drink and then let his left hand drop down into the grass. A fly buzzed around his face, landing on his forehead. He tried to kill it with his right hand and smashed the glass bottle onto his forehead and screamed out loud, clutching his face in both hands.

"What did you hit me for? Woman I'm glad I divorced you! Best thing I ever done."

Spunky was so involved with his pain, that he didn't notice the old man walk up behind the plane, and he tried to jump to his feet when he finally saw him but instead flopped over to one side on the grass, trying desperately to keep his booze from spilling.

"Afternoon Spunk! How's it going?"

"Confound it Rock! Hellfire and damnation! What you doing sneaking up on a man like that? I coulda' been relieving myself or some such thing. Don't you know nothin' about privacy?"

Rock laughed out loud.

"Well, I don't know. You did just land an airplane in my back yard. Mind if I sit for a spell?"

"Go ahead. I don't care. Is this yer field?."

Rock laughed again and sat down on the grass next to the drunken pilot, picking a blade of alfalfa and chewing on it.

"Yes, it's mine. I was thinking of planting corn in it next year. But I . . . ."

But Spunky was already interrupting.

"What'dya think you are, a cow or somethin'? Why you always eatin' grass like that for?"

"I need the vitamins."

Spunky laughed, took a drink and then handed the bottle over to the old man. Rock took a tiny sip then handed it back to him. He never had been much of a drinker.

"Hey, you want vitamins, eat an apple. The cows depend on this grass, but you keep eating it all the time and they're gonna starve to death. That stuff'll go clean through ya. Might as well eat a bale of hay!"

Rock looked over thoughtfully. He was used to his friend's drunken ravings and knew how to handle it.

"I suppose you're right Spunky. I'll have one as soon as I get back to the house."

"Have what? A bale of hay?"

Lance laughed again and shook his head from side to side.

"Pronoun problems. No, I mean an apple. I'll eat an apple when I get back up to the house."

"Yeah you do that. The cow's need all the grass fer themselves."

"So what's the problem?"

Spunky took a drink.

"Problem? I'll tell you the problem! I can't get this bird in the air! Worse than that, I'm almost out of supplies."

He took the last drink and then handed the bottle to Rock, who just stared at the few tiny drops left in the bottom.

"Thanks Spunk. How did you know I was thirsty?"

"It's all that grass you eat, that's how. Cows drink a lot too. I know, I've seen 'em do it."

"Yeah, I bet you see a lot of cows in your line of work."

"Oh yeah. Herds of 'em. Ever notice how cows are always having sex? Horniest little buggers I ever seen. Those bulls just go from one heifer to the next, jump up, climb aboard, do their job and move on to the next. Like a production line."

Rock smiled.

"Like a reproduction line you mean."

Spunky squinted and looked the old man straight in the eyes.

"Tell me the truth now, Rock. Was that a joke?"

The old man nodded.

"Why you horny old son of a gun, you. I can see your pilot light's still lit. I get laid every week ya know."

Rock feigned interest.

"Is that so? Why you must be very proud."

Spunky cocked his head to one side.

"Are you funnin' me again?"

Rock laughed out loud and tossed the chewed-up grass stem off to one side.

"Ya know Spunk, I can't fool you even when you're drunk. You up to a game of chess?"

"You kiddin' me, I'll wipe the board with you ever day and twice on Sundays!"

"Oh I bet you will. But I've been practicing since last time. I think I can take you now."

"In yer dreams old man. I'll clean yer clock drunk or sober. I play better when I'm drunk."

"Is that so? Then you must be feeling pretty intellectual right about now eh?"

"Einstein's a retard next to me, buddy."

Rock stood slowly to his feet and extended his hand down to the drunken pilot.

"Come on up to the house and we'll crack open a few and play some chess. After all, you know what they say, friends don't let friends fly drunk."

Spunky raised his hand and Rock was barely able to lift him to his feet.

"I never said that. Who told you I said that? Did Bink Brewster tell you I said that? I fly better when I'm drunk, everybody knows that. But I ain't drunk now."

"Yeah I know. Let's just get on up to the house and I'll spot you a bishop."

Spunky cleared his throat and spit off to one side.

"Yeah right! I'll spot you a queen old man!"

Rock laughed and walked slowly so the teetering man could keep up without falling.

"Oh I bet you will. Probably whip me too!"

"Oh yeah. I'll wipe the board with ya!"

"Why of course you will."

All the way up to his old farmhouse, the two men talked, saying absolutely nothing. Rock told him to sit on the couch while he went to get the beer and the chess board. When he came back, Spunky was passed out and snoring.

Rock looked down sympathetically, went to the cedar chest, pulled out a blanket and draped it over his friend's unmoving body.

"Maybe next time partner. And I'll take you up on that queen."

He went back to the kitchen and fixed a pot of strong coffee while Spunky slept it off. Then, from the rocking chair on the porch, he watched the sun dip down and touch the trees, the last light and warmth of day fading second by second, minute by minute, heartbeat by heartbeat.

It was good to have friends again. Friends of little pretense.

Chapter 12

The events of nine-eleven had changed everything for Hank. He'd had to stay up all night long reworking the whole layout of the paper, pulling in stories from off the wire, interviewing the locals to get their reaction, that sort of thing. Circulation was way up, because people wanted to know what was happening on the outside, but, for the most part, life in Iroquois county pretty much had stayed the same. Yeah, sure, there was the initial shock, then grief, then anger, and people were glued to their television sets for several days, but life in a small town goes on. After all, what choice is there? Most of the townsfolk were farmers, and the corn doesn't just get up and walk in out of the fields on its own, now does it.

So eventually, the everyday events of life returned to normal, but there were certain things, things core to life and basic to humanity that would never be the same. People thought differently now. No longer did they take the important things in life for granted, like God, Family, and Country. Almost overnight American flags had gone up all over town, and it was considered unpatriotic to not fly one from your house and your car. People started going to church again too, and Hank was one of them. But there was one thing that didn't change, and perhaps never would. Hank Simmons remained a lonely man – a single parent, a man alone, craving a mate, needing a partner, but with little prospect or hope of ever meeting those needs.

On the Sunday immediately following nine-eleven, Hank and his four kids had joined the crowd and attended the service at Freidham Ridge Community Church and had been going ever since. Hank had gone to church while growing up, but had stopped as an adult, primarily just because he didn't have the time to spare. When you work 6 days a week, you just don't want to get up early on your only day off and listen to someone tell you that you're going to burn in hell unless you do things his way.

At least that's the way Hank remembered it as a child, but Freidham Ridge Community wasn't like that at all. It was a small church, and they were very accepting and kind. His kids even liked the Sunday School. In fact, Hank liked it so much that he started going every week, and then at the end of October, Pastor McCullen invited them over for dinner to get to know them better.

"So Hank, tell me about yourself."

The Pastor's wife gave her husband an annoyed stare.

"Now Josh, at least let him get some food down him before you start with the interrogation. Hank, you'd think he was in the CIA or something the way my husband pries."

She put down her fork and looked over at him with inquisitive eyes, before asking a question of her own.

"So why aren't you married Hank?"

Hank's spoon of mashed potatoes stood poised in mid-delivery. He wasn't expecting the direct approach. Hank didn't have time to answer before his 5-year old son chirped in for him.

"We're not married. We're avorced."

Hank shot his son his best red-flag warning look, but it was too late. Kids just don't shut up, and, apparently, neither do preacher's wives.

"Oh, I'm so sorry honey! Do you miss your mommy?"

Little Micah shrugged his tiny shoulders before answering.

"Nope. Mommy's a drunken hoe. I don't know what that is. But Daddy says he'll tell me when I'm bigger."

Hank's face turned beet red, and he opened his mouth to speak, but nothing came out but voiceless, empty air.

"Mommy sleeped a lot. Just sleeped and yelled, sleeped and yelled, sleeped and yelled. Daddy said she sleeped with a lot of people."

Finally, Hank found his voice and in his most impressive, condescending parental tone began to correct his son.

"Now Micah, we don't talk that way about your mother!"

A confused look came over the little boy's face.

"We stopped doin' it?"

Hank lowered his head in shame.

"That's right Micah. We stopped."

"Okey dokey."

Then the little boy went back to eating as if the conversation had never taken place, leaving Hank to pick up the pieces and bask alone in the embarrassment and humiliation.

At last, after what seemed like hours, but was really only a few seconds, the Pastor broke the clumsy silence.

"So what did you think about the sermon today Hank?"

Hank couldn't even hear himself answering. He just talked on and on in an attempt to monopolize the conversation, all the while knowing that he was being rude and boorish, but he didn't care. Besides, the more he talked, the less that his four children could reveal.

Eventually, the meal ended, and Hank and the pastor went into another room. By the looks of it, it was a large, walk-in closet that had been converted into an office. There were papers and books piled on the desk and on the floor, and an old banana peel was drying and turning black on the floor in one corner. Hank was relieved to finally see someone else's flaws come to light. Pastor McCullen was the first to speak.

"Sorry about that, Hank. Sometimes Louise misspeaks herself. She means well. It's just that she's curious about things that she knows nothing about. I hope you won't let this keep you from worship."

Hank let his muscles relax a little.

"I'm sorry pastor, I think I'm the one who should apologize for my son. I can't believe he picked up on that. I only called her that just the one time and I had no idea he was listening."

"Please, call me Josh. Kids hear everything, even when you think they don't. Sometimes I think they follow us around and take notes."

Hank nodded his head and looked down at the cluttered floor.

"Of course, my kids are all grown up and moved away now, but I remember one time about 25 years ago that my son embarrassed me so bad I thought I'd have to move to another state."

Hank looked back up.

"Really?"

Josh smiled and leaned back in his chair. He was about 50 years old and his hair was half-gray and cut fairly short.

"Now I don't mind telling you the story, but you'll have to promise me it never gets printed in your newspaper."

That was the first time Hank smiled all day.

"No problem Josh. Go ahead. It's off the record."

The pastor gave him a trusting look before he launched into his narration.

"Well, Louise and I were at our very first church, and we really wanted to make a good impression. We were so young and excited, full of ideals and all. You know how it is when you're young and first starting out. You want to conquer the world."

Hank nodded. He knew exactly what he meant. He had been the same way as a cub reporter.

"So Louise and I were living in the parsonage. It was just a little three-room house out in the middle of nowhere, and there were only about 50 people in the whole church. Anyways, Louise had all the ladies over for tea and cookies one morning and things weren't going too well. Women in a small church can be real cliquish you know?"

Hank didn't know, but he nodded nonetheless. He wanted to hear the story.

"There were about 5 women, all fundamental, conservative, dressed in long dresses and wearing their hair up in buns. Real hard-core domestic kind of people. Most of them had that Ex-lax look on their faces. You know, like they'd been sucking on green persimmons all day?"

Once again, Hank didn't know what he meant, but he wished he'd been there to see it.

"It painted quite a picture, like something Norman Rockwell would have created after 20 years without sex."

Hank looked up and his mouth dropped open. Then he slowly smiled.

"You just said sex."

The pastor nodded.

"Well, yes. Not only am I familiar with it as a concept, but I've also practiced it throughout my marriage. I've got five kids you know. But don't tell Louise I said that. I'd never hear the end of it. The "S" word embarrasses her."

Then Pastor McCullen smiled before adding, "At least in public it does."

Hank was starting to feel more and more at home with the pastor and he leaned back in his chair anxious to hear the story.

"So these five church ladies are in my living room and I'm over in a corner by myself studying the sermon for Sunday when my oldest son, he was only 2 years old at the time, toddles on in and right up to the head Deacon's wife. I just glanced up a moment but didn't think much of it. I was pretty absorbed in my sermon outline."

He paused here to take a drink of his coffee, then he went on.

"Then I heard the old lady, I think her name was Prudence or some such puritanical nonsense. She said to my son, 'Why hello there little fellow. What's that you're chewing on?' And then there was a moment's silence before I heard this blood-curdling scream!"

Hank's eyes perked up.

"What was it?"

Josh motioned with his hands for him to be patient.

"Well now, just hold on. I'm getting to that part. But you can't rush a good story."

He settled back in his chair and put his coffee on the desk.

"So I heard this blood-curdling scream from Prudence the head deacon's wife and then another from the lady next to her, and another and another and another. And my son was so scared he started crying and ran into the other room and I jumped up because I didn't know what was going on. So I ran over there, and already four of the ladies were standing up and putting on their coats as if they were going to leave real quick like. My wife, she just sat there in her chair in shock with this cemetery look on her face, and poor old Prudence was sitting in her chair stunned into silence, holding onto a pair of neon green underwear, dripping wet with my son's saliva. She just dropped them on the floor and walked out."

Hank couldn't help himself and started busting out laughing.

"You're right! That is worse than calling your wife a drunken sl-u-. Well, . . . you know."

Josh nodded, glancing out the window at a passing car.

"The deacon's board met that same night and we were on the road within 24 hours. Apparently there was something about bright green that really bothered them. Danged if I knew what it was."

Hank was still smiling, and he remained quiet for a moment, relishing the image in his mind. Then he looked up and made eye contact with the pastor.

"Ya know, Josh. I don't think I've ever talked this way with a pastor before. You just don't seem to fit the stereotype I have on men of the cloth. You seem . . . well . . . very real."

Josh smiled.

"Well, I'm not surprised. The last church that fired me said the same thing, in a manner of speaking."

A rare, playful look came into Hank's eyes.

"In fact, I think that when the sunlight strikes you just right, you seem . . . almost lifelike."

It was Josh's turn to laugh, and then the two men talked for the next hour about everything: life, religion, philosophy, nine-eleven, even about some of the more eccentric characters in Freidham Ridge. But not once after that did Hank ever feel uncomfortable in the presence of Pastor Josh McCullen, and over the next several weeks, they got to be good friends and had many personal conversations. By December, Hank and his four kids had become part of the landscape at Freidham Ridge Community Church. They blended right in.

Chapter 13

Angela pulled into her Aunt's driveway just as the moon was peeking up over the horizon. She turned off the engine and sat there behind the wheel watching the moon's slow and silent ascent. All the way here, she'd been wrestling with the rightness and wrongness of her decision, and once she had even stopped the car and turned around. But now, in the faint light of the rising orange, harvest moon, she realized that coming back home had been the best thing to do.

She saw her Aunt Millie run out of the old farmhouse in her house-coat.

"Angela!"

Angela smiled. Yes, Aunt Millie was glad she came. She opened the car door and ran to meet the woman who had raised her like a mother. They embraced amidst the gravel in the driveway and cried without shame. All the while, the moon shone brightly, rising like a shining star, approving of every smile and every tear they shed.

§ § §

"Forgive me Father, for I have sinned. It has been 42 years since my last confession."

Hank squirmed on his knees, and shifted his bottom to a more comfortable position. He felt cramped and out of place in the tiny confession booth. Then he heard the man on the other side turn his body toward him in interest, and thought he heard the bumping of glass, but couldn't be sure.

"My son, why so long since your last confession?"

Hank peered through the little window, trying to get a good look at the other man's face, but the screen jaded his view. The Father's voice was old, very old - very old and very raspy - like the broad blade of a bastard file and the sound of metal on metal. Hank felt a little intimidated by the gravelly tone of the old man's voice.

"Well, because I'm 42 and this is my first confession. I've never been in a Catholic church before. This is something I saw on TV when I was a kid. I was raised a Baptist."

For a moment the old man was silent.

"I see. Then why not go to a Baptist church? Perhaps you would feel more comfortable there."

Hank shook his head.

"No Father, the Baptists I grew up with don't have confession. Hardly believe in forgiveness as near as I can tell. At least not for divorced people. They simply judge you and send you straight off to hell. Do not pass go; do not collect grace, they just shoot you straight on down!"

The old man smiled behind the screen.

"I see. Well, then, in that case, I am ready to hear your confession, and I promise not to judge you too harshly."

Hank bowed his head into his hands as if praying and began to confess his sins to the unseen stranger beside him.

"Well, okay, sometimes I have unclean thoughts, you know, about women and all. I'm a bachelor, a single dad, and I'm not sure it's possible not to think about the sex thing sometimes. But I try not to dwell on it at least. I know I was supposed to keep track of how many times, but after a while you lose count, and you see I didn't really anticipate coming here, especially being raised a Baptist and all. I'm not sure, but I think that's one of the main differences between Protestants and Catholics: All of us enjoy sin, but the Protestants won't admit to it and the Catholics just do it so they can brag about it later on in confession."

The man behind the screen smiled again, but maintained a serious tone.

"That's alright, my son. Please continue."

"Okay. There was that, plus some lying, a little stealing, mostly pencils and things when I was a kid. Once I cheated on my timecard at work. I murdered my wife. I made 50 dollars one year that I didn't pay taxes on. Plus I . . . ."

The raspy voice interrupted him.

"I'm sorry. What was that last one again?"

"Tax evasion?"

"No, no. The one before that!"

"Murdering my wife?"

"Yeah, that one. You murdered your wife?"

Hank lifted his head up.

"Yes. I shot her in the head with a pistol six times. I guess I would have shot her more, but that's all the gun held was six bullets."

The old man peeked through the screen window to get a better look at his confessor.

"Why did you kill your wife?"

"Well, I didn't actually kill her."

"You shot her in the head six times and she lived?"

Hank shook his head.

"No, no Father, you don't understand. I didn't really shoot her. I only imagined that I shot her. But according to the Bible to do something in your heart is just as bad as actually doing it."

The old man leaned back away from the window and breathed a sigh of relief.

"I see. So why did you imagine shooting your wife?"

Hank took a deep breath and continued.

"Well, I came home from the newspaper and found her in bed with my boss. They were naked, and they didn't have any clothes on at all, and they were having sex, penetration and everything right there in our bed. My four kids were right in the next room. I couldn't believe it! Is it okay to talk about sex in here?"

The old man chuckled under his breath.

"You may speak your heart in the confession booth, even about sex. I'm glad you didn't really shoot your wife. What happened after you walked in on them?"

Hank leaned back against the wood.

"Well, I was pretty shocked at first, so I couldn't do anything for a few seconds except stand there and stare. I trusted her so much. I knew she drank too much, but I never dreamed she'd betray me like that. I felt so hurt that I couldn't talk. I couldn't even move."

Hank rubbed his wet eyes with one hand.

"Yes, my son, it must have hurt a lot."

"It did, Father. I just stood there for a few seconds with my mouth hanging open. Then Caroline started yelling at me, screaming at me to get out. She said she was divorcing me, that she no longer loved me. She said that it was all my fault because I didn't make her feel loved enough. She stood up on the bed naked, and yelled all this to me while my boss put his pants on. She told me to get out so they could finish, and I guess that's when I cracked."

"You cracked?"

"Yes Father. I reached over to the dresser drawer where my wife kept her pistol. I took it out and aimed it right at her head. She just kept on screaming and screaming, and she wouldn't shut up. I guess that's when I fired the first shot."

"So you did shoot her."

"No, I shot the wall behind her. I could never shoot her, Father! I don't even like guns. They terrify me! I just wanted to scare her so she would shut up. But it didn't work. She just kept swearing at me, so I pumped a few rounds over my boss's head and then a few more into the waterbed. By then the gun was empty, and they both ran out into the hall screaming. My wife was still naked. The kids woke up and they were crying. Needless to say I haven't slept on a waterbed since."

The old man leaned toward the window again.

"So no one ever died? You never shot anyone?"

Hank brushed some more water away from his eyes.

"No sir. I never hurt anyone."

Hank buried his face into his hands again.

"My boss fired me the very next day."

"Ouch! That must have hurt. Losing your wife and your job at the same time."

Hank answered as if ashamed.

"Father I used to be so strong, so independent. People looked up to me, respected me. They liked me. I liked me! I don't know what happened. I wish I did, but I just don't know what went wrong with me. My confidence is gone."

The old man interrupted.

"Well, I'm very sorry. So how long ago did this happen, my son?"

"Almost three years ago, sir."

"And where have you been since then?"

"I moved away to this little hick town about 20 miles from here. I divorced Caroline and got custody of the kids. They live with me now."

The old man pressed his face up against the wooden screen.

"How did that happen? Usually the mother gets the kids."

Hank wiped his nose on his sleeve before answering.

"She's an alcoholic."

The man nodded knowingly.

"I see. I'm familiar with the problem. Come closer my son."

Hank obeyed him.

"My son. Your sins are not against God, and they are not against your former wife. They are against you alone. You are a child of God, and you have forgotten yourself. You have forgotten your own worth. You have forgotten the value that God breathes into every man, woman and child at birth."

He hesitated, as if deep in momentary thought.

"So now you must take measures to ensure your own happiness. You must forgive yourself for your past mistakes. Start over fresh, right now, tonight."

The old man stopped and thought for a moment before continuing.

"That's right, you must love yourself. Stop this self loathing. You must start a new life, a happier one. Right now, while you still can."

Hank leaned back away from the screen.

"I don't know if I can Father. Women scare me now. And . . . I just can't bring myself to . . . you know."

"Can't bring yourself to do what? Are you talking about sex again?"

Hank hesitated a moment before blurting it out.

"No, not that! I can't bring myself to trust them! I can't trust women anymore, even when they've given me no reason not to. I just can't do it! Every time I start to feel close to a woman, I start thinking that they're cheating on me. It drives me crazy! I hate it!"

The man across from him nodded.

"Hmmm, I see. Well, I'm no therapist, so I won't comment on that.

It's just my job to issue your penance and to absolve your sins. Are you ready to receive your penance my son?"

Hank looked through the window, but couldn't hold the man's shadowed gaze.

"Oh, I suppose so. Never had a penance before. I'm, not sure what to expect."

The old man laughed softly.

"Well, don't be afraid. There's a first time for everything I suppose. Sit up straight and take it like a man. Are you ready?"

Hank straightened his back and leaned hard against the wall. He nodded his head.

"I can't hear your head nod son."

"Yes sir. I'm ready."

"This is your penance: to be a good father to your children, to forgive your ex-wife and show her kindness, and to find a woman you can love and trust and be happy with. When you have completed this penance, your sins will be absolved."

Hank looked wide-eyed over at the black screen.

"What! That could take years! I thought maybe I could just say "Hail Mary" or something like that. That's what happened on TV!"

"This isn't television. This is real life. Bless you my son. Go with God."

The screen slid shut.

Hank sat there for a moment, disappointed.

"Hello?"

But no one answered, and the window remained closed, separating him from absolution. Hank bowed his head in deep despair.

"God. Help me! I'm lonely. Please help me!"

Hank's prayer floated slowly up through the roof of the booth, and out into space. After taking a moment to regain his composure, Hank dried his eyes and got up and walked out of the booth, into the high-ceilinged cathedral and then back out to the cold, deserted street.

§ § §

Back inside the confession booth, behind the closed window, the old man sat nestled with his bottle of cheap wine. Catholics were crazy, leaving a nice warm building like this unlocked and unguarded all night long. He came here sometimes to escape the cold, and sometimes just for fun. Slowly, he uncapped the bottle and raised it toward the heavens.

"Thank God for crazy Catholics."

He drank deeply from the bottle, communing with God, remembering the blood of Christ.

Chapter 14

The wind was blowing hard when Hank walked out of the cathedral, and it whipped down into the space between his collar and his neck. He pulled the hood up over his head and tied the strings together, then he shoved his hands into his pockets as he walked down the sidewalk. He couldn't believe what he was doing. He should be home with his kids, but sometimes, he just got in these lonely, melancholy moods and he had to get out and get away. They hit him about once a month, usually on a Friday night when he knew all the other single people were going out on dates. That's when the loneliness seemed to overwhelm him the most. Usually, he could throw himself into his kids, and the service and selflessness of single parenthood left him no time for his own feelings. But sometimes . . . sometimes he couldn't hold the wolves at bay . . . sometimes, the lone wolves ate him alive from the inside out. And that's when he had to get away. On those nights, he left his kids with Freida, telling her he was going to see a movie in Bentley, and sometimes he did actually see a movie. But not tonight.

There was a wino leaning up against an apartment building, and he leaned forward when he saw Hank.

"Hey buddy. Got a dollar? I haven't eaten in 2 days."

Hank knew he was lying, but he stopped nonetheless and fished a dollar out of his pocket and held it out to the man.

"Hey, thanks buddy. God will bless you for this. I'll pray for you. God listens to me you know. He talks to me all the time."

Hank walked away unbelieving. But what if the man wasn't lying? What if he really needed food? That same question of "what if" had nagged him all through the divorce proceedings over three years ago. What if Caroline had been right? What if it really was his fault? What if, what if, what if - the dreadful what ifs, and should have dones. What if I'd done this? I should have done that. It had been in his power to heal her alcoholism if he'd only loved her better; if he'd only spent more time at home; if he'd only been more romantic, more emotional, more intimate. If he'd only been more of a man, then she would never have sought out affection from someone else. That's what she had told him.

A bar loomed up ahead and Hank hesitated at the entrance. There was no point in going in. He knew from experience that nothing good would happen in there. But some unseen force tucked at him. The sirens of his loneliness beckoned, and he walked through the cold, heavy, wooden door.

Once inside he went over to the corner table. No one was sitting there because it was so isolated, but that's why Hank chose it, why he indeed sought out the solace of the empty space. He was in one of those strange, ambivalent moods where his heart ached for company, yet . . . somehow, he just couldn't bring himself to face another human. Sometimes he confused himself. He had . . . issues.

When he'd been a kid, Hank had loved to climb way up on the rooftop of their house and look down onto his community, catching them unaware. He had always been content to experience relationships from a distance, to merely look on as an observer, passively watching the things of life: the dances, the rituals, the loves and lives and lingering hopes of everyone he'd watched. Maybe that's why he'd become a journalist; it was easier to write about other people's lives than to live your own. Perhaps that's why Caroline had left him as well. Maybe she didn't like being watched from a distance, being worshipped, admired, exalted like a holy, untouchable deity. But, at the time, Hank had been incapable of anything deeper. He'd been wrapped up in his work, too busy trying to win the Pulitzer prize.

The low-ceilinged room was dimly lit, and the smoke that filled it drifted up towards the stained ceiling tiles where it hit and then bounced back down like curling, rolling fog in a big city fall. Hank didn't like that about bars. Actually, he didn't like anything about bars. He didn't even like the big city anymore. He'd only come here tonight to commiserate in anonymity. That was probably the hardest part for him about Freidham Ridge. There were no secrets; there was no hiding. If he walked into the Mudhen Grille looking sad, then every person he passed would stop and ask him what was wrong.

Thank God for Freida – loyal, frumpy Freida. She was watching the kids until late, so that he could go out and feel sorry for himself. His newspaper was doing better. Circulation was way up since nine-eleven. Perhaps he should give her a raise.

The waitress saw him and trudged on over. She wore thick-soled tennis shoes and a dirty white skirt that came up well above her knees. Hank remembered her from last month. She was in her forties, and Hank intuitively felt sorry for her.

"Whatch ya want honey?"

Hank looked over at her and smiled softly.

"Bourbon please. Bring the bottle."

She looked at him a little surprised and snapped her gum.

"Really? You look more like a Grape Nehi kinda guy. Isn't that what you drank last time you come in here?"

Hank looked up impatiently.

"No! Last time I had a Coke."

He squirmed in his chair before completing the full truth.

"It was the time before that I had the Grape Nehi."

The waitress chuckled to herself.

"I thought so. We don't get a lot of Grape Nehi drinkers in here. Especially on Friday night."

Hank then turned his attention to the people dancing on the floor. He envied all of them, with their ability to stand in a crowd and block out all else except the music and the feel and flow of their own bodies as they moved across the floor in a feverish act of self-fulfillment. They were oblivious to all else save their own passions and emotions. The waitress walked away.

Hank's parents had never let him dance, had indeed never allowed him to attend a dance during high school, and he would always resent that. Indeed, his feet would not and could not dance, and he felt too old to force them to learn now. But, just for tonight, he was here to watch them, to admire them, to encourage them with his jealousy, and perhaps absorb a bit of their passion and confidence. It was his only way of connecting - his only way of sharing the loneliness. At least he was sharing something with someone.

Caroline had loved to dance, but Hank had been afraid to learn. Perhaps if he had learned to dance, she would not have . . . . He let the sentence die unended. Finally, the waitress came back with his Bourbon, and set it down on the Formica table.

"You don't have to drink it all if you don't want. I won't charge you for what's left over. Just don't drink out of the bottle."

Hank looked up at her. There were wrinkles around her eyes, the kind not caused by age. Hank tried to smile, but could tell by the look on her face that he'd failed. On a normal day, he would have her laughing in 5 seconds flat. But not today; it just wasn't in him. She walked over to another table.

The Daddy part of him wondered about his kids. Were they okay? Were they crying? Did they need him? Should he call? Should he run home and forget about this silly self-indulgent night on the town? He wasn't having any fun anyways. Maybe he needed a psychiatrist? The priest sure wasn't any help. One by one, those thoughts slowly floated away like the cigarette smoke around him, and his mind moved on.

Suddenly, he was reminded of a scene from the movie "It's a Wonderful Life" where Clarence the Angel had written in a book, "No man is a failure who has friends." And then it suddenly occurred to him – he had no friends.

Yes! That was it! That was the reason for his loneliness. It was, indeed, merited! He couldn't think of a single adult who truly loved him, maybe not even one who liked him, except perhaps for Freida. Well, no, Josh McCullen liked him too. Must be something else. He just couldn't figure things out in his monthly funk.

Hank took a drink of the Bourbon and coughed. Cigarette smoke and alcohol - they both made him wheeze. He saw a woman at the bar in a short, black, leather skirt and stared at her crossed legs. She looked back at him and smiled. Hank turned away involuntarily and took another drink. Just looking at the softness of her enhanced his loneliness, enfleshed it, breathed into it, gave it life, and feeling, and with the feeling . . . a multitude of pain.

"You kiddin' me? My divorce was ten times worse than that!"

The word "divorce" caught Hank's ear and pulled his attention to the table directly to his right where two men were talking.

"I don't believe it! What could be worse than being left for another man?"

Hank nodded his head involuntarily. Nothing could be worse. He knew that firsthand.

The man's laugh roared above the clamor of the crowded bar. Then he grew silent, waiting, building the suspense as the skinny man scooted his chair up closer to the table. The big man took a drink and then wiped the foam off his beard with his sleeve.

"Dora and I were married for 23 years. Twenty-three very long and very happy years. Never once did she ever let on that she was dissatisfied. We never fought, and we never disagreed. We raised four beautiful children together. It was the perfect marriage. We were the perfect family, or so I thought."

Hank leaned over toward the man's voice, wanting to get closer, wanting to hear every word. The reporter in him was tempted to take out a pen and paper and take notes, but he just listened.

"Then two years ago, after the last of the kids went away to college, I came home and my key no longer fit in the lock of the front door. I was shocked. I had no idea what was going on. I could see Dora peeking out at me from the living room window and I waved at her and yelled, but she just closed the drape, and that's the last time I ever saw her."

The other man, the skinny one, interrupted him.

"What in the world are you talking about? That's crazy! What do you mean you never saw her again?"

The big man nodded.

"As I was standing on the porch, this pencil-necked guy in a suit walked up the porch steps and handed me some papers. He walked away and I opened the envelope. They were divorce papers."

The short, skinny man interrupted again.

"The ultimate in "Dear John" letters."

He shook his head solemnly from side to side.

They both took another drink, and the man continued his story.

"Anyways, I was mad as a hornet. I wound up and punched that solid steel security door as hard as I could. Shattered my hand to pieces. I was so mad though I couldn't feel the pain. I dented the door, though, a little bit anyway."

His drinking partner nodded his head in approval.

"That's good. At least you dented the door."

"When the police got there, I was throwing my body up against it over and over again. But you know that thing just wouldn't give. She'd had me install it the week before along with a home security system. I do good work ya know."

The skinny man nodded and then looked down into his beer.

"Man, she knew all along she was going to divorce you. She planned it out!"

"The police had no idea who I was, and I didn't have my wallet. That morning before work I couldn't find it. Dora mailed it to me several weeks later. She had it all planned out, right down to the last detail. I was arrested and thrown in jail for punching my own door. She had a restraining order put on me too. It all makes sense now. She'd been planning that divorce for over 5 years."

The big man took a long swallow of his beer.

"I never had a prayer. Dora was the best."

The other man nodded his head.

"No kidding. I feel lucky next to you. Why did she say she divorced you?"

"She didn't."

"What?"

"She sent me a letter and said that she didn't love me anymore, that she didn't even like me. She said she felt like a prostitute living with me because she had no feelings for me at all. She said it was nothing personal, just that she didn't like who I was. A few months later I found out she'd left me for another woman."

The other man whistled.

"What! A woman! You mean she turned to the dark side? Ouch! That's gotta leave a mark!"

The big man slouched over the table and nodded in shame.

"Yep! I drove her into the arms of another woman."

The skinny man shook his head in disgust.

"At least I've got someone to blame, someone to strangle in my dreams. I'm so glad my Sally had the decency to fall in love with another man. I guess she wasn't so bad after all."

He took a drink of his beer.

"Yep. That Sally made a pretty mean meatloaf."

The two men grew quiet, and Hank leaned back over his table, contemplating all they'd said.

"Sound familiar, does it?"

Hank looked up and saw the waitress standing there with a glass of dark liquid.

"I hear those same stories a million times a night. They're all different, but they're always the same. I spotted you the first time you came in. I knew it was a woman that done ya."

She set the glass down on the table on a funny little napkin.

"Grape Nehi. Just in case you change your mind about the bourbon. It's on me this time."

She smiled sadly.

"So what's your sob story?"

Hank shook his head and looked away. She laughed lightly.

"Oh come on fella. You wouldn't be here if you didn't have a sob story. You were gonna drink that whole bottle of Bourbon, and you don't even drink. I can see right through ya."

She sat down beside him, and Hank leaned away from her.

"Mind if I sit down? My feet are killing me. I hate this job!"

She turned back to Hank.

"So spit it out. What's the problem?"

Hank looked at her. Oh well, none of this night was proceeding as planned, so why should the bar-room scene be any different?

"I'd really prefer not to talk about it, if you don't mind."

She laughed out loud.

"You are so incredibly polite! I just love the way you talk. Even when you're mad, you still force yourself to be patient and nice."

She smiled and reached over for his bourbon glass.

"Aw, come on now! I'm studying to be a bartender. Humor me! Besides, what difference does it make? You'll never get over her until you talk about it, and I'm willing to listen. Be smart. You can either tell me now, or you can pay some shrink in a tweed suit with a pipe a hundred dollars an hour. It's your money fella!"

She took a sip of his bourbon.

"Besides, you don't belong here. You just don't fit in. All these other guys are jerks. I bet you never hurt another person in your whole life, except maybe yourself."

Hank remembered the words of the priest. "Your sins are not against God, they are against you alone."

He looked at her eyes; they were bloodshot, bloodshot and old, older than the rest of her.

"How long's it been?"

He hesitated a moment, and then came to his decision.

"Three years."

The woman whistled.

"Wow! My old man stopped grieving over me when the door hit him on his way out."

A faraway look settled over her eyes.

"I haven't seen him since."

Hank looked away from her. He shouldn't have said anything. He didn't want to encourage her.

"You're not alone fella. Every last man that comes in here has been through the same thing. People just can't get along anymore. There's no commitment, no loyalty, no trust."

The words pierced Hank's soul. No commitment! No loyalty! No trust!

"I wish it wasn't true. But it is. It's the truth. And the truth can be so hard to swallow nowadays."

She took another drink of bourbon, then looked back at him. He could feel her stare, probing into him, looking for things he wanted hidden, deep, dark, festering things that hadn't seen the light of day in years. He slouched down in his chair, and she laughed.

"Oh, forget it. You're not ready yet are you?"

She set the glass back down on the table.

"Too bad. You're kinda cute."

She stood up and walked away. Hank looked after her again, and then down at the lipstick stain on the edge of the wet glass. Suddenly he wasn't thirsty for bourbon anymore. He took a few minutes to finish his grape Nehi, then he got up, paid his bill, and left through the cold, wooden door.

The waitress watched Hank leave from across the room and nodded her head in approval. She didn't notice the two men beside her, the old man in the wheelchair, and the tall one, dressed in white.

She smiled to herself. Every once in a while she did something right. But, then, even a busted clock was right twice a day. Then she returned to delivering cold beer, while the black-skirted woman at the bar left with a man who liked to dress up in lady's underclothes.

Chapter 15

"The United States and its allies continued to close in around the fortified mountain strongholds of Al-Qaeda forces near Tora Bora today, while U.S. forces continued its relentless bombing in the Malawa Mountains. Meanwhile, in southern Afghanistan, United States Marines seal the escape routes out of Kandahar. In a concerted effort to capture Osama Bin Laden, the Pakistani military deployed helicopter gun ships and troops along the Afghan border."

"In related events, the Washington Post revealed today that the United States has, in its possession, a videotape in which Osama Bin Laden describes the damage to the World Trade Center as being much greater than he had hoped for. In the tape, Bin Laden praises Allah for the success of the attack and uses language indicating that he was familiar with the planning of the attacks. Bin Laden explained in the tape how he had expected only the top of the World Trade Center to collapse. He also indicated in the tape that more destruction is coming."

Angela had never been one to listen to the news, but now she couldn't tear herself away from it. She had become a regular news hound, and she rarely missed an hourly update, either on the radio or on the Fox News Channel.

Her Aunt Millie had become concerned with her niece's obsession, but Angela just didn't know how to explain it to her in any way that she might understand. It had become personal to her, and she was involved on a firsthand level. Indeed, she had been there when it had all started on nine-eleven, and she was determined to follow it through to the end. The news stories were more than just words to her; they were alive, because she had been there amidst the smoke and ash and rubble and ruin of the twin towers when they were hit and while they burned and melted and fell to the ground. Without realizing it, she had become a child of ground zero.

The hourly news broadcast ended and the music on her car radio came back on. She reached down and turned it off just as she pulled into the tiny parking lot of the Iroquois County Gazette. She couldn't believe she was doing this, and she really didn't understand her overwhelming desire to apply for a job as Advertising Director of this little dog and pony show, but she was doing it nonetheless. For some strange reason, she just felt like she was supposed to, like the suggestion was coming from someone greater than herself. So, after a week of trying to talk herself out of it, here she was.

Her car came to a stop on the gravel drive, and, for a moment, she sat there, wondering if she'd overdressed. Then she got out and walked through the front door, letting it slam shut behind her. There was no turning back now.

§ § §

"In related events, the Washington Post revealed today that the United States has, in its possession, a videotape in which Osama Bin Laden describes the damage to the World Trade Center as being much greater than he had hoped for."

The radio blared out the news while Hank walked over to Freida's desk.

"In the tape, Bin Laden praises Allah for the success of the attack and uses language indicating that he was familiar with the planning of the attacks. Bin Laden explained in the tape how he had expected only the top of the World Trade Center to collapse. He also indicated in the tape that more destruction is coming."

The newscast ended and an older song by Hank Williams filled the air. "Now tell me Hank why do ya drink?"

Freida had gone out for mid-morning donuts, and Hank, taking advantage of her absence, had finally given in to the chronic desire to try on her gas mask. It was in her top left drawer as always, and it slid easily onto his head. Hank cinched down the straps and then covered the filters with both palms the way he'd read in the instructions. He breathed in deeply to make sure he had a good seal, just like he used to do when he still scuba dived.

That was easy enough. Then he saw Freida's pistol lying next to the gas mask case in the same drawer. It was like forbidden candy to a kid – so alluring, so tempting – he had to, just pick it up, just touch it, only once. It wouldn't hurt. He would be careful. It couldn't hurt to just touch it.

Hank reached down and touched the dark blue gun metal slide of the big pistol. It was cold and smooth. Just then, the bell over the door rang and Angela Benning walked in and strode confidently up to the counter. Hank jerked his hand back like a kid getting caught in the cookie jar. He looked up and saw Angela. His first thought was – she's beautiful – followed quickly by his second thought, I'm wearing a gas mask.

Despite the adrenaline coursing through his veins, Hank forced himself to remain calm. Slowly, he reached down and closed Freida's desk drawer. Then, with mock pomp and confidence, he strode on over to the counter.

"Yes, mam. How may I help you today?"

Hank's voice was muffled inside the mask, and was hard for Angela to understand. That, plus she didn't quite know how to respond. As Marketing Director for a major corporation in New York City, she had helped to broker multi-million dollar contracts, negotiated six-figure salaries, and wined and dined with CEOs and politicians from all over the country. But none of that had quite prepared her to be alone with a lunatic in a gas mask. She was amazed at how natural it all seemed. But then, this was Freidham Ridge. Why not?

She quickly regained her composure and pressed on with her agenda. She was in business mode now.

"Yes, I'm here to apply for your advertising position, and I'd like to speak with Mr. Simmons please."

She tried to look inside the man's mask at his eyes, but the plastic lenses were fogging up quickly. Without missing a beat, the man nodded.

"Yes Mam. I'll go see if he's in."

Angela looked on in amazement as the man turned away and walked into what appeared to be a cleaning closet. She hesitated before lifting her briefcase up onto the counter and taking out a copy of her resume. She heard a broom fall and then the clutter of a mop bucket from inside the cleaning room. And then, as she was deciding whether or not to turn around and leave, a man walked out of the closet and on over to the counter.

"Well hi. How ya doing? I'm Hank Simmons, owner of the Gazette. My janitor tells me you're here regarding the Advertising Director's position?"

She nodded her head slowly, wanting to speak her mind, but still not sure what had exactly transpired.

"Does he always wear a gas mask?"

Hank hesitated a moment and then laughed out loud.

"Oh, you mean that mask he was wearing?"

Angela nodded. Hank laughed nervously.

"No, no, no. That would be crazy. Only crazy people walk around wearing gas masks. He only does that once in a while. You know, special occasions when he's working with toxic cleaning fluids. We've got a pretty nasty clog in the bathroom and he's been working on it all morning. He's just about got it licked though. Nothing to worry about."

Angela cocked her head slightly to one side. Hank saw her skepticism, so he renewed his deceptive effort.

"Yes, Jake's more than just a janitor around here. Why I don't know what I'd do without him. He's my right hand, and my left hand. Why, without him, this paper couldn't even run efficiently."

Angela smiled for the first time all day.

"Wow, that's quite a janitor you have there. Maybe you should just put him in charge of advertising as well. I bet he'd do a great job! Waxing floors, fixing toilets, selling ads!"

Then she looked down at the counter as if trying to think of a way out of this clumsy situation. None came to mind.

"Mr. Simmons. Is it just coincidence that you and the janitor wear the same clothes?"

Hank's forehead began to perspire, and against his wishes, he reached up with his sleeve to wipe it away. He was busted and he knew it. Might as well go all the way.

"That's right. We all wear the same clothes around here. Part of the journalistic uniform code you might say. Did you know that recent studies have shown that people are more open and honest when being interviewed by journalists wearing faded blue jeans, tennis shoes, and Sesame Street t-shirts?"

Angela bit her lower lip to keep from laughing.

"Mr. Simmons, I can still see the lines on your face where the gas mask was touching your skin."

Hank's face turned red.

"Oh. I didn't know that. This is indeed clumsy now isn't it."

He was silent a moment. Then he looked down at the counter.

"How do you suggest we proceed?"

Angela thought a moment before speaking. On the one hand, it would be incredibly easy to manipulate this man. He had set the groundwork for her already, and she definitely had the upper hand in any salary negotiations that might ensue. He would probably give her a job just so she wouldn't repeat this story to anyone. On the other hand, there was something about him that she liked. He was kind of a cross between a Border Collie and a game-show host. Without trying to, he had made her want to stick around just to see what might happen next. She made her decision.

"Well, Mr. Simmons, pretending is great fun and I really have enjoyed this little game, but I believe the employee-employer relationship is based on mutual trust and respect. So I think we should just start over. How about if I turn around and walk out for 10 seconds. Then I'll walk back in and we can try it again. Agreed?"

Hank felt totally humiliated and embarrassed, but he saw the look of compassion in her eyes. So, without hesitating, he looked up from the counter and nodded his head.

"Mam, if you did that, I would be eternally grateful. In fact, I'd even take you out for a steak dinner and try to explain what in the world just happened to us. As it is, I may be in therapy for the next 10 years trying to understand why I was wearing a gas mask to work in the first place."

Angela laughed out loud for the first time since nine-eleven.

"Well, then, let's save you all that time and money for therapy and steak. Besides, I'm really more of a French fries and hamburger kind of gal. Shall we head on over to the Mudhen and talk about this Advertising Director's position?"

Hank smiled inside. Barring some unseen malady like schizophrenia or dementia, this woman already had the job.

Hank turned his back. He listened to her footsteps, then heard the bell ring as she left. He waited 10 seconds – the bell over the door rang again, and when he turned around, she was there, brand new, at her best, though a little overdressed, and, this time, he no longer wore a gas mask.

She smiled. He smiled.

Chapter 16

"Bottom line is, I never should have married her. I knew it was a bad match from the start. I should have questioned her drinking more than I did. I should have sensed her wandering eyes. I should have sensed a lot of things I suppose. At best I was incredibly naïve. At worst, very, very foolish. At any rate, the final outcome is always the same. I ignored all those yellow flags and I shot myself in the foot and it caused a lot of pain. For me, and for my kids."

Hank had no idea why he was spilling his guts to this woman. He'd only met her an hour ago, and already she knew his entire life history.

"We've all made mistakes Mr. Simmons. You can trust me on that one."

She smiled when she spoke, and Hank could tell she was sincere and that she was not judging him.

"Call me Hank, please. We're not real formal around here. It's not like in the city where you can hide things and no one is the wiser. Out here everyone knows everything about everybody. I think there must be something in the water out here that makes people want to talk too much."

"I know. I was born and raised here, remember? Do you think you're talking too much, Hank?"

The question reminded Hank of the waitress at the big city bar. She had tried to get him to open up and he'd refused, so why was he spilling his guts to this woman? There was so much about life that he no longer understood. His face turned red, and he looked down at the table top. Angela wasn't sure why, but for some reason, she found that incredibly endearing and attractive.

"I don't know. I've been needing to talk to someone about these things for a long time I guess. I'm not sure why I'm opening up to you about it."

Angela laughed out loud.

"Well, Hank, maybe you're just tired of hiding behind that mask."

Looking up again, he saw the playful twinkle in her pretty, green eyes, and they both laughed out loud together.

"You must've thought I was a total idiot when you saw me in that gas mask. You handled it well though."

Angela signaled with a nod of her head to the waitress. Ruthie came over and filled both their coffee cups.

"Good to have you back in town, Angela. Glad you made it through nine-eleven okay. We were worried about you for a while. Your Aunt had you on the prayer list until we knew you were okay."

Hank watched as a sudden cloud came over the fair skin of Angela's face. She nodded to Ruthie, but said nothing. Ruthie wandered off to fill other coffee cups, leaving Hank to wonder. His reporter's instinct kicked into overdrive and he asked the obvious question.

"So you must've been in New York City on nine-eleven. What was it like?"

The question made Angela squirm in the cheap, dining room chair of the Mudhen, and Hank immediately regretted asking the question.

"I'm sorry. Should I not have asked that?"

"Don't be silly, Hank. You're a reporter. You had to ask. It's pathological I suppose. Besides, like you said, you can't hide anything in this town. You'd probably find out sooner or later anyways."

Now Hank was curious as to what could be so discomfiting about her whereabouts on nine-eleven. It had become a normal topic of conversation within a few weeks after the bombing. In fact, he had run a special nine-eleven issue and had interviewed quite a few people about it.

"Why don't you go first, Hank? Where were you on nine-eleven? What were you doing?"

Yes, that was the question he'd asked everyone else. Hank nodded. He was curious, but he wouldn't push her. He remembered it like it was only yesterday, and he doubted that he would ever forget it.

"I had just dropped all my kids off to school that morning. It's quite a job you know, dropping off all those kids. They keep me busy."

Hank hesitated, but Angela encouraged him with a friendly nod. He was a good man. She could tell that.

"My first thought was disbelief, then shock, then outrage, then absolute terror and fear for my kids. I drove back to school and got my kids right away. I know most reporters probably wouldn't do it that way, but I couldn't help myself. I had to see them and make sure they were safe. After that, we went home and they played while I sat glued to the TV screen. I worked at home all day. That night, I slept on the floor in the hallway between the kid's rooms."

Angela was interested in his story, but Hank stopped talking. His mouth remained half open, but he said nothing, deep in thought, but speechless. She prodded him on.

"Why did you do that? Sleep in the hall I mean."

Hank shrugged his shoulders.

"I don't know. I couldn't sleep in my room. I was too far away from them. I just wanted to make sure they were safe. That's what dad's do. They keep their kids safe. They protect them and take care of them."

Angela was suddenly reminded of the old man at the hospital chapel.

What had he told her about fathers? “You will be given an opportunity to understand fatherhood. And then, your relationship with God can be restored.” Angela didn’t say anything. She couldn’t. A tear welled up in her eye, and it wouldn’t go away. She wanted to talk, but the lump in her throat was huge and wouldn’t let any words pass by. She took a large swallow of her coffee to push the lump back down and burned her mouth in the process.

“That is so much nicer than my story, Hank. I was alone on nine-eleven, alone in my office. That’s about it. Not much of a story I’m afraid.”

Hank knew there was more, but he nodded in acceptance. This was the weirdest job interview he’d ever been through. Something told him this wasn’t going to be a normal employer-employee relationship. But then, nothing was really normal in Freidham Ridge, at least not “his” kind of normal.

“It wasn’t a good day to be alone. I’m sorry there was no one there for you.”

Angela could tell that Hank knew she was hiding things, but she didn’t care. It was really none of his business anyways. This was supposed to be a job interview, and here he was grilling her about her personal life. Angela knew her words were unfair even as she thought them, but she couldn’t help herself. This conversation had exceeded her comfort zone by miles, and she wanted to back away from the intimacy of that personal precipice.

“No, I suppose it wasn’t. But, I’m here now and ready to work for you if you want me.”

Hank thought a moment. She had some wounds. He recognized that. The father part of him wanted to put his arm around her and give her a reassuring squeeze, but the man part of him wanted to go even further. She was beautiful, witty, smart, and funny. He admired her long, dark brown hair for a moment. He liked the way it curled and draped over her shoulders. She was mysterious. He liked that. But he brushed all those feelings aside now and returned to business.

"Of course I want you, Angela. I'd be a fool not to."

Angela's pulse quickened at his words. Why had he chosen to say it that way? Hank looked down a moment, and she quickly brushed the lone tear from her eye before he looked back up again. Hank reached his right hand out over the table and extended it there for her.

"Do we have a deal, Ms. Benning?"

Angela smiled and slowly met his hand with her own. When they touched, a pleasant, tingling sensation ran up her arm and into her body. Hank felt the same sensation.

"Yes, Mr. Simmons. We have a deal."

Chapter 17

It was early November, and Freida was taking down the Halloween decorations while Hank worked on writing a story and Angela busied herself reading through old copies of the Gazette. Freida found it humorous, observing the two of them as they watched each other. First, Hank would look up and study Angela from a distance, then, just before Angela looked up to watch him, he would put his head back down just in time to keep from being caught. There was no doubt in her mind, if these two had any more chemistry between them, they'd be Louis Pasteur and Madame Curie.

However, Freida had mixed feelings about their new ivy league employee. On the one hand, Freida was jealous. Of course, she had long harbored her own secret desire for Hank, but she was realistic and perceptive enough to realize that he wasn't interested in her in that way. Another part of her, the stronger part she thought, wanted the best for Hank and his four children. They deserved it, and maybe Angela was the one for them. She would just have to wait and see. Freida prayed that the stronger part of her would win out.

Once she had put away the Halloween things, she brought out the box of Thanksgiving decorations and began to put them up all around the office. She loved the holidays.

"Do you need some help, Freida?"

Freida looked up and was surprised to see Angela suddenly standing beside her. She hadn't even seen her get up and walk over.

"No, it's okay. I can get it."

"Are you sure? I'd love to help out."

Freida hesitated and then made an important decision.

"I suppose I could use some help putting up this tabletop turkey ornament. I can never seem to get the crepe paper tail feathers to fan out the way they're supposed to."

Angela smiled.

"All right then. The turkey feathers are all mine."

Freida watched her smile again, and it was infectious. She'd never seen a woman smile so much.

"You know what bothers me most about this turkey bottom?"

Angela shook her head no.

"It looks too much like my own!"

Angela picked up the cardboard turkey and fiddled with it.

"I can relate to that. I eat an ounce of dark chocolate and I gain ten pounds right in my bottom. You ever wonder why that happens, Freida? Is there some cruel, higher force at work with the things we eat? Like a calorie god who immediately transforms all we eat into excess fat? And it always seems to multiply exponentially too. Life is so cruel that way. I never understood how one ounce of chocolate could magically transform itself into ten pounds of fat!"

Freida had no idea what exponentially meant, but she had to laugh regardless, just because of the way Angela said it.

"Oh yeah! Dark chocolate is the best! Why do they put so much fat in it if it's not good for you? Doesn't make any sense to me. I love a dark chocolate cake, with dark chocolate frosting and dark chocolate chips sprinkled on top."

Angela covered her mouth with her left hand as she laughed out loud at Freida's comment.

"I'm with you all the way girl! I get those endorphins pumping through my blood like a freight train and I'm happy as a lark. Dark chocolate is the best kind of comfort food. What else do you like?"

Hank chuckled under his breath. He doubted very much if Freida knew anything about endorphins. She was an expert on NASCAR, monster trucks, and deer hunting, but then, so was everyone else around these parts. He pretended not to be listening as the two women chattered back and forth at each other, about food, then clothes, then perfume, then Freida started talking about how old Zeke down at the Mudhen shamelessly passed gas, even in church.

Hank was impressed with the way Angela seemed to fit in at the office. She was equally comfortable in the ivy league and in redneck heaven. He took out a notebook and jotted down something in the margin. "Likes dark chocolate." That would turn out to be the first of many such notes.

He looked up at her again. This was only the first day, and already she was distracting his work. Once again, he looked back down at the empty paper and tried to focus on the story, but it was no good. He kept listening to their conversation. Finally he gave up and pushed his chair back away from the desk.

"Okay ladies. I'm heading over to the Mudhen for some lunch. Can I bring anything back for either of you?"

Freida shot back a reply without missing a beat.

"How about a six-pack and some chocolate-covered donuts?"

Hank hesitated in mid stride and raised his left eyebrow at her in mock condescension. He pretended to ignore her request.

"What about you Angela?"

Angela smiled.

"Sure. A 6-pack with a donut chaser sounds like a great lunch!"

Freida and Angela laughed out loud as Hank continued walking toward the door. The bell rang as he opened the door. He paused and looked back in. Angela glanced over and saw him staring. Their eyes locked for a moment and she smiled while Freida kept right on talking. Yes, he was a good man.

"Hey Hank. I was meaning to ask you. Do you know where my gas mask went? I can't find it anywhere. I could have sworn I left it in my desk drawer, but it's gone."

"I think I saw it in the cleaning closet, Freida."

Freida looked confused.

"What's it doing in there?"

Hank tore his eyes away from Angela and answered as he turned away from them.

"I saw Jake wearing it yesterday. Ask him."

Her brow furrowed when she heard his answer.

"Who's Jake?"

Angela covered her mouth to hide her growing smile, before answering for Hank.

"He's the make-believe janitor. He borrowed it yesterday to work with toxic cleaning fluids. I think he's done with it now though."

Angela winked discreetly at Freida.

"Yes, I don't know what we'd do without make-believe Jake. Why, he's Hank's right-hand, and his left hand too. Why I don't think we could even run the paper without him."

The door slammed behind Hank as he contemplated the age-old question: Why do women enjoy talking so much? He didn't understand it and doubted that no man did. He strongly suspected that his days of peace and quiet at the office were over forever. He pulled up his collar to fight off the cold as he walked to the car. Hank smiled, then he wrestled the car door shut behind him. It wasn't so bad though.

Chapter 18

"Load your firearms. All ready on the firing line? Commence firing!"

A score of gunshots rang out, and the sound of the blasts reverberated off the side of the hill before echoing back at the men and women standing on the firing line.

Angela, Freida, and Hank, were all on the far left end of the shooters, standing about 5 feet apart, and facing the same direction. Angela's .38 revolver barked out 5 times in rapid succession, and all 5 bullets hit the target, either close to, or inside the bulls eye. It was the same story with Freida and her large-framed 10 millimeter Glock semi-auto. The big gun's recoil jerked her hands upward with each shot, until all 10 rounds were launched toward the target. Freida smiled as she shot. She loved the feeling of power it gave her.

However, it was not so with Hank. He gripped the little .22 caliber Ruger revolver gingerly, as if it had teeth and it would bite him if he squeezed it too hard or offended it.

"Cease fire! Unload!"

Lance Stuart and Pastor Josh McCullen moved down the firing line, inspecting each firearm to make sure it was safe before sending all the shooters back to the staging area for their next round of instruction. They both reached Hank at the same time and hesitated. Lance looked at Josh, but quickly turned away, signaling that he should handle the problem shooter. They'd been shooting for over an hour, and Hank had yet to hit the target. Josh checked Hank's revolver for safety and asked him to remain on the line for a moment.

"Hey Rock, let me talk to you a minute."

"Lance Stuart and Josh walked off to one side where no one else could hear them and spoke in hushed tones. Everyone else watched from a distance or talked and joked with one another.

"This guy's the worst shot I've ever seen!"

Rock nodded his head in agreement.

"I've seen some bad shots in my time, but this guy couldn't hit the broad side of a barn – from the inside."

Josh tried to keep from smiling but couldn't. He enjoyed Rock's blunt way of putting it. It was true, despite all their attempts at teaching him, Hank Simmons couldn't hit the target to save his life. Josh ran down everything they'd tried so far.

"He's got a good grip, not flinching, good trigger squeeze, breath control seems okay. He understands sight alignment and sight picture pretty good."

Josh was stymied. Throughout the course of his life, he'd taught thousands of people to safely and properly shoot a pistol, but Hank was by far the most challenging.

"Got any ideas Rock?"

Rock shook his head and looked down at the dead, brown grass of late autumn.

"Beats me, Josh. It's almost like he doesn't even want to be here. He's either got bad eyesight, or firearm dyslexia, one of the two."

Josh smiled again at his humor, but once again refrained from laughing. This was serious.

"Well, I've never met the willing student I couldn't teach, and I'm not about to lose this one now."

Rock nodded.

"I'm with you all the way on that one. Hank's got 4 kids to protect. He's got more need to learn how to shoot than anyone else here."

A light went off in Josh's head and he smiled and nodded.

"You're right. You want to go back and talk to the rest of the class about proper utilization of cover and concealment while I give it another try with Hank?"

Rock quickly nodded in agreement and started walking back to the staging area. He was out of ideas. Josh hesitated a moment as he whispered a short prayer under his breath. Rock was probably the best pistol shooter that Josh had ever seen, and he had tried everything he knew to correct Hank's errant shooting, but it was to no avail. However, Josh wasn't willing to give up yet. He had an idea. He put on his happy, confident face and smiled as he strode over and stood by his student.

Angela and Freida watched from a distance with looks of obvious concern on both their faces. Freida shook her head helplessly from side to side.

"Man, he must really be embarrassed. He hasn't hit the target yet."

Angela removed her hearing protection and set the heavy blue muffs down on the staging table.

"Oh, it's not that bad Freida. He just hasn't caught on yet, that's all."

Freida laughed.

"Yeah, right. Everybody's caught on but him. Even Margaret Howard is hitting the paper and she's 87 years old! Hank's shooting the smallest gun here! That is so humiliating! Let's face it, Angela, our boss is no Clint Eastwood."

Angela took off her shooting glasses and nodded involuntarily. She was concerned for Hank at a deeper level. They had been spending a lot of time together the past two weeks, and she was really starting to become attached to him. They had even been attending church together, so when

Pastor McCullen had announced this personal protection class, it had only seemed right that they take it together. At first, she'd been confused by his hesitancy, but then, after a little female prodding he'd agreed to go with her and Freida. In fact, he was even going to write a human interest story about it, so that he could write it off on his taxes.

Lance Stuart was talking to them now, but she didn't hear him. Poor Hank. She felt bad for him.

"So Hank, why did you decide to take the class?"

Hank looked up from the ground and seemed to be impatient with the question.

"Why are you asking me for, Josh. You didn't ask anyone else that."

Josh nodded.

"That's because everyone else is hitting the target."

Hank kicked the dirt with the boot of his left foot.

"That's pretty cruel Pastor, considering I'm already being humiliated in front of half the town. It's bad enough that everybody calls me a city slicker behind my back. Now it'll just get worse."

Josh smiled sympathetically. He'd heard several people call him that at the Mudhen, but hadn't realized until now just how hard Hank was trying to fit in with the rest of them. He thought for a moment before speaking.

"Is that why you took the class, Hank. To try and fit in with everyone else?"

Hank fidgeted nervously with his pistol, and Josh responded out of habit as an instructor.

"Keep your finger off the trigger and the muzzle pointed in a safe direction please. Even when it's not loaded."

Hank nodded before answering.

"You know how I feel about firearms, Josh. I didn't even want to take the class, but Angela and Freida kept bugging me about it, so I felt like I had to in order to save face."

Josh smiled.

"Yes, Angela can be quite persuasive can't she?"

Hank's face turned a little pink and he looked back down at the dirt and dead grass on the ground. He shifted his feet back and forth nervously.

"Is it that obvious, Josh?"

"Oh yeah. But who cares what other people think. She's a good woman, and if I were single I'd be all over her like a chicken on a June Bug myself!"

Hank looked up and smiled.

"Really?"

Josh nodded. Good, he was starting to loosen up a bit. Hank had been wound tight all day long.

"But we can talk more about that later. For right now, why don't you tell me what's eating you, so I can get your bullets on target."

Hank looked back down at the ground, but didn't speak.

"Come on Hank! I'm your friend. Just spill it!"

When Hank looked back up, Josh saw the conflict etched all over his face. He looked like the little engine that wanted to, but couldn't. But Josh waited him out.

"I just don't think I could ever kill a man, Josh. That's all."

"But these aren't people. These are just paper plates we're shooting at. It's just a simulation."

"Maybe for you it is. But not me. All day long you've been talking about protecting yourself from crime and violence, and I suppose that's good for you and for Angela and Freida. But not for me."

Josh was silent for a moment. He didn't understand.

"Why not? You could be a victim of violent crime just as easy as the next guy. What are you going to do if someone sticks a knife in your face? Just let him kill you? You have to be prepared to defend yourself!"

Hank shook his head back and forth in disagreement.

"No I don't. I can just let him kill me. Doesn't the Bible say to turn the other cheek, love your enemies, do good to those who persecute you?"

Josh nodded. He thought about countering his argument with a dozen different scripture verses. He knew them all, but decided against it. He seemed to sense that this wasn't really about the Bible, and that quoting scripture would not win this argument for him. Besides, he could win this battle and still lose the war.

"Hank, is there any situation where you could take the life of another human being to save your own?"

Hank responded without hesitation by shaking his head no.

"Are you sure?"

Hank nodded.

"I'd rather die than take another life. I can't even shoot a squirrel."

Josh smiled resolutely.

"Well, okay then. That's it. I respect your views and won't try to convince you otherwise. Besides, if you can't pull the trigger, then you've got no business carrying a gun. It would become a liability instead of an asset."

Hank cocked his head slightly to one side. He wasn't quite sure he fully believed what Josh was telling him.

"Really?"

"Of course. I got no problem with a man who loves his fellow man so much that he would rather die than kill someone. Wouldn't be much of a pastor if I did, now would I?"

Hank smiled.

"I guess not."

Josh reached over and placed his hand on Hank's shoulder and gave it a reassuring squeeze.

"Go ahead and load your firearm up and let's try it one more time though just for appearances. After all, everyone's watching."

Hank laughed out loud for the first time that day, then he loaded 6 shots into the revolver he'd borrowed from Lance Stuart.

"Okay now. This time we'll try something different. Let's use a training technique called visualization. Here's the scenario. I want you to close your eyes and imagine this picture with me."

Hank nodded and closed his eyes.

"You and your four kids are in Bentley shopping at the Wal-Mart. On the way home, you stop out front to get gas. A man drives up and stops next to your car. He gets out and walks over to your car, opens the car door, removes Cathy from your car and places her inside his own car."

Hank's face clouded over, and the lines in his brow deepened like furrows in the ground.

"What are you doing, Josh? Don't even talk like that!"

But Josh interrupted him.

"Close your eyes!"

Hank hesitated before complying. Josh continued.

"Cathy is crying now. She's terrified. The other kids are screaming. Phillip is begging you to do something. 'Save my sister' he cries out. And Cathy begins screaming now too. 'Daddy, save me. Daddy, help me! Help me Daddy! I'm scared Daddy!'"

Josh's voice had crescendoed and everyone back at the staging area turned to watch. Angela looked on with concern.

"Stop him Hank! Save your daughter! The man has a gun and you have to save your daughter! What will he do to her if you can't protect her? What will happen to your daughter, Hank?"

Hank opened his eyes and tears flowed reluctantly down both his cheeks.

"Stop it, Josh! Stop it! Leave me alone!"

Josh took a step behind Hank and stood there.

"No Hank. The man won't stop. He won't stop. He has your daughter.

Criminals don't stop just because you tell them to. Now go ahead and stop him! Save your daughter Hank! Save her! She needs you!"

Hank looked down range at the paper plate. He gripped the pistol firmly in his right hand.

"Save your daughter Hank! Commence firing!"

All Hank saw was the face of the imaginary man, laughing at him as he drove away with his daughter. Cathy screamed again, and her cries echoed back and forth between Hank's ears. He watched as she turned around in the seat and looked up through the window, pleading with her father to protect her.

"Please Daddy! Help me! Help me Daddy! Help me!"

The shots rang out in quick succession, and Hank watched with anger and determination as the bullets slammed into the face of the man stealing his daughter.

"Cease fire!"

Hank kept squeezing the trigger, over and over, again and again, but now all the gun did was click. Josh reached over from behind him and placed his right hand on Hank's forearm and gripped it tightly. He placed his left hand on Hank's shoulder and squeezed it like an old friend.

"It's okay, Hank. You got him. Cathy is safe. You saved your daughter and she's home with the others now watching cartoons at the house."

Hank looked down range and the man's face slowly turned back into a white, paper plate, with 6 small holes inside the paper, grinning their approval back at him.

"Make your firearm safe."

Hank lowered the pistol and mechanically ejected the empty casings. He stood looking down range as Josh checked to make sure all six cylinders of his revolver were empty.

"Okay Hank. You're good to go. Nice shooting."

Hank turned slowly and faced his instructor.

"I don't understand. What just happened?"

Josh smiled.

"You just saved your daughter's life. No big deal. That's what fathers are supposed to do. Protect their children."

Hank stood motionless for a moment. Then he nodded and turned around. A smile was beginning to widen across his face.

"Yeah. I guess I did."

A serious look came over Josh's face before he spoke again.

"Remember Hank. To be defenseless is irresponsible. But to be defenseless as a parent, is complicity with those who would hurt your children."

Both men turned around and walked back to the staging area, and rejoined the others. Angela came over to him.

"You okay, Hank?"

He smiled.

"Yeah. Sure. I'm okay. We're just out here throwin' lead. No big deal."

Angela smiled and nodded in agreement.

"That's right boss. No big deal. We're just throwin' lead."

She hesitated a moment.

"I sure am proud of you though."

Hank holstered his pistol and blushed out loud.

"Let's go girls. We have to learn all about the proper utilization of cover and concealment."

He turned and walked away, and Angela followed him. She saw him now through different eyes. And she liked it.

Freida waited a moment longer, then she took off after them, struggling to catch up, her frumpy, fat body bouncing along in the dirt.

"Wait for me, Mr. Eastwood!"

Chapter 19

"See Hank. It only took half as long to lay out the paper using the computer."

Hank looked on nervously from over Angela's shoulder at the big screen. He wasn't convinced. True, she'd proved her point, and it was fruitless to argue about it – still – he just hated computers, had, indeed, avoided them like the plague his whole career. He just didn't believe that people had been created to stare at a computer screen all day long watching excited electrons dance around on a screen. It just didn't seem natural. After all, the whole idea of computers was to allow you to do more in less time, and, when one followed that to its natural conclusion, people ended up so busy that they had no time for the important things in life like God, Family, and Country. Instead of people running the machines, the machines ended up running the people. Hank didn't like that at all. Moving out to Freidham Ridge from the big city was one way he'd slowed his life down, and he was hesitant to incorporate anything into his routine that might accelerate his slow-paced paradise.

"I don't know, Angela . . . ."

"Hank, we timed it! It was faster! You can't deny that!"

He leaned farther over her shoulder, pretending to look at the screen, and soaking in the smell of the skin lotion she used on her hands. He loved everything about her, including her smell. It was difficult to find something wrong with this woman, though he was desperately trying to do so. On the one hand, he loved being around her. She was witty, intelligent, kind, and a lot of fun. On the other hand . . . she was still a woman, and women had always hurt him before. Hank was just very hesitant to let her in. If he shut her out, then she couldn't hurt him. Besides, his kids were his first priority - he had to watch out for the kids – that was job one!

But . . . the smell of her skin pulled him in even closer.

"Do you want to sit down and take a closer look at it, Hank?"

Hank backed up a step.

"No. That won't be necessary. I can see it just fine from here."

Angela turned around in the chair and faced him.

"Hank, you're acting weird. Everything okay with you?"

Hank stood up straight and turned slightly away from her, trying to create distance and safety. There it was again, staring him straight into his mind's eye, obvious and big as life, calling out to him like some stubborn muse that just wouldn't shut up! She was just too nice! But . . . he must resist. Any means necessary.

"Hank, are you okay?"

Movement. He needed movement. Just change the situation.

"Hey, I'd better get on home to the kids. Freida wanted me back before 8 o'clock so she could make her nightly cyber chat with the other right-wing fringe lunatics."

Angela's voice took on an anxious tone.

"That's right, Hank! That's my point! We're done with the layout and it's still only 6 o'clock. No more late nights at the office! You can go home to your kids early and spend more time with them, and all because of the wonders of computer technology."

Hank hesitated. This woman was tough. She just seemed to care so much about the people around her. It was dastardly! Then he remembered the plan again – movement – change the situation.

“Can I get you a cup of coffee, Angela?”

She looked at him suspiciously.

“Sure, that would be great. two sugars, one . . .”

“I know, I know, two sugars and one cream.”

She watched him make the coffee while she talked, impressed that he seemed to remember the smallest details about her. Then she looked down into her lap, and her voice took on a melancholy tone.

“Hank, it’s okay with me if you want to do the layout by hand. This is your newspaper and I was only trying to help. I just thought it might make it easier for you. I was just trying to help you out.”

Something in the sound of her voice made him turn around and look at her. She almost sounded hurt, and he’d never heard her like that before. When he saw her, Angela was looking down at her lap with a disconcerted expression on her face. He felt like a heel.

“Well . . . maybe you’re right.”

She looked up quickly.

“Really? You think so.”

Hank didn’t like to lie, but it tore him up inside to make people sad, especially women and small children.

“Let’s just try it for a few weeks and see what happens.”

She smiled and Hank followed suit. He thought it odd that he felt better when she felt better.

“Thanks Hank. You’re a good boss. I like working for you. You have a way that makes everything, even work, so much fun.”

He realized that his plan was failing. He was no longer moving.

“Kind of like Mary Poppins you mean?”

Angela looked at him a little confused.

“Mary Poppins?”

“You know. Julie Andrews. My kids watch it all the time.

J-u-s-t . . . a . . . spoonful of sugar helps the medicine go down, the medicine go down, medicine go down!"

She laughed when Hank started using hand motions to coincide with his singing. He even moved his feet a little.

"Oh my, Hank! You're a regular John Travolta! You and I will have to go out dancing sometime. It's so hard to find a good man who's willing to dance."

Hank pointed one arm straight up over his head and the other down toward the floor in his best John Travolta pose. He changed his song and dance routine without missing a beat.

"Burn baby burn! - Disco inferno! Burn baby burn!"

Angela laughed louder than ever before, and it made Hank happy to see her this way. He hated dancing. It made him feel incredibly stupid, but if it made her happy, then he would dance his way to the moon and back on his knees. Did she just say she wanted to go out dancing with him? Then he realized that he was no longer moving again. But she was moving. She was coming straight for him.

Angela stood up and walked over to Hank and gave him a big hug. Suddenly he felt very uncomfortable. Inside his head, he was reminded of that old science fiction movie, "Lost in Space" that he had always watched as a kid. He saw the robot rotating back and forth, waving his mechanical arms up and down, all the while sounding out his classic intergalactic clarion call. "Warning! Warning! Danger Will Robinson! Danger! Danger!" Angela was talking now, but he didn't hear her. All he could make out was the robot's warning, and then the feel of her arms around him, the softness of her flesh pressing closely against his chest, and the incessant, unrelenting aroma of her hand lotion. For a moment he thought that it must be coursing through her veins and secreting itself out through her skin. But he liked it. He liked it all.

She said something again and Hank tried to clear the fuzz from his brain.

"I'm sorry. What did you say?"

She moved back a step and held him at arm's length and looked him straight in the eyes.

"How could you miss that? I whispered it right into your ear."

Oh no! She'd caught him daydreaming. Women hated not being listened to. He'd missed something important and now he was in trouble. Why did he always get in a bind when women were around? He had to think of something fast. Jimmy Stuart – "It's A Wonderful Life" – his favorite movie. The fib rolled passed his lips before he could stop it.

"I'm sorry Angela. That was my bad ear. I couldn't quite make out what you said."

She smiled and hugged him again. Hank smiled. All better. This time, she whispered into the opposite ear.

"I said, sometimes you make me want to tell you all my hidden, deep, dark secrets."

Hank started to get nervous again. He knew that this was a potentially romantic moment, and that most middle-aged men, with or without hair on their backs, would jump at an opportunity like this, but his reporter's instinct kicked into overdrive, and he wanted to pull away from her, get a pencil and notebook and start taking notes. Deep dark secrets – reporters live for stuff like this.

"You have secrets?"

Angela leaned slightly away from him.

"Well, yes, everyone has secrets. Don't you?"

Hank backed up and bumped into the coffee counter. They were no longer touching, and the magic had come and gone.

"Let me get that coffee for you now. I think it's done."

She moved back over to the computer and sat down again. She was confused. Hank was not acting like himself tonight. Normally he was so open, so predictable, so honest. But Angela was not one to back off, so she decided to call him on it.

"You never answered my question about secrets. You have them too don't you? Things that you don't tell others because it would embarrass you or make you feel uncomfortable. Stuff like that."

He poured her coffee.

"I suppose so. Everyone has secrets. Can you give me an example of one of yours?"

Angela smiled discreetly. This guy was clever.

"Well, I suppose a good example would be your bad ear. I never knew that about you until just a moment ago when you shared it with me. Until then, it was a secret to me."

She watched his body stiffen, and his hand stopped in mid stir. Hank thought to himself. "How does she always know when I'm lying to her? Can she read my mind?" He turned around slowly. He wanted to just be himself, but that would mean opening up in so many ways, and that would leave him vulnerable. He'd have to trust her. He'd have to take a risk. He might get hurt. He reached deep inside himself looking for a measure of fortitude. When he found a small handful of courage, he came back up.

"I'm a liar, Angela."

She looked shocked.

"What?"

Hank pressed on. Lying made him feel dirty, and he desperately needed a bath. He wanted to get his cleanness back.

"I don't have a bad ear. I was just daydreaming, and I didn't want you to know about it, so I said I had a bad ear."

Angela shook her head back and forth in disbelief.

"Why did you lie about such a stupid thing as that?"

Hank answered quickly. His courage was almost gone now.

"Because I didn't want you to know that I was feeling overwhelmed by your hug, the way you were touching me, the smell of your hand lotion. Oh everything! It was discombobulating me, and I felt really stupid and clumsy. But I didn't want you to know that I was feeling stupid and clumsy so I just made up that story about my ear so I wouldn't get in trouble for not hearing what you said."

Angela needed time to think about that one.

"Will you bring me my coffee now, please, Hank?"

Hank brought it over and held it out to her.

"You know, Hank, I think a million psychiatrists could probably spend their entire careers trying to unravel all the complexities of what you just said, and in the end, they would still die unsatisfied."

She reached out for her coffee cup.

"That was really stupid, Hank. Really, really stupid."

She touched the glass mug, felt its warmth and went out of her way to brush her fingers across Hank's quivering hand.

"And it was also very sweet. Thank you for telling me the truth. I appreciate honesty. I insist on having it from all my friends."

Hank started breathing again.

"Can I just be myself again?"

"Of course. Why did you ever stop?"

Hank shrugged. He wouldn't lie again, but he had to find some safe middle ground.

"I can't tell you why. It's too personal. But someday I'd like to share it with you. Just not tonight."

He paused and looked at her as if totally at her mercy. She smiled softly and nodded.

"I can live with that, Hank. You take your time. And when Hank Simmons is ready to come on out and play, you just let me know, and I'll meet you at the swing set."

She blew the steam away from the rim of her coffee mug.

"And it's okay if you don't like to dance. I understand that most men feel stupid when they do it. Just always be honest. Otherwise I can't trust you. And two things are necessary for any kind of relationship: trust and respect."

She took a sip of her coffee. It burned her upper lip.

"And now I feel like I need to be honest with you as well."

Hank poured himself a cup of coffee and walked over next to her. He sat down and made eye contact.

"Did you lie to me?"

Angela shrugged.

"Depends on how you look at it. If it was a lie, then it was a lie of omission I suppose. Do you remember the day you hired me, when we were at the Mudhen having lunch?"

Hank nodded. He remembered it like it was yesterday.

"You asked me where I was on nine-eleven, and I told you I was all alone, and that it was really no big deal. Do you remember?"

"Yes, I remember. I felt like you were hiding something painful. So I just let it go, and didn't pry into your personal affairs."

She looked down at her coffee cup and traced her right forefinger across the rim of the steaming cup.

"Would you like a better answer to that question now?"

Hank hesitated, as if waiting in front of a very important door. He wasn't sure what was on the other side, or how his life would change if he entered in, but, intuitively, he suspected that once entered, he could never leave, and that the act of entering would change his life forever, in very profound ways. He couldn't speak the words, so he just nodded his head for her to continue.

She hesitated, thought for a moment, and took a deep breath before telling her story.

"It's true that I was alone, from a certain point of view. I was alone with 5 million other people in New York City. And, more to the point, I was alone in my office at the World Trade Center when the first airliner slammed into it."

Hank leaned forward to hear better. He wanted to record this, but knew better than to try.

"It shook the whole building so hard that it knocked me off my chair and on to the carpet. It was really plush, thick, soft carpet, so it didn't hurt at all. But I never got up."

Hank wondered what she meant by that, but didn't want to interrupt her story. He wanted to hear it all.

"I just lay there, listening to the flames eat their way up. They sounded alive, like a freight train, like an angry, malevolent train that would consume everything in its way, and I was in its path."

She paused long enough to take a sip of her coffee.

"I'm not sure how long I lay there. Probably just a few seconds. But the place filled up with smoke really fast, and people were screaming outside my office. They're all dead now. I was the only one to get out. Just me. And I have no idea why. Why would God save me and let all those other people die?"

She looked up at Hank as if expecting an answer, but he had nothing to say. He had no answer.

"Many of them were better people than me. But they still died."

She looked down.

"Burned to death!"

Then she remembered her secretary.

"I recall feeling the terror."

She looked back up at Hank, straight into his eyes, and he made compassionate eye contact with her and held it.

"That's what the terrorists wanted wasn't it? To make us afraid? To kill as many of us as they could and to destroy any peace that we may have had?"

Hank wasn't sure she wanted an answer, so he just nodded.

"Well, they got their wish. I was terrified then, and there's not a day goes by that I don't feel terrified at some level. They really got to me, Hank. They really did."

Hank wanted to say something to make her feel better, but he had no idea what words could possibly heal her wounds. He remained silent, impotent, and helplessly listening to every word.

"When I finally realized that I was going to die if I didn't get out of there, I started to crawl towards the door of my office. I think it was off its hinges, because I can't remember opening it. And I remember the smells most of all, because it wasn't just one smell, but a mixture of millions. Everything in that building was being melted and fused together, so that it came out as one smell, but I could still sense that it was something new. Something new and terrible."

Then Hank watched as Angela's hands tightened on her coffee mug. Her knuckles turned white, and Hank was afraid she would crush the thick glass in her hands and cut herself.

"And then I found Marge, my secretary. I smelled her first, because the smoke rising up from below had already blotted out the sun, making everything in my office dark. I smelled her blood. And when I saw her, I think I screamed. But the other sounds, the sounds of the building dying, were so loud, that I couldn't hear myself. My one, tiny, little scream, was just but a drop of rain on the ocean. It was swept away on a wave, and I never saw it again."

She looked over at Hank.

"Does that make sense, Hank?"

Hank didn't answer. He just swallowed real hard and tried to give her an empathetic look. She looked back down again.

"There was a big shard of glass in her throat. It was sticking up out of her like a glass tower, dripping red with her blood. Blood looks creepy when you're seeing it through smoke and dark. Did you know that Hank? It seems surreal. Even though I knew it was very real, and I believed it with all my heart, it still seemed like a fantasy land, a harsh, terrifying, but yet, incredibly esoteric and interesting world of dark fantasy."

She shook her head from side to side.

"And I never want to experience it ever again.."

Once more she shook her head from side to side.

"By rights, I should already be dead, like Marge, and Bill Collins, the guy in purchasing who was always hitting on me at the copy machine. He was married and I kept telling him no, but he just kept right on hitting on me. And Lisa at the front desk. I don't even know her last name. I never did. If I'd known she was going to die that day, I would have gone out of my way to talk to her, to at least find out her name so I could properly mourn her and remember her. But I didn't. I was too caught up in my own push for success. Lisa died and I can't even remember her properly. I know she had a fiancé though, because I heard her talking to someone about it one morning. She seemed so in love with him. You could tell by the sound of her voice. It had that feel about it. I was waiting there, wanting to ask her a question, and I can remember feeling so perturbed at her for making me wait while she spoke about the man she loved and was going to marry."

She looked up at Hank with pleading eyes, as if begging him to argue with her.

"I was a jerk, Hank! A big jerk! And I didn't even know it. I thought I was the good guy. But I didn't even know what life was all about. I didn't even believe in God."

Hank spoke before thinking.

"You didn't believe in God?"

She took a sip of her coffee and laughed out loud. But it wasn't laughter of happiness, or even of nervousness. It was a laughter teetering on the border between insanity and despair. Hank didn't know why, but listening to all this had made his hands turn cold, so he wrapped them around his coffee cup for warmth, but to no avail.

"Why didn't you believe in God?"

Suddenly, Angela shifted in her chair uncomfortably.

"My coffee got cold."

Hank stood up without speaking and retrieved her cup. He quietly placed both cups of coffee in the microwave for 33 seconds on medium heat. Normally, 33 seconds would seem like a long time for two people to say nothing, but it passed quickly now, as if some unseen threshold had been crossed, or some new door had been opened and passed through. It was an old, cheap microwave that Hank had bought at a yard sale for 5 dollars. The bell on the timer dinged, and the next round of talk began. He turned around and handed Angela her hot coffee before sitting down again next to her.

"Thank you Hank. You're very reliable."

Hank smiled softly.

"You're welcome. My kids call me the energizer bunny."

But he said nothing more and just waited for her to talk. He suspected that she needed to talk, and he needed to listen. At this moment in time, nothing else existed. Talking and listening – it was the way of all things.

"The day after nine-eleven, I began to believe in God. Not only in His existence, but also in His compassion, in His power, and in His complexity. At the time, I didn't understand why I'd been able to go through so much of life just ignoring the Creator of all things. But after nine-eleven, I couldn't go on denying Him anymore. Because on nine-eleven, I was several floors above the flames, Hank."

Hank watched as the intensity returned to her face and she continued on with the story.

"I can remember lying next to Marge, smelling her blood, realizing that I was about to die, knowing that I had totally wasted my life, that no one had ever benefited from the blood I'd pumped or the air I'd breathed. I was a waste of time."

She sipped her coffee and burned her lip again, but this time she didn't feel it.

"It was at that moment, that moment right before my certain death, that I finally realized that nothing done in selfish or vain ambition will ever last. Anything that you do solely for yourself, will rot away, decompose, turn to dust and blow away at the moment of your passing."

She looked out into Hank's face, but he got the feeling that she couldn't see him, that she was deep inside herself, reliving those final moments in the Twin Towers.

"I can remember the heat on the left side of my face, right here on my cheek."

She moved her hand up and touched her skin.

"There's still a tiny scar there where the carpet had melted onto my skin. And my hands were burned too. I remember squeezing the plush shag between my fingers and feeling it melt and ooze like thick liquid between my fingertips."

She turned her head off to one side and looked down at the stark linoleum floor of the newspaper office.

"Have you ever had surgery Hank? Do you remember what the anesthesia felt like? Do you remember them asking you to count to ten? It felt like that, Hank. I remember when it all went black. I remember my final moment on this earth. I think I died. At least a part of me. I can't explain it, and I know how crazy that sounds. But I believe it with all my being. I should be dead right now."

She looked up and made eye contact again.

"You don't understand this do you? You can't."

Hank shrugged his shoulders.

"I wasn't there. I'll never understand it the way you do. But friends don't always have to understand. Sometimes . . . they just have to be understanding."

Angela smiled, making Hank feel warm and good inside.

"That's enough for now. I'll take it."

She sipped her coffee and so did Hank.

"I guess the point is, Hank, that I went to sleep above the inferno, and when the firemen found me, I was several stories below it. There is no explanation for that outside of God. He saved me. And I'm grateful and hateful all at the same time. I'm grateful that He saved me, but I hate Him for making me live through all this guilt and pain. Because I was supposed to die that day and I didn't. I'm alive, and all the others are dead."

She was done with her story. Her shoulders sagged with fatigue and she bowed her head down. Hank's paternal instincts seemed to kick in, and he talked to her now, as if she were his own daughter.

"Earlier you told me that on the day after nine-eleven, you began to believe in God, not only in His existence, but also in His compassion, in His power, and in His complexity. But you left out one very important aspect of God – His grace. I don't think you hate God at all. I think you feel anger and guilt. God isn't making you live through all this guilt and pain. That's something people choose for themselves. I've learned that most of the pain in life is self inflicted. I used to blame God for all of that, but one day, I don't remember exactly when, I realized and admitted that it was mostly my fault. I was where I was because of the choices I'd made, the words I'd spoken, and the things I'd done. I was sick, and I was hurting, and I needed God to heal my wounds."

He paused to see if he was losing her, to consider whether or not he should go on, or leave well enough alone. She seemed receptive.

"When I was little, and I fell down and scratched my knee. I remember I cried because I was scared, because blood was coming out of me and because I was hurt. That happened more times than I can count. And, every single time, without exception, my mom and dad were there for me. They picked me up; they held me; they told me how much they loved me, and, little by little, the hurt went away. And that's who God is, Angela. He's the world's most perfect parent. He's always there, and He'll never leave you. It says that in the Bible somewhere, and I believe it with all my heart. I believe it because God is my father, and that's what father's are like."

He reached over and put his arm around her.

"Trust me Angela. If there's one thing I know, it's fatherhood."

Angela looked up with tears in her eyes.

"My father is gone. I never knew him."

A large lump formed in Hank's throat. He tried to swallow it, but it wouldn't go away. He squeezed her harder and held her tight. She responded by turning in her chair and laying her head on his shoulder.

"I'm sorry, Angela. I wish I could change that."

Five minutes later, she was still on his shoulder, and all the crying had soaked his shirt. But Hank had remained silent the whole time, instinctively knowing that Angela's needs transcended the spoken word. Finally, she lifted her head and Hank reached over and wiped away her tears with the tattered sleeve of his sweatshirt.

"It's going to be okay. You are going to be okay. No matter what happens, no matter what you do in life, you are never beyond the grace and love of God the Father. Forgiveness and love are within your reach, now, and forever more."

Hank held her at arm's reach, as if she were his own child, and he brushed the dark brown hair away from her forehead and placed his right hand on her brow. He closed his eyes, and he spoke.

"Dear God. Please be with Angela. Protect her and keep her safe.

Amen."

The prayer seemed simple and childlike to Angela, but she liked it anyway. She looked up and smiled.

"Hank, you have a way of reducing complicated things to their barest minimum and making them easier to understand."

Hank returned her smile.

"It's a talent derived from raising four children all by yourself. You learn to avoid complication and to appreciate simplicity."

They both leaned back away from each other and dropped their arms in unison, as if on cue and agreement. The moment, which had seemed so tender and natural just a few minutes ago, now crumbled to clumsiness.

"Okay boss. What now?"

Hank laughed out loud.

"Well isn't it obvious? Of course it is. Now we go over to my house, put the kids in bed, and Freida goes home to cyber space. Then you and I order a pizza and watch "Mary Poppins!"

Angela smiled and nodded her head.

"Well, okay. You're the boss."

Chapter 20

"Despite reports today of an imminent Taliban surrender in Konduz, advancing Northern Alliance troops were hit hard with a sustained volley of Taliban artillery shells. The Alliance responded with a barrage of long-range rockets. As American soldiers celebrated Thanksgiving Day on the battlefield, U.S. forces continued to bomb Taliban front line positions in Konduz."

Immediately after nine-eleven, it had become commonplace to listen to the war news. Even people who had never before taken an interest in world events, Hank called them the ostrich people, perked up their ears when a news broadcast came on radio or television. Hank's children, who were eating Thanksgiving Day dinner at a smaller table adjoining the dining room, instinctively knew that it was time to be quiet when the news came on. Serious looks came over the faces of the adults who sat quietly around the long table, which was covered with a traditional American Thanksgiving Day dinner. Hank loved it – holidays in the heartland of America. He hadn't experienced anything like this since he was a kid.

"Contradictions continue as Alliance and Taliban commanders, meeting in Mazar-e-Sharif, say both the Afghan and the foreign Taliban fighters will lay down their arms. Amidst the turmoil and confusion, aid agencies in Afghanistan attempt to move in supplies for millions of war weary civilians, as winter draws near."

"I hope we kill every one of those terrorists! Especially that Bin Laden son of a . . . .!"

But the pastor's wife interrupted Spunky's irreverent diatribe before it came to full steam.

"Now, now Mr. Cannon. Let's not get all worked up into a tizzy before we eat. This is the Lord's Day you know."

Hank and Angela gave each other a secret glance and smiled. This was probably the most diverse mix of dinner guests assembled since the original Thanksgiving Day dinner with pilgrims and Indians. Angela had taken great care to seat them in places where arguments were least likely to break out. She had placed Hank at the head of the table, herself to his right, with Aunt Millie beside her. Spunky Cannon was to Hank's left, with Rock Stuart beside him. Then came frumpy Freida, who had been overjoyed at the prospect of sitting beside a famous writer. Rounding out the table on the far end was Josh McCullen and his wife Louise.

"Well hell then. Shouldn't somebody pray so we can eat. I'm in a hurry to wash it all down with some ice cold beer!"

Josh watched the shocked look on his wife's face and laughed delightfully inside. She started to rebuke Spunky for cussing, but he quickly reached over and squeezed her hand in his own. Their eyes met and she nodded to him in a determined, but temporary truce. She had promised her husband that she wouldn't argue with anyone about anything. She thought to herself, "That's okay, I'll just catch Mr. Cannon after dinner when everyone else is distracted." She was already forming the sermon in her mind. Josh diffused the situation with a suggestion.

"That's a good idea Spunky. Hank, you're the head of the house. How about it?"

Hank felt a little uncomfortable at the prospect of praying in front of people, so he stalled for time.

"Angela will you turn that radio off please. I think we can do without that distraction for a while."

Angela got up and walked into the next room to turn it off.

"Well damn it! I'll pray if nobody else wants to. I'm half starved!"

Louise McCullen bit her lower lip so hard it almost bled. Aunt Millie's frail, old voice broke in unexpectedly.

"You listen to me young man. If'n you cuss one more time, I'll be jumpin' outta this chair and over this here table and I'll be slappin' y'all into next week!"

The room became deathly silent. The pastor's wife had never heard language like this before, and while she approved of Millie's fiery rebuke, she was shocked that a lady her age would even think to use violence.

"Y'all? Now what does y'all mean anyways? I never did understand all that southern fried dialect!"

Aunt Millie stood slowly and resolutely to her feet, causing Hank to shift uncomfortably in his chair. Angela came back in and seated herself beside Hank. Everyone seemed to be moving in slow motion. Professor Lance Stuart looked on in fascination and awe. He could never have compiled such a dysfunctional group of characters even if he had written the novel himself. He was extremely anxious to see what would happen next, but, when little Cathy spoke up out of nowhere, even the Pulitzer prize winning author seemed surprised.

"Dear Jesus. Thank you for all this good food. Except the carrots. Please make all the big people stop fighting and saying bad words. Please keep us safe from the bad persons in Ganistan." Her little voice hesitated. "And please help daddy to marry Angela. Amen!"

Angela's jaw dropped open. Hank's heart froze in his chest. Aunt Millie sat back down. Spunky Cannon waited a moment, and then leaned back in his chair and laughed out loud.

"Amen sister! You preach it!"

Louise McCullen began to breathe again, while Josh smiled and thought to himself, “From the mouths of babes.”

Rock Stuart had become strangely quiet. He was totally lost in thought. He felt something break free inside his mind, like a door that had been rusted shut for decades. And when the door swung open again, he recognized it with all its power and might and wondrous beauty. For the first time since the death of his wife, he felt . . . inspired to write.

“Give me those mashed potatoes over there will ya Millie?”

Aunt Millie contemplated Spunky’s request like an old woman who had nothing but time. Then she smiled decisively.

“Here ya go youngster. Eat ‘em up. This be the Lord’s day! Try to chew before ya’ll swallow.”

Off in the corner of the next room, as if in a world all their own, the four little children held their own conversation.

“Why do they make us eat carrots?”

Phillip answered Cathy’s question without hesitation.

“Cuz they’re orange, that’s why.”

“So why we gotta eat orange food?”

“So you get a balanced meal dummy! Ya gotta eat all your colors if you want to grow up big and strong!”

Susan nodded her head.

“Yup. It’s true. You gotta eat all your colors.”

Lance Stuart heard it all from a distance and smiled inside. He couldn’t wait to get home and write again.

Chapter 21

"Daddy! Daddy! Let's play the lava game!"

Hank felt the familiar tug of his 6-year old daughter, Cathy, on one arm and another from his 4-year old son, Micah, on the other. He was totally exhausted from working at the paper all day, but he forced himself to act excited at the prospect of wrestling on the living room floor after a long, hard day's work.

Not that Hank didn't love his children, because he did. Hank loved his family more than life itself, and he would do anything for them. He loved kids, and in the days of computers, abortion on demand, and physician-assisted suicide, Hank Simmons was fast becoming a dinosaur – but a happy dinosaur nonetheless.

He let the two kids pull him into the living room where Angela was absorbed in the nightly news. She looked up and smiled.

"Well hi! Did you get the newspaper layout done?"

Hank smiled and nodded. There was something odd about coming home and being greeted so warmly by a beautiful woman. It was a feeling he didn't altogether dislike.

"Yeah, we're good to go. Freida took it all over to the print shop in Bentley. The paper will go out on schedule."

Angela looked pleased.

"Good."

Hank picked up on the distant tone of her voice and the faraway look in her eyes.

"Everything okay Angela?"

She smiled again and nodded.

"Yeah. Everything's great. I was just thinking."

"About what?"

Her head went down and she smiled even wider.

"Sure you want to know?"

Hank thought for a moment. He thought he wanted to know, but her hesitance to talk about it made him a little unsure.

"Of course. What's up?"

"Well, I was just thinking that if a few months ago someone had told me that today I'd be babysitting for my bosses' four kids, I would have told them they were crazy as loons?"

Hank's heart sank. He knew it! He knew it was too much to ask of her, but he'd been desperate for help, so he'd taken the easy way out of his childcare dilemma. In the big city, he might have been sued for sexual harassment for something like this. But he'd hoped she was different, that they had grown close enough as friends for him to ask a favor of this magnitude.

"I'm sorry Angela. I know you're the Marketing Director and this isn't in your job description, but I was really desperate. I won't ask again. I'm very sorry if I offended you."

She analyzed him hard and ascertained that he was sincere before she answered. He was. In fact, she'd come to admire his sensitivity and his apologetic manner. Sometimes she wondered how a man like Hank had ever been divorced. That woman must have been crazy.

"No Hank. It's not that at all. I was just amazed that my life took such a radical turn and that it's so much different now than I thought it would be."

Hank was relieved to hear that's all it was. He cocked his head to one side.

"How so?"

"Well, think about it. A few months ago I was the Marketing Director for a major New York firm. I had a plush, corner office, a six-figure salary, and I had access to just about anything money could buy. And now look at me. Instead of business dinners at 5-star restaurants, I'm eating at the Mudhen Grille, I earn . . . considerably less, and instead of going out to fancy nightclubs after work, I'm reading Dr. Seuss, cooking pancakes shaped like Mickey Mouse and monster trucks, and watching Barney the purple dinosaur."

Hank's heart sank again. He knew when he'd seen her resume that she wouldn't stay long. She had an MBA from Princeton, and her business credentials far exceeded his own.

"I know Angela. This must be a big disappointment for you. You only came back here while your company made the move to Rochester. I knew you wouldn't be able to stay forever. I just wanted to make you happy while you were here, and secretly, I was hoping . . . ."

She smiled softly.

"Hoping what?"

Hank shook his head and turned away.

"Nothing."

Just then Cathy grabbed his arm and pulled Hank down onto the floor and Micah jumped onto his stomach. Hank let out a tired groan. Angela's heart leaped for joy every time she watched him play with the kids. He was such a good father. He loved them so much. She believed that Hank would die for them without hesitation, and she wondered what it felt like to be the object of so much love.

Cathy was sitting on the left side of his face and his lips squished together when he talked, making his words slurred together.

"So where are the two big ones?"

Angela was slightly perturbed because she'd been interrupted during a speech that she'd been practicing all day long.

"Phillip is upstairs putting a model airplane together for history class, and Susan is playing Barbie."

Hank roared like a lion and pretended to be angry at Micah for jumping on his stomach.

"The lava monster is going to eat you up!"

The two kids immediately screamed and ran around the room trying to get away, but Hank was too fast. He grabbed onto 6-year old Cathy and pretended to eat her face.

"No Daddy no! You can't eat raw meat! You'll get sick. Cook me first!"

Angela stood to her feet and shook her head from side to side. Sometimes she was amazed by her own complexity. On the one hand, she loved it when Hank played with the kids, on the other, it made her jealous, because she wanted all of his time.

"I can't believe you play that game with them. Child Protective Services would throw you in jail if they found out you were eating your children."

"Ah, the government. Bless their souls. What would we do without them."

Angela stood up and walked toward the door.

"See you in the morning, Hank. I need some sleep."

Micah took a running jump onto Hank's back and wrapped both his little arms around his father's neck.

"Thanks Angela. I'd show you out, but I'm a little tied up at the moment."

Hank heard the door open and close. He didn't like her abrupt departure, and he didn't like that she'd be leaving the paper either. Circulation was up, as well as income generated from ad space, and most of it was due to Angela's efforts and her new ideas. He didn't want her to go. And there were other reasons too – other more personal reasons that he dared not think, much less utter out loud. But he forced Angela out of his mind. The kids were his number one priority, and they needed him to play with them before bed time.

"All right you guys. Now you've made the lava monster mad!"

Micah held on tight, flopping around like a rag doll as Hank gently pressed Cathy's face to the carpet and made a hissing sound.

"There! Now you're cooked and ready to eat."

Cathy squealed with delight.

"No Daddy no! Help me Micah. Don't let the lava monster eat my face off!"

Micah responded with a loud growl and bit Hank on the ear.

"Ouch! That hurt, you little runt!"

He let go of Cathy and reached up and swung Micah around by his legs, repeating the same lava-cooking procedure with his son. Micah screamed and Cathy saved him, then Cathy screamed and Micah saved her. Over and over the game played itself out until Hank could barely move.

"Okay you two. The lava monster isn't hungry anymore. Kiss daddy good night."

After several more minutes of winding down, Hank ended up carrying them both upstairs to their room. He kissed them both good night and made them close their eyes and fold their hands while he prayed for them.

"Dear Lord, please bless Cathy and Micah. Give them happy dreams and keep them safe. We love you and thank you for everything. Amen."

Micah said "Amen" in his little boy voice, and Cathy echoed her own

6-year old version. Hank kissed them one more time, turned on the night-light and closed the door softly behind them.

As he walked down the hall, his older son Phillip called out from his room.

"Hey Dad! I need help with this."

Hank trudged on over and walked into his son's room.

"What do you need son?"

Phillip held up the fuselage of a plastic model P-51 Mustang.

"Looks great. What's the problem?"

Phillip looked down sheepishly and let go of the fuselage. It stuck to his fingers, and Hank laughed out loud.

"You glued yourself to the airplane again?"

Phillip nodded.

"I'm sorry dad. I couldn't find the airplane glue so I used the Crazy Glue instead. That stuff dries really fast!"

Hank tried to remember if he'd done silly things like that when he was 10 years old.

"Let me see if your sister still has that nail polish remover. That'll do the trick."

Phillip smiled.

"Thanks Dad."

Hank went to the bathroom and found the nail polish remover. Life with kids was never boring. It was a lot of work, but never boring and he wouldn't trade it for the world. He thought of the priest at the confessional and just assumed this was part of his penance. The easy part.

"Okay son, hold out your hand."

Phillip complied and a few seconds later was free. Hank sent him into the bathroom to clean off the remainder of the residue and went in to say good night to his oldest daughter Susan.

He found her asleep on the carpet, surrounded by a mound of Barbie dolls and tiny clothes. Her cat, Cheshire, was laying on her neck, straddling it like the saddle on a horse. Hank smiled and reached down, pushed away the cat, and then, with love and care, he picked up his daughter and placed her gently onto the bed and pulled the blankets up over her 8-year old body. He placed his right hand on her forehead, closed his eyes and prayed.

"Dear God, Please bless my daughter and give her happy dreams. Keep her safe forever. Amen."

Hank then said good night to his son, and prayed with him as well, then he went downstairs.

This was Hank's favorite part of the day. He was alone, finally. He could think without interruption; there was no pressure, no screaming children, no crisis to be averted, no fights to referee, no homework to do, no blood, no foul. He could relax. As much as he hated being a single parent, it was still better than being married to the wrong person. Marriage to an alcoholic had been like leading his family uphill with a boat anchor tied to his neck. Now, it was still all uphill, but at least the anchor was gone.

Life was more predictable this way. He could plan and organize, even accomplish things. But there were many things he didn't like. He didn't like feeling tired all the time, having no one to count on, no one to help him, no one he could share the load with. And he was lonely. That was probably the worst part of it all. He had no mate, no match, no one to tell him it would be all right, no one to scratch his neck when he got tense, or to just smile reassuringly.

Hank laughed at his own thoughts. He was living in a fantasy world. All those things were imagined. He'd never had them during his marriage, indeed, never had them during his whole life. But he thought he'd seen them in other couples before, unless of course they were just faking it. But, a big part of him wanted it to be real, to be out there for him, waiting, seeking him out. He wanted to be part of a team, to be part of something special.

Unfortunately, no self-respecting woman would ever touch him again. He was an outcast, unclean, a social leper. What woman in her right mind would want a 42-year old man with 4 kids and a lousy job? On nights like this, he felt like damaged goods.

And now, Angela was leaving, and that made it hurt all the more. Deep down inside, from the moment she'd walked into the office, he'd secretly harbored a desire for her. She was so beautiful, and funny, and competent to boot. Life with her as an employee and friend had become so much easier and even . . . enjoyable . . . exciting . . . unpredictable.

Hank shook his head and shoved his hands deep into the front pockets of his jeans. But, for the most part, he was a reality-based personality, always had been, and he didn't have the luxury of crazy hopes and dreams. She was 10 years younger than him. Besides, the kids needed him with both feet planted firmly on the ground, not with his head and his heart way up in the clouds.

He put on his jacket and walked out onto the front porch. When he saw the giant, white moon down close to the horizon, his mouth dropped open in amazement. It was beautiful. He sat down on the porch swing, folded his arms across his chest and began to rock himself back and forth in the chilly, night air. He knew he should go inside and wash the dishes, sweep the floors, pack the kid's lunches for school, get their backpacks all around – the list was endless.

Instead, he just sat there, staring up into the giant globe of white, letting it fill his heart and his mind, basking in the tainted light of its hope. He watched a single snowflake float on down, spiraling in the cold night air. Angela was leaving, but, perhaps, just maybe, there was someone out there, looking at this very same moon, lonely, searching, in need of a man like him, someone yearning for a middle-aged man; someone who liked hairy backs and balding heads, and thickening waist lines. Then he laughed out loud and let his chin drop down onto his chest. Who was he fooling? There were no women like that in the world – at least none here in Freidham Ridge. He didn't even know any single women except for Freida. This entire countryside was infested with healthy, happy families, all staring at him accusingly as if he and his single-parent home was a boil on the otherwise perfect landscape.

He stood up and walked back inside. It did no good to dream, no good to hope for things unseen and non-existing. He would just keep his eyes on what he had for sure, on the real things in life, on the tangibles that he could reach out and touch and feel and that drove him on from day to day, and day after day, to day after unending day.

As he walked up the stairs, he was bone-tired and brain weary, but he drug himself on nonetheless, knowing that he had no choice. Too many people depended on him, little people that loved him and were still too young to recognize his failings.

He paused at Cathy's door and watched her sleep in the faint light from the hall. Then he walked over and stood by her bed. Out of habit, he watched to make sure she was still breathing, then, after a moment of focusing, could hear the air entering and leaving her tiny chest. Sometimes he felt more like a woman than a man, and he wondered where all this nurturing instinct had come from.

He lay down on the bed beside her and kissed her gently on the forehead. Then he reached over and brushed the hair out of her face. She always let it fall down into her eyes, no matter what he told her.

"Hi Daddy."

Her little voice sounded half asleep.

"I'm sorry honey. I didn't mean to wake you. Daddy just wanted to make sure you were all right."

She smiled and put her little hands on his cheeks.

"Are you going to marry Angela?"

The question made a lump rise in Hank's throat.

"Why would you ask that, Honey?"

Her soft little hands patted his whiskered cheeks softly.

"Just 'cuz she likes you. So I figured you liked her too."

Hank smiled and squeezed her tight.

"You're a smart girl, Cathy. I do like her . . . very much. But I'm just her boss and I don't think she'll be staying around much longer. It's almost time for Angela to go back to the city to her other job."

"But I don't want her to go! She plays with me and watches Barney! Can't you just give her more money?"

A concerned look came over Hank's face. He'd underestimated how much the kids needed a woman in their lives. Their own mother hadn't come to see them in over a year.

"I'm sorry honey. Daddy doesn't have enough money to make her stay."

"Can't you just sell some extra papers?"

Hank smiled. He admired the simplicity of a child. Their view of life was so pure and simple and basic. Sometimes he yearned for childhood again.

"It's not that easy honey. Angela has her own life to lead, and Daddy's already selling as many papers as he can."

"Would you keep her if you could?"

Her innocent, but probing questions were making him feel uncomfortable now. But he was a father, a patient father.

"Sweetheart, it's just not that simple. I don't know if Angela could ever be happy here. She's from the city."

"We're from the city too, Daddy. We just moved here, member?"

Hank shifted his hips and shoulder uncomfortably on the twin bed. He wanted out of this conversation.

"Tell you what little one. If she asks me to marry her, I'll do it right away!"

Cathy's bright, brown eyes opened wide.

"Really? Good! I'm going to pray that God makes her want to stay and marry us."

Hank laughed out loud.

Okay punkin'. But let's get some sleep now. Morning comes way too early for little girls and tired daddys."

"Okay Daddy. Ya know what?"

"What's that little one?"

"I love you Daddy."

Then she snuggled up next to him and fell fast asleep. A tiny glow of warmth and a faint glimmer of hope came alive, deep down inside him. And, all of a sudden, things didn't seem quite so bad. He would clean the house tomorrow.

Outside, the moon slowly departed the horizon, casting light and hope to everything it touched. Inside, Hank slumbered with his family, dreaming the dreams of hope and faith and love.

Chapter 22

Angela pulled into Aunt Millie's driveway and turned off the car engine. She didn't quite know what was going on. Things had happened so fast lately – too fast – way too fast, and her head just kept spinning and swimming with all the changes in her life. She had come to Freidham Ridge to regain her center, to get back to her roots, her family, to find the answers to so many nagging questions. Instead, all she'd gotten for her trouble was more confusion and a host of more unanswered questions.

She opened the car door and stepped out. All the New York City boys had found her attractive, so why didn't Hank? What was he waiting for, an engraved invitation? He hadn't so much as laid a finger on her, or even hinted at his feelings. Were her instincts that skewed? The first time they'd met, she was certain he'd been attracted to her. So why not move on it? What was stopping him? Or was she just plain wrong? Was her ego that gargantuan?

Then there was still the bigger question: Why had God saved her? She was no closer to that question than on the day she'd left New York City. And to complicate things further, her home office had called her today. They were almost finished moving the business to Rochester and they wanted her back, and soon. She was mysteriously torn. Torn between a dead-end job in a one-horse town on the one hand, and her plush, corner office and her golden-girl career on the other. There was no choice. This was a no brainer. So why was she hesitating? There it was, another infernal question without an answer!

But she was just fooling herself. Deep down inside, she knew the answer to that one. She just didn't want to admit it.

She enjoyed babysitting Hank's children. She enjoyed selling ad space for 50 cents a word to Zeke Tyler so he could advertise his alfalfa for 2 dollars a bale. That was weird. She enjoyed that? Amazing.

Most of all, she enjoyed working with Hank. She enjoyed his nervous sense of humor; she enjoyed their lunches together; she enjoyed the way he treated her, the way he made her feel so special using his own brand of clumsy chivalry. He opened and closed doors for her, complimented her at every opportunity, and she didn't want that to end. He was a perfect gentleman, noble and dignified to the core of his being. But – there was something hidden, something holding him back - and she yearned to discover it.

Unfortunately, she seemed destined to never find out. She had to make a decision soon, and the only sensible, practical decision was to return to her job, her corner office, her six figures, all the clout, all the success, all the boring blah, blah, blah, blah, blah.

She looked up at the hugeness of the bright, white orb of the winter moon now rising over her Aunt Millie's old two-story farmhouse. It seemed to stare down at her, looking at her reprovingly as if to say. "Fess up Angela. You know what to do! Don't blow this opportunity!"

Then she remembered what the old man in the wheelchair had told her in the hospital chapel.

"He will provide you with what you need. He is your heavenly Father – you are his child. God is the provider, He has already anticipated your need and made provisions. You will be given an opportunity to understand fatherhood. And then, your relationship with Him can be restored."

She heard the front door open and close. Aunt Millie came out and stood beside her in the moonlight.

"Hello Sweetheart. It's cold out here. Aren't ya comin' inside? Y'all doin' okay?"

Her Aunt Millie followed her gaze on up to the moon and she nodded as if understanding her unseen thoughts.

"Yep, it's beautiful ain't it. I like it too. It's a thinkin' moon tonight. Gets you to wondering don't it?"

Angela looked back down and smiled softly at the woman who had raised her. Her Aunt Millie had been raised in Kentucky and then moved up here with her husband early in their marriage. She had never quite lost all of her lazy, southern accent. Where would she be without her?

"I love you Aunt Millie."

She reached down and hugged the old woman's fragile frame with a tender conviction that transcended any satisfaction she'd ever felt from her golden-girl career. She realized that someday, Aunt Millie would die and leave her here all alone. Her family would be gone.

"I love you too, honey. You okay child? What ya'll thinkin' 'bout tonight?"

Angela stepped back and let her arms drop down to her sides.

"I'm thinking about life. About everything that's happened to me the past 3 months. I never would have guessed I'd end up back here. It was the farthest thing from my mind. How did it happen? What's going on Aunt Millie?"

The tired old woman laughed with a twinkle in her eyes and a smile on her face, and when she answered, there was compassion and courage in her southern-fried voice.

"It was just life, child. Just life. Few things we got are predictable. Mostly it's outta are control. Ya just gotta close yer eyes and hang on fer the ride sometimes. But there's this one thing I know over all my years.

I stay close to God, and I never regret a friendship, if'n it's a man or a woman or a child; they're all so special in their own way. And sometimes they hurt, and sometimes they're happy, but I done learned never to regret 'em. The only regrets I have are the times when I got scared and took the safe way, even when God told me not to. I did it a few times, and I always knew it was a mistake afterwards. And, eventually, I learned not to let my fears make my decisions for me. Cuz every time I did it, for the rest of my born days, I always wondered what might of been – what could of been, if I'd of been strong instead of weak." Aunt Millie laughed softly again. "That's one thing I like about God. That old boy just never asked me to do nothin' He knows I can't. He always says, 'Hey Millie! You do this thing and I'll be helpin' ya all the way there.'"

She looked down and then back up again, and when she spoke, it was resolutely, with a firmness and a power belying her age.

"I don't know what's been eatin' ya lately child, but it must be somethin' big to have y'all twisted up in knots the way you are. But I just want ya to take care of one thing. Never make choices from the weakest part of you. Cuz you'll regret it for the rest of your days. But if you act outta the strongest part of yer soul, then no one can stop you! You hear me child? And you'll never, ever regret it!"

Angela saw the moon shining down on her Aunt Millie's old, weather-stricken face and smiled. Faith. Yes. Faith. Simple, childlike faith. And suddenly, the veil was lifted, and she knew her own heart. It became more clear to her than anything else she'd ever been sure of. She looked the moon in the eye and nodded her head. She reached over and hugged the old woman again.

"I have to go see someone Aunt Millie. Don't wait up for me!"

Angela got back in her car and drove away, leaving her Aunt Millie standing in the driveway. The old woman watched until the tail lights faded into the distance, then she laughed softly and hobbled slowly back up to the porch. Kids. Why do they make everything so difficult? She opened the door and went back to her crossword puzzle - still looking for a five-letter word that meant “to believe in something without evidence”. She sat down in the old wooden rocker. She was patient; it would come to her – in time – in the Lord’s good time. She closed her eyes, and she rocked.

Chapter 23

Hank was in the back yard tending burgers on the grill. The little ones were scattered all around him on the grass, playing with balls, Tinker Toys, and horse shoes. Then he felt a woman's hand move around to the front of his waist and then pull herself close to him. Gentle, tender lips kissed his neck, sending shivers down the length of his spine, arousing and awakening deep places inside him that had been lying safely dormant for many years. Angela spun him around, threw her arms around his neck and kissed him gently on the lips, then more firmly. Hank responded by dropping the spatula to the ground. His first thoughts were of his children. "I shouldn't be doing this in front of my kids." He looked over at them playing in the grass, but they were absorbed in their play and oblivious to his presence.

He put his empty arms around her slender waist and pulled her closer to his body. There was a warm, ancient surge that flushed the surface of his skin, and a desperate, primal fire that coursed through his veins to every part of his body aching for release.

But his children, not in front of his children! They must not see him like this! Angela went slack in his arms and her weight pulled him gently down to the grass. His legs straddled her own, pressing down on her thigh like a raging beast. Suddenly, when he was at the verge of losing all self control, a tiny finger tapped him on the shoulder. He ignored the tapping, but it grew harder and more insistent. Then words took form and invaded the slumber of his dreams. When he awoke, Micah was standing over his bed. He was naked from the waist down.

"Daddy, will you come wipe my butt? It's all yucky and I need help."

Hank wiped the dream sweat from his brow and yearned to go back to sleep. Though it had only been a fantasy, he still remembered Angela's touch, as if it had been real and not a dream at all.

"Sure honey. Let's get back into the bathroom and take care of it."

Hank drug his tired body out of bed, took Micah by the hand and staggered into the bathroom. Five minutes later, he was back in bed, struggling to return to Angela and his dream. He found himself wondering if it were possible to pause a dream like a DVD, then come back to it later. But the images wouldn't come. They were hindered by his own inhibitions and insecurities.

Then, just as he was beginning to drift off, he heard pounding at the front door. He shrugged it off at first, hoping it was part of another dream, but instead of going away, it intensified, dragging him kicking and screaming back into the conscious world.

Hank sat up and rotated his body slowly, at the same time swinging his feet around to the floor. A higher level of consciousness rushed over his brain when his bare feet hit the cold linoleum floor. He slowly got up and walked downstairs, glancing at the hallway clock as he passed – 1AM.

When he opened the door, he saw Angela. She walked in without an invitation. It was then that Hank noticed he was wearing nothing but boxer shorts. He made a quick check down south, ensuring that everything supposed to be covered, still was. Angela seemed nervous when she spoke.

"Did I wake you?"

Hank remembered his dream, but quickly beat the thought down like an uninvited demon. That was dream; this was reality.

Hank couldn't think of anything to say. Finally, after a few moments of clumsy silence he answered her.

"Well, at least I'm not wearing a gas mask this time."

She smiled and looked down. Conversations with Hank never seemed to go as planned.

"I'm sorry, I woke you didn't I. I'll come back tomorrow. I'm sorry Hank."

Angela turned and started to walk back out, but Hank reached over and touched her shoulder, freezing her in mid stride. With the other hand, he closed the door.

"It's okay Angela. We're friends. You've earned the right to wake me up at 1AM. Please, sit down at the kitchen table while I run upstairs and put some clothes on. Okay?"

Angela nodded sheepishly while Hank turned and tried to walk away sideways so she couldn't see the hair on his back. She sat down at the table and waited. Part of her wanted to run out the door and never come back, but, another part, couldn't be dragged away by wild horses.

When Hank entered the room again, he was wearing gray, cotton sweat pants and a plain white t-shirt. She could tell that he had tried to comb his hair, but to no avail; it still stuck up at odd angles all around his head.

"Can I get you some coffee?"

She nodded.

"That would be wonderful Hank. Thank you."

While Hank busied himself with the water and the grounds, Angela studied him carefully. Even at 1AM he was still the polite gentleman. She noticed that he had kept in pretty good shape for a man his age. Then, as she often did when she felt an urgent need to break the silence, she said the wrong thing.

"How old are you, Hank?"

His hands stopped moving and he glanced over his shoulder.

"You woke me at 1AM to ask my age?"

Angela fidgeted with her hands atop the Formica table top.

"No! No! I'm sorry. That was the wrong question again."

But Hank interrupted her.

"I'm 42 and proud of it."

She moved her hands up to her face and covered them in embarrassment.

"I'm sorry again Hank. I just get so nervous around you."

Hank turned around.

"Really? I didn't know that. You always seem so in control to me. I've listened to you at work, when you're on the phone selling ads. It's like you have this mesmerizing control over people. Sometimes I think you could sell a newspaper ad to just about anyone. You're amazing Angela. You really are."

Her hands involuntarily inched down from her face.

"Really? You think that about me?"

"Of course. It's obvious. You're a natural, Angela."

"I didn't know you thought that about me. Why didn't you ever tell me that?"

Hank turned on the drip coffee maker and smiled.

"I didn't think anything that intuitively obvious needed telling."

She smiled and a little of her nervousness melted away.

"What else do you think about me?"

Hank sat down at the table across from her.

"Well now, not so fast Angela. I'm not saying another word until I know how old you are."

"You're asking my age?"

"Well, you asked me and I told you, so it only seems fair."

Angela turned her head away.

"Well I don't think a gentleman should ask a lady her age. It doesn't seem proper to me!"

Hank laughed out loud.

"I can't believe you just woke me up at 1AM in my underwear, and then told me I was being inappropriate."

She looked down at the table top and let a tiny smile slip onto her lips.

"Well, I suppose you have a small point there."

"A small point? Who are you kidding Angela? It's a big point, it's valid and you know it."

She threw up her hands in final surrender.

"Okay, fine! I'm 31 years old okay? What difference does it make how old I am anyways?"

"It makes no difference, Angela. Not to me."

Hank got up and opened the cupboard searching for mugs without broken handles. He found two and proceeded to fix her coffee exactly the way she liked it: two sugars, one cream. Angela watched in fascination. If he worked this hard to please her as only her boss, how much better would he treat her as a . . . . She didn't finish the thought. When he was done, he handed her the steaming cup and sat back down across from her.

"So, do you still want an answer to your question?"

She looked up at him blankly.

"What question?"

"Do you still want to know what else I think of you?"

"Oh, that question. Is it good? I only want to know if it's good."

Hank thought for a moment. He had been burned and betrayed so many times before, and he felt that old familiar fear creeping back in. Instinctively, he knew in his heart of hearts, that tonight, at this very moment, he was at a strange crossroads in his life. If he blew it, and took the wrong turn, life would go on as it always had. But, if he took a chance, then maybe, just maybe. . . .

"I think you're wonderful, Angela. You're beautiful. You're smart. You're warm and kind. You treat my kids with compassion, even though I can tell you've never been around kids before. You're patient with them, and that says a lot about your character. You can always tell the full measure of a person by the way they treat children, and you treat my kids with dignity and respect, the same way you treat everyone else you come in contact with. I respect you very much. And I like you."

Hank watched her, trying to ascertain what she was thinking, but she said nothing. He was almost afraid to ask, but he forced himself. No sense in going half way.

"So what do you think about me?"

Angela hesitated, wondering what to say and how far to go. In the end, she threw caution to the wind.

"I have never been treated so kindly by anyone as I've been treated by you. You are the nicest man I've ever known."

Like a balloon losing its air, Hank's heart flew around the room, slowly deflating. He'd heard these words before. "You're a nice man, but . . . ." Sometimes he hated being a nice man. If the next word out of her mouth was "but" then he would wait until morning and throw himself off a cliff.

"And . . . sometimes, I just catch myself thinking, that, what would I do if you weren't in my life anymore? What would it be like if you stopped being nice to me. I like everything about you Hank. You have a servant's heart, and sometimes you put me to shame. I watch the selfless way you care for your children, the way you love them, and I long to be loved that much by someone, to be cherished and protected and warded from harm the way you stand guard over your family."

Hank's heart slowly began to re-inflate.

"You like that stuff?"

Angela nodded.

"I love it. I never thought I would love watching kids, but I do. You have great kids, Hank. You really do. You've done a good job with them. You sacrificed your own needs for theirs. You've got character Hank. Real character. And I want to become more like you. And the only way I can think of doing that is to spend more time with you."

Hank's heart was bursting at the seams. He smiled and blew the steam away from his coffee. This was better than the dream. This was real!

"I want to stay at the Gazette, Hank. If it's okay with you, I'm going to call my old company and give them my notice. I want to stay here in Freidham Ridge. And I'd love to watch your kids anytime you like."

Hank smiled and nodded.

"I would like that, Angela. I would like that very much."

Chapter 24

Folks around town called him the crap duster, and Hank watched him now from the safe distance of two tables away inside the Mudhen Grille. He was a burly enough looking fellow, and Hank guessed that he was the kind of guy who women seldom ever brought home to their mother. Hank had been told that the man's real name was Eldon Cannon and that he had moved to Freidham Ridge about the same time as Lance Stuart, but that everyone just called him Spunky.

Spunky's greasy, graying hair was matted down and laying flat and close against the sides of his head, and even from two tables away, that rotted sweat and stale alcohol smell often characteristic of alcoholics was more than evident. His faded blue jeans were dirty and torn and they hung down at the waist low enough to show his plumber's vertical smile as he sat haphazardly on the old barstool.

Hank had been watching him curiously ever since that Thanksgiving Day dinner at his house, and the man fascinated him. That had always been one of Hank's greatest fascinations: the eccentric, the insane, the downright weird. Hmmm, a light suddenly went off in Hank's brain. That certainly explained his errant taste in women. Hank made a mental note: "Next time, marry a 'normal' woman."

Spunky flew a crop dusting plane all over Iroquois county, and his services were in semi-moderate demand, but instead of spraying insecticide and chemical fertilizers like everyone else, Spunky took the organic approach. He also owned a septic tank service and spent half his time sucking out septic tanks. He called the waste-product liquid gold, and it went straight into the tank on his crop duster and from there onto farmer's fields all over the county. Thus, he was dubbed Iroquois County's one and only "Crap Duster".

Hank had all but made up his mind to go over and talk to Spunky when he saw Lance Stuart come through the door and walk straight over to Spunky's table. Hank's interest became even more intense, and it was only a matter of time before the same curiosity and fascination which had prompted him to marry a drunken lunatic, swelled and surfaced, and he was uncontrollably overcome by his own woebegone lack of common sense. He slowly got up and began the walk over to Spunky and Lance.

"Did ya bring the board, Rock?"

The Pulitzer prize winning author nodded and smiled as he took off his winter coat and hung it on the chair behind him.

"Got it right here Spunk. And I feel pretty cocky today! Man it's cold out there tonight!"

Spunky Cannon straightened his large frame in the chair and pretended to spit off to one side.

"Bring it on old man!"

When Hank reached the table, they were both setting up the chess pieces, preparing for their game. Neither of them appeared to see him.

"Hi guys. How's it going?"

Lance Stuart glanced up, but didn't stop putting his chess pieces on the board.

"Not too bad there Mr. Simmons."

But Spunky Cannon looked up at him as if Hank had just drowned a whole litter of the cutest kittens on earth.

"What'd ya want jerkweed!"

His tone was pure venom, and Hank was taken aback for a moment. Was this the same man he had invited into his home on Thanksgiving Day? Then his reporter's instincts took over and he came back with a quick retort.

"What do I want? I want to marry a super model. But I doubt it'll happen. Didn't happen yesterday or the day before either. What'd you want?"

A subtle smile came over Lance's face, but he didn't look up and he continued to set up the game. He thought it funny the way Hank got so nervous around Spunky. But there was no need for it – Spunky's bark was much worse than his bite. It had always been that way. Spunky sat staring at him for a moment, and Hank knew that either he was about to be welcomed into the fold, or be bludgeoned to death. Finally, Spunky burst out laughing and motioned for Hank to sit down.

"You play chess, city boy?"

Hank nodded slightly.

"Used to, but it's been a while. I thought all you rednecks played was checkers on top of wooden barrels and ate pickled pig's feet and chitlins."

This time it was the Rock's turn to laugh. He reached over and shook Hank's hand in formal greeting and recognition.

"Good to see you again Hank. I enjoyed Thanksgiving at your house by the way. You can play the winner. That would be me of course as soon as I wipe the board with this old codger."

"Old! Who are you calling old? Why yer so old you spawned the first dirt!"

Rock's eyes twinkled playfully.

"Why thank you Spunk, but I think you're confusing me with another elderly gentleman named God."

"Yeah, right. Just make yer move college boy!"

Lance put his hand on his king's pawn but then drew it back.

"Last time we talked, you said you were going to spot me a queen?

You reneging on the deal?"

A cocky, confident air came over Spunky's face as he reached up ceremoniously and pushed his black queen over onto its side.

"In the immortal words of King Ramses the second, 'So let it be said, so let it be done.' Now move before I change my mind."

Lance moved his king's pawn, and then Spunky countered by moving his own king's pawn. And then they moved back and forth, back and forth, quickly, like a jig they'd been dancing for years, and a song they'd been singing since they were kids.

Hank found himself intrigued with Spunky's style, who seemed to sacrifice and trade chess pieces with great confidence and poise for a man steeped and controlled by addiction. Finally, 30 minutes later, almost out of nowhere, Spunky let out a loud bellow.

"Checkmate! Ah you stupid college boy I got ya again!"

Lance meticulously looked over his options and found none. He quietly smiled and conceded his loss.

"Blast it! I thought I had you this time."

"Yeah, well you thought wrong old man! I can't believe you fell for that one. I thought you were supposed to be educated? What's that school you taught at again? Harvard wasn't it?"

Lance appeared to be a little annoyed.

"Oh just shut up about it. You beat me every time we play. Can't you win graciously just for once?"

Spunky, with a huge childlike grin on his face cocked his head to one side and pretended to spit off to one side again.

"What for? No fun in that. What good's winning if ya can't rub it in. What's the matter old man, are ya losin' yer edge?"

Lance yelled over to the waitress for some coffee.

"You're assuming I once had an edge. And no I'm not losing my edge!"

By now the waitress had reached the table. She saw the look on Lance's face and guessed the game's outcome.

"Lost again, eh Rock?"

Lance nodded.

"Go ahead, Ruthie. Put his bill on my tab again. A bet's a bet. And bring me some coffee please. Decaf this time. Caffeine makes me cranky, especially after I lose."

The waitress looked over to Hank.

"Anything for you, Mr. Simmons?"

Hank was still looking down at the board, trying to figure out how a Harvard Professor and Pulitzer prize winner had just lost in Chess to an alcoholic crap duster.

"Oh, yeah. Coffee's fine for me. Some fries too please."

Then he looked over at Spunky, who was already pushing back his chair to get up. Rock tried to talk him out of it.

"Hey where are you going? Aren't you going to give me a chance to even it up?"

Spunky waved him off.

"Nah, you've suffered enough for one day old man. Besides, I got a date with a septic tank. She's a real honey too!"

He laughed alone at his own humor. On his way out the door, Spunky called back to Ruthie who was pouring coffee.

"Hey Ruthie! Hank over there needs to get laid. Go ahead and put it on Rock's tab."

She gave him an annoyed stare, and then the door slammed shut behind him, leaving Hank and Lance alone at the table.

"Wow! You just got beat in chess by a septic tank man that quotes Ramses! I can't believe it! This town just keeps getting better everyday!"

Ruthie set down their coffee and left without speaking.

"Hush up city boy! Don't you start in on me too. He wasn't always a septic tank man you know."

"Oh really?"

Lance put his wrinkled old hands around the hot mug to warm them.

"You'd think a nosey, old reporter like you would be better informed."

Hank sensed a keen edge in the old man's voice and backed off a bit.

"Hey, I'm sorry. He would've beaten me in half as many moves. Where do you think he learned how to play like that?"

Lance picked up his coffee and blew on it. Steam wafted out and away from him.

"I taught him 20 years ago. He was one of my students at Harvard. He's a natural."

Hank was silent for a moment, trying to figure out whether or not to believe him.

"Harvard?"

"Yeah. Harvard. You've heard of it. A prestigious institution of higher learning over on the east coast? It was in all the papers."

Hank regained his composure and slowly smiled. He was taken aback. It wasn't like the professor to be so coarse. Best not to perturb a man who carried such a big gun.

"I thought he was just a redneck."

"Well, you were right on that count. He is a redneck. But you also thought he was a dumb redneck. You judged him by his cover. He was Captain of the Harvard Chess Team for two years, until his wife came down with cancer. He dropped out of school and held her hand while it slowly ate her down to the bone. Then he moved here and took up drinking. He hasn't been the same since. But I don't judge him. Some pain is more than a man can take and justifies capitulation. So, can I talk you into giving the man some slack?"

Hank looked down and frowned.

"Ah, yeah. Sure. I just didn't know that's all."

"I know. Don't worry about it. I used to make the same mistake."

Then he put his coffee mug down on the table, and hesitated for a moment as if weighing his words carefully.

"Every man, woman, and child is a story. We are all books waiting to be written. And inside the cover of each man, beneath the surface, we discover what makes him laugh and cry. Sometimes it's best to hold off on first impressions. That's what I've done with you."

Hank looked up, his eyes revealing a million and one questions. Dare he ask?

"So what exactly do you think of me?"

Lance looked back down at his coffee, watching the steam drift up and fade away into nothing.

"Guess I fell right into that one didn't I?"

Once again he hesitated, weighing his words as if each one were an irretrievable bullet.

"There's a lot I like about you, Hank. You're witty, you're clever, you're smart. You say what's on your mind, and for the most part you have integrity. But there's just one thing that bothers me. Sometimes you think you're better than other people. You feel superior to all these dumb farmers and rednecks around here. And that one thing is what keeps you from becoming a great reporter and a great writer, because it keeps you from seeing the value of those around you. The people in this little hick town are some of the most interesting on earth. You just don't see it because you already have them stereotyped. And I guess I recognize it in you, because I used to be the same way. But I have to tell you straight from the hip, that I've learned more from these lowly rednecks in the past 10 years than all my stay in the ivy league. Harvard teaches books, but Freidham Ridge teaches life!"

Lance looked up at Ruthie who was just now turning on the television.

The 24-hour news channel was reporting on the war on terror as usual.

"And all that advice plus fifty cents will get you a cup of coffee at the Mudhen Grille!"

Hank's face turned red. At first he was angry, but deep down inside, he knew that the old man had hit the nail on the head. He didn't want to respond based only on his emotions, so he thought about it for a minute. Then Ruthie came over with his fries and that helped to distract him and diffuse the tension in the air."

"Need ketchup for that Hank?"

He looked up from deep contemplation and answered.

"Ah, yeah Ruthie. Better bring a whole bottle. This is a little hard to swallow."

Ruthie sensed something was wrong but didn't want to pry.

"Sure thing. Be right back."

Hank picked up one of his fries, but it burned his fingers and he quickly dropped it.

"I know you're right Rock. I'm not sure why I do it though. I pride myself in being open minded, so why can't I be open minded and tolerant about all these folks? It doesn't make sense."

"Doesn't it? Think about it for a minute. And the question you have to ask yourself is this: What does it give you? What need does it fill? If you can be honest with yourself about that, then you'll be halfway there. Just my opinion."

Hank picked up the fry again. This time it was cool enough and he popped it into his mouth.

"Ya know what Rock?"

Lance took a sip of his coffee and grunted.

"For a guy who just got wiped out by a septic tank man, you're pretty smart!"

Rock tried to stay serious, but he couldn't, and soon both men were laughing out loud. Suddenly, Hank's ears perked up and he motioned with his hands for Rock to be quiet. They both swiveled simultaneously in their chairs and looked at the images coming over the newscast. Together, they listened intently as the newscaster read off the news of the day.

"U.S. Government sources revealed today that they believe Osama Bin Laden's terrorist network has been actively seeking to develop and procure nuclear devices for use against the United States and the West. They said that the source of their belief is rooted in key documents which were left behind after Al-Qaeda's swift departure from Kabul, Afghanistan. For a more in depth look at this frightening possibility, we bring you now to Nuclear terrorist expert, Dr. Harry Donovan, from Georgetown University."

Lance Stuart scoffed out loud.

"Where do they get off calling 'him' an expert on anything! I used to teach with that guy when he was at Harvard. He's an arrogant moron!"

The newscaster's voice continued. The TV screen was split, one showed the newscaster, and the other showed Dr. Donovan from Georgetown University.

"So, Dr. Donovan, what can you tell us about the possibilities of a nuclear terrorist attack on the United States? Do we really have anything to fear, or is all this being blown out of proportion?"

Dr. Donovan appeared to be in his early sixties, bald on top, and boasting very large ears. He wore a grey suit with a white shirt and black tie.

"Well, Steve, I think I can say with the utmost certainty, that there is absolutely no reason for the United States to fear this type of attack from Al-Qaeda or any other terrorist network."

"But how do you know that to be true, Dr. Donovan?"

"It's quite simple, Steve. Show me the evidence. Show me the proof! All we have here are a few documents that speculate that Al-Qaeda might be in the market for a weapon of mass destruction. Where's the real human intel? Where's the other corroborating evidence? This is nothing but conjecture, hype and pure speculation on the part of the administration."

"But why would they do that? Why would they raise this question if it wasn't real?"

Dr. Donovan threw up his hands and rolled his eyes in disgust.

"Why does the far right do anything, Steve? For personal and political gain of course! They have to justify this invasion of Afghanistan, so they're looking for anything they can to bolster their case. They have to create fear in the American public. Once that is done, the citizenry will line up behind the President like lemmings on a cliff."

Steve interrupted him with another question.

"But isn't it true that several nuclear suitcase bombs developed by the former Soviet Union are now confirmed as missing by Russia?"

"Absolutely not, Steve. Those were not solid confirmations, just off the record quotes by unidentified Russian sources. Those reports have no credibility whatsoever, and shouldn't really even be reported as such. And even if those suitcase bombs did exist, even if they were in the hands of terrorists, they are relatively low-yield devices."

"So how many people could one of these bombs kill?"

Dr. Donovan seemed perturbed by the question, but thought for a moment before answering.

"Well, Steve, there's no real way of answering that question. There are just way too many variables: size of the bomb, wind direction, time of day, population density, even delivery method; they all come into play here."

"So just take a guess. A hundred – a thousand – a million?"

Dr. Donovan wiped his left hand nervously over the top of his bald head. It was obvious that this interview wasn't progressing according to his plans.

"Depending on population density, anywhere from 1,000 to 30,000 could die in the initial blast, on the first day that is. After that, it would depend on all of the variables I mentioned."

The newscaster raised his eyebrows in surprise.

"Thirty thousand on the first day? From one bomb the size of a suitcase?"

Dr. Donovan nodded his head.

"Yes, and that would be followed over the ensuing days and weeks with tens of thousands of more deaths caused by fallout, disease, radiation sickness, not to mention casualties caused by the breakdown in police, medical and emergency services. But like I said before, Steve. I don't believe any of that will happen."

"So if this were to happen, then hundreds of thousands of Americans could die from just one of these little suitcase bombs."

"I didn't say that Steve!"

"Well thank you for your expert opinion, Dr. Donovan. We appreciate your willingness to come on the air with us."

The split screen went away just as the doctor was trying to speak. But the newscaster had already moved on to other topics.

Lance and Hank turned back toward each other. Hank looked down at his cooling French fries, while Lance blew uneasily on his cold coffee.

"Do you think that could really happen?"

Lance shrugged.

"My degrees are all in English and Literature. But one thing's for certain, if Harry Donovan says it can't happen, then you can bet the farm that it's entirely possible. I can't remember that guy ever being right about anything. That guy would say anything to keep himself in the limelight. Makes me wish I had a fallout shelter."

"You're kidding, right?"

Lance smiled.

"Mostly kidding, but not all. Have you ever read a novel called "Alas Babylon", written by Pat Frank?"

Hank shook his head from side to side.

"Go to the library tomorrow and check it out. It'll make you think twice, that's for sure."

Hank shrugged his shoulders.

"I'm not really into that kind of stuff."

Lance Stuart looked down and sighed.

"Well, you can bet the terrorists are into it."

Hank pushed back his chair and started to get up.

"Well, you're the Professor, so I'll just leave all the thinking up to you. I gotta get home. I promised Angela I'd be back early. We're all going to watch "It's a Wonderful Life" tonight with Jimmy Stewart. The kids and I love that movie."

Lance raised his eyebrows and smiled.

"Yes, I heard you two were fast becoming good friends. How is it going?"

Hank lifted the heavy wool coat off the back of his chair and pulled on first one sleeve and then the other.

"Can't anyone keep a secret in this town, Rock?"

"It's no secret, Hank. I've seen the two of you in here over lunch everyday this week, staring at each other, all lost in each other's eyes. You're a lucky man Hank."

Hank zipped his coat and nodded.

"God has blessed my family. She's an incredible woman. And the amazing part is, she thinks I'm incredible too! I can't believe it."

Rock took a sip of his coffee and set the cup back down on the table with a gentle thud. Rock remembered his own wife, gone these many years. He had been blessed too, at one time.

"Have a good night, Hank."

Hank walked back out into the cold, anxious to get home to his family.

Chapter 25

"Buffalo gal can't ya come out tonight, can't ya come out tonight, can't ya come out tonight. Buffalo gal can't ya come out tonight. And, dance by the light of the moon."

The kids were already tucked in bed, and Hank and Angela sat on the couch watching Jimmy Stuart and Donna Reed flirt with one another. Toto was curled up on the floor, sleeping between Hank's feet. He liked having the little dog there. It kept his feet warm.

"I have no idea what a buffalo gal is. Do you?"

Hank shook his head no. He seemed surprised by the question, but nonetheless tried to answer it.

"I never really thought about it before. I suppose it must be a woman cowboy or something. Maybe it's a woman who likes to buffalo hunt?"

Angela laughed out loud at him, and he looked hurt.

"What? Why are you laughing at me?"

Angela looked over at him. He was 2 feet away on the couch, and it seemed unnatural that he didn't just move on over and put his arm around her. But she knew that he wouldn't. He was too much of a gentleman, and, as far as Angela could tell, that was his only flaw.

"Oh nothing. I just wondered why men always think they have to be able to answer every impossible question us women ask."

Hank moved his right hand up to his chin and held it there, totally lost in thought.

"Hmm, I'm not sure. Maybe we're just trying to be helpful. Maybe, we're just . . . ."

But Angela was quick to interrupt him.

"You're doing it again Hank!"

"Doing what?"

"I just asked a question you couldn't possibly answer, and now you're trying to answer it for me."

He let his hand drop down off his chin and fall to his empty lap. He lifted his left foot up off the floor and crossed it over his right leg. Toto whined softly at the disturbance, before shifting his body slightly and returning to slumber.

"Well if you don't want me to answer the questions, then why do you keep asking them?"

Angela's eyes sparkled in the faint light of the television screen.

"Are you kidding?"

Hank hesitated a moment.

"Is that one of the questions I'm supposed to answer or one I'm not supposed to answer?"

Angela laughed out loud again, until she realized that his question was more serious than she'd first imagined.

"You're serious aren't you?"

This time Hank remained silent. He was starting to feel a bit foolish.

"I'm sorry Hank. Us women are terrible sometimes."

She paused for a moment, trying to think of the best way to describe this to him. Hank had dropped his head down, and Angela couldn't help but think of him as a confused little boy who'd just gotten his feelings hurt. She smiled softly, then very slowly, reached over and touched the side of his cheek with her left hand. Hank looked up slowly and gazed into her eyes.

"We don't want you to answer all of our silly questions, Hank. We don't want you to solve all our problems. We're not broken, and you don't have to fix us. Okay?"

Hank nodded as if he were the first man in history to suddenly understand this most basic of life's truths.

"Oh. I see. Really?"

Angela smiled.

"We just want our man to listen to us. That's all. No more, No less."

Hank nodded again.

"Well, okay. I can do that. I guess."

Hank turned back to the television but didn't notice that Angela kept looking at him. Her hand had moved away now and was safely back on her own lap.

"Oh no, not just one wish, but a whole hatful! I know what I'm gonna do tomorrow and the next day and the next day after that. I'm gonna shake the dust of this crummy little town off my feet, and I'm gonna see the world!"

Hank nodded his head, involuntarily agreeing with Jimmy Stuart's words. Angela immediately wanted to know what he was thinking.

"What was that?"

Hank looked confused again.

"What was what?"

Angela was impatient when she replied.

"I mean what were you just thinking when you nodded your head? If you and I are going to spend time together, then you're simply going to have to learn how to read my mind. I see no other option. You shouldn't have to ask 'what was what'. You should intuitively know what I want you to tell me."

This time Hank raised his eyebrows in surprise. On the one hand, it seemed crazy to believe she was serious, but something inside him cried out for more detailed information.

"Now doesn't that seem a bit one-sided? If you were better at reading 'my' mind, then why should I have to tell you what 'I'm' thinking?"

Angela smiled.

"Okay Hank. That impressed me."

Hank smiled too.

"Good. It's about time I impressed you. I've been trying for weeks."

"Really?"

Hank nodded.

"Ya know what Hank?"

Hank thought about making a sly comment about reading her mind, but the magic of the moment intervened, and he just shook his head no.

"You started impressing me the first time we talked and you haven't looked back."

Suddenly, Hank's ego grew three sizes, and he felt 10 feet tall and bulletproof. He wondered how Angela could make him feel that way.

"I was nodding at what Jimmy Stuart just said. I once thought like him. I thought I wanted to get out and see the world, to conquer it." His voice took on the tone of mock pomp and importance. "To bravely go where no man has gone before!"

Angela leaned closer.

"So what happened?"

"I had kids. And that changed everything. It changed me mostly I suppose."

"How so?"

"Well, I'm not sure. It just seems like from the first moment I held Phillip in my arms, that life was no longer the same. One moment I was lost in my career and my ego, worried about how many points I scored, how much money I made, what kind of car I drove. And the next, I looked down and I was a daddy. And I knew at that moment that I'd found my calling in life. I'd suddenly reached out and touched someone greater than myself. From that moment on, I became a servant and a protector. My kids were bigger than me and anything else in life I may have thought I wanted. They became my reason for being."

Angela once more remembered the man in the wheelchair and his words. "Angela, you will never understand God, until you understand firsthand, what it is to know a kind, loving, strong, father."

Angela's heart flooded with emotions, and suddenly, she realized just how much she loved this man. She leaned over and kissed him on the cheek.

Hank looked surprised.

"What was that for?"

Angela smiled and leaned back against the throw pillow on the couch.

"Just for being you."

Hank smiled softly.

"Well, I guess I'll have to be myself more often then."

He hesitated a moment, as if collecting inner strength.

"So who do you think I am, Angela?"

Angela leaned closer again, and Hank grew a little uneasy at the scent of her.

"I know who you are, Hank. I know everything about you. You're faithful. You're loyal. You're kind. You protect and serve the ones you love. You seek the truth. You are the embodiment of every Boy Scout who ever lived. Sometimes you lack confidence, and you make silly jokes, but that's okay, because even then you try to do the right thing. You have a humility about you that is very attractive. Your strength is subtle. You seem like an ordinary guy, but you're anything but ordinary. I've been watching you Hank. I watch the way you treat people around you. I watch the way you play with your kids. There's a lot of love inside you, more than I've ever seen inside anyone else. And everything I see in you just draws me closer. You're almost selfless, and that's hard to find now days. Most people spend their whole lives feeding and worshipping their own egos. They live to please themselves."

She stopped a moment when she saw that Hank's face had turned red with embarrassment.

"You're a great man, Hank. But you don't know you're a great man. And I think that's what I like about you the most."

Hank uncrossed his legs and then looked down at the couch and scratched the back of his neck the way he always did when he got embarrassed. When he looked up again, his face was no longer red, and his eyes met her gaze and held it solidly.

"No one has ever told me anything like that before, and I don't really quite know what to say. I don't know how to respond. I feel very clumsy right now." He threw his hands up. "I just feel clumsy, that's all. Just clumsy."

Angela nodded her head, all the while afraid she would burst inside if she couldn't comfort him. Hank noticed that the television was still on. This was the scene where Jimmy Stuart and Donna Reed were walking back home from Harry's school prom. They had just thrown rocks at the old Grandville place. Hank watched as the fat, balding old man in the white t-shirt stood up from the porch rocker.

"Why don't you kiss her instead of talking her to death?"

Jimmy Stuart cocked his head to one side.

"How's that?"

"Why don't you kiss her instead of talking her to death!"

"You want me to kiss her, huh?"

The old man's exasperated look grew stronger.

"Aw-w, youth is wasted on the wrong people!"

Hank looked back over at Angela. She was beautiful, her long, flowing brown hair, curling at the ends and cascading down the side of the pillow.

"Angela, am I talking too much?"

Angela smiled and leaned slightly forward. She reached her hand over, gently closed it around his own and waited patiently. Hank glanced over at Jimmy Stuart, as if asking him what he should do next.

"Hey, come on back here mister! I'll show you some kisses that'll put hair back on your head!"

Hank leaned closer, touched Angela's cheek with his free hand, and kissed her gently on the lips. Angela responded, and they soon held each other safely for the remainder of the movie.

Afterwards, Hank walked Angela to the door and kissed her good night. And as he watched the glowing red tail lights outlined against the pure white snow fade away into the night, he reached up and touched his mouth. He recalled last month at the confession booth in Bentley, how he had told the priest that whenever he started to get close to a woman, that he thought she was going to cheat on him. It was odd, but after so short a time, he knew in his heart that Angela would never cheat on him. And he found himself suddenly ready and willing to take a risk. He smiled.

Then Toto walked up and brushed against his leg. Angela's tail lights were gone now, and he spoke to the quiet, December chill of the night.

"Well, Toto. I don't think we're in Kansas anymore."

His words echoed softly into the night, bouncing off the front porch and on out into the white-frosted snow of his lawn.

"I never liked Kansas much anyways."

Then he closed the door and went to bed.

Chapter 26

"Nurse, has the anastasia taken effect yet?"

Phillip was dressed in one of his father's baggy white dress shirts, and it hung down to his knees. There was a white dish towel wrapped and duct-taped to his head, and he was the perfect picture of a budding young surgeon.

"Let me check Doctor Philly."

Susan was dressed in similar garb, with a toy stethoscope around her neck, and a bowl full of kitchen utensils in her right hand. She walked around her four-year old brother, Micah, who was staring up Hank's nose from only 6 inches away.

"He sure gots a lot of hair up there."

Hank started to snore, and Micah moved back a few inches.

"What's he doin' Phillip?"

Phillip gave him an annoyed stare.

"He's snoring. I told you to call me Dr. Phil!"

Micah moved closer to the sound again and tried to look further up his father's nostrils.

"Can't we make it stop?"

Phillip's voice took on a confident, superior tone.

"Of course we can. I'm a doctor! I'll simply remove his snoring gland up there inside his naval cavity. But first we've got to take out his guts, 'cuz they're all inflected."

Cathy was wearing her favorite pink pajamas and laying on the back of the couch looking down on her father's sleeping body. She always liked it when he held still for them.

"Is it going to hurt, Doctor Phil?"

Phillip dug through the kitchen utensils and pulled out an egg beater and held it up to the light as if to inspect it.

"Only if he wakes up, Nurse Cathy."

Susan was bending over his face now and prying open his eyelids. She looked deep into Hank's bloodshot orbs.

"I think he's dead!"

"Don't be stupid, Nurse Susan! Dead people don't snore!"

Her father's eyelids slammed shut as she walked back to take her place beside Dr. Phillip. He put the egg beater back in the bowl.

"Nurse, I'm ready to make the indecision."

He held out his right hand.

"Scalpel!"

A serious look came over Susan's face.

"Be careful Doctor. He's the only daddy we got."

Hank's flannel shirt was pulled up to his armpits, and Micah, whose attention to Hank's nose hair had been temporarily interrupted, was now drawing on Hank's chest with colorful felt markers.

Cathy propped her head up on her elbow and looked on with interest while Phillip took the grey rubber hunting knife and began the imaginary cut across Hank's stomach. First, he cut out all the "inflection", then, one by one, each of Hank's organs were removed and handed to Nurse Susan who pretended to place them delicately in a 5-gallon bucket behind them.

"What happens to all these parts when we're done Dr. Phil?"

Phillip looked up long enough to answer her, and as he did, Susan swabbed imaginary sweat from his brow with a dirty dish rag.

First, we take 'em to the lab and look at 'em under a telescope. Then we give 'em to the pigs. Freida says pigs will eat anything."

Susan nodded her head knowingly.

"I guess he don't need 'em anymore anyways."

No one saw Micah reach over and take the small metal spoon out of the plastic bowl.

"All we got left is the ruptured tumor, and then we can do the circumspection."

Phillip handed the rubber knife back to Nurse Susan, who took it and quickly swabbed his forehead.

Suddenly, Hank awoke with a piercing scream and jumped up off the couch, all the while holding onto the spoon shoved deep inside his nose. Cathy fell off the back of the couch, and Micah, who had been straddling his chest was thrown completely clear.

"What are you guys doing!"

Hank pulled his hand away from his face and Phillip could barely see the end of the spoon through all the blood coming from the patient's nose. But the 10-year old doctor maintained his composure.

"Nurse! More anastasia!"

Hank fell down to the carpet, tugging at the end of the spoon, but it was firmly fixed to his snoring gland and wouldn't budge.

Nurse Susan ran screaming to her room and hid under the bed while Cathy peeked out from behind the couch, and little Micah looked on with joy at all the excitement caused by his handiwork. Angela, who had been washing the dishes in the kitchen, heard the screaming and ran in dripping dishwater with every step.

Phillip alone remained calm.

"Sir, I think we're going to have to operate."

Chapter 27

There was a cold, icy feel in the air tonight, so Special Agent Resnik waited patiently outside the apartment from the inside of his car, with the heater turned on, watching every movement, every shadow that passed by the shaded windows on the second floor where Momin and his comrades were staying.

He had just found out that Momin had flown to Russia yesterday, and there was no telling when he would be back. But, instinctively, Richard knew that he would be back, and no telling what manner of evil he would bring back with him to unleash on the general populace of America.

It was Christmas Eve, and he had been watching this terrorist cell for almost 3 months now, but still possessed no hard evidence to link them to terrorist activity. His orders, were to find out their orders, and how they were planning to carry them out. So, he had decided that tonight he would risk going into the apartment. It was very important that no one saw him, that they suspected nothing.

After waiting for over two hours, the four men came out of the front door together and walked away. Agent Resnik watched until they were out of sight. Then he quietly exited his car and walked through the front door and on up the stairs. No one saw him, and within 30 seconds he was inside the apartment.

The first thing he did was to quickly plant two bugs: one in the kitchen and another in the living room by the computer. Then he began to search for evidence, first in the dressers, then in the suitcases that were stacked against the wall. He found nothing, so he went to the computer in the corner of the living area and quickly booted it up. It was password protected, so he would have to come back for that later.

He saw a box of newspapers and magazines partially sticking out from under the coffee table. He pulled them out and began leafing through them. The ones on top were hard-core pornography and he tossed them to one side on the coffee table. Then, towards the bottom, he saw a manila envelope. He quickly opened it up and slid out the contents. They were printouts from the internet on crop dusting planes. One immediately caught his eye and he read the first two paragraphs.

Crop Duster Terrorism

What could a single suicide pilot do with a gasoline-laden crop duster? Crash into a people-packed baseball Stadium during the World Series, or into the Superbowl. The deaths would no doubt exceed those at the World Trade Center by the tens of thousands. Those not burned to death or killed by smoke inhalation, would certainly be trampled trying to escape the flames. And the most attractive part to a terrorist is, the entire event would be broadcast live on international TV. Free publicity! Electronic proliferation of terror, worldwide!

An Air Tractor 502 Crop Duster airplane is a lot smaller than an airliner, but it has one thing an airliner doesn't: fertilizer containers capable of holding about 1,200 liters of liquid, with a 500-liter fuel tank to boot. That is approximately the blast equivalent of 34 tons of TNT. A crop duster would also be able to fly close to the ground, where it could avoid radar, and no one would think anything of it, until it was in the city. But by then, it would be too late to stop.

Richard's mouth dropped open and he let the sheets of paper slip through his fingers and fall to the floor. He had seen a report on that possibility several years ago, but no one had taken it seriously. Nonetheless, they had warned all crop duster associations and pilots unions just as a precaution. Richard had come to the point where he took everything seriously now. After all, no one had expected them to fly airliners into the Twin Towers either. But they had done it. They had killed 3,000 people, but this crop duster plan could kill even more.

He quickly leafed through the rest of the papers and they confirmed what he had just read. He found flying instructions, a list of crop dusting pilots and their addresses in Michigan, and other articles on the different types of crop dusting planes.

A green spiral notebook on the bottom caught his eye, and he picked it up and let it fall open. What he read, took his breath away.

> *Effects of Radiation on Humans*
> *Nuclear radiation produces many negative health effects, appearing over a long span of time following exposure. The severity of the damage to the human body varies, depending on two things: duration of exposure and the volume of radiation dosage.*
>
> *Initially, humans experience nausea, headache, vomiting, and dizziness. As the final phase of radiation sickness sets in, the human subject suffers from diarrhea, hair loss, bleeding eyes, and skin hemorrhaging. And, finally, a slow, painful death ensues.*
>
> *The long-term results of overexposure*

to nuclear radiation include: genetic mutations and birth defects, increased levels of cancer in the exposed population, and the creation of new bacteria, viruses and diseases.

Richard's face paled and a shiver ran over his entire body. This discovery was both good and bad, because now he had evidence to show his superiors. Now they would give him the resources and authority he needed to shut these people down. Perhaps now they would take him seriously. On the other hand, if these animals succeeded in their plans . . . . He didn't even dare to end the thought. He just couldn't let that happen.

Just then he heard the door downstairs slam shut and the voices of men and laughter. As fast as he could, Richard took pictures of the papers and then put them back the way they were. Footsteps were coming up the stairs. It was too late to get out the way he'd come in.

He retreated to the bedroom and closed the door softly behind him, just as the apartment door opened and the others walked in. Richard's mind raced wildly! If they caught him here . . . he was a Jew and they were Moslems; they would not be content to kill him quickly. At best, he would have to fight his way out, then they would flee and the fifth terrorist, the leader, would no doubt be tipped off as well. They would all go into hiding and resurface somewhere else at a different place, in a different time, and, this time they may get away with their plans.

The room was dark and smelled rank and dirty. Light poured in from around the dirty window shade, casting a single ray of light onto the bed. And what he saw there stunned him, causing his pulse to race wildly and adrenaline to pump through his veins out of control. There was a naked woman tied to the bed. And she wasn't moving.

Chapter 28

The children were nestled all snug on the floor at Hank and Angela's feet. Micah was dressed in Sponge Bob pajamas, Phillip garbed in monster truck Hot Wheels, Susan in Barbie night-time fashion attire, and Cathy in plain, red flannel with white lace for trim. They were all bunched together on the floor, sprawled arm over arm and leg over leg, intertwined like several strands of a single hyphal unit.

Hank and Angela had fallen asleep on the couch just above them, arm in arm, snuggled as close together as the law of Moses would allow, with a blanket pulled up over them to take off the chill. None of the six had meant to fall asleep, but their combined peace had lured them here, and each of them, one by one, had quietly and contentedly, slowly drifted off to slumber.

To the left of the television set, the 6-feet tall Christmas tree, with its mismatched conglomeration of colored lights, tinsel, candy canes, and homemade adornments, had been decorated beyond repair. To the right of the television, the children had put their creative talents and water color paints to good use, by creating a Christmas fresco fireplace, and now, their stockings hung there quietly, waiting to be filled with nuts and fruit and candy.

Hank's breathing was louder than the others, with his nose still slightly red on one side and a little puffy, but most of the pain had subsided and he could breathe a little easier. For the first week, it had been grossly obvious, so Angela had tried to help ease his embarrassment by not staring at his swollen nostril. Now, on Christmas Eve, two weeks after Micah had shoved the spoon up his nose, Hank was almost back to normal.

Fuzzy little Toto was at their feet, the only one still awake, curled up between Hank's legs, staring blankly at the television, purporting to watch the movie. It was the second time this week they had all fallen asleep watching "It's a Wonderful Life".

Angela's breathing began to gradually accelerate as she started to dream, and like most dreams, it was mixture of reality and fantasy, the weird and the stable, of cosmos and chaos, and all were struggling for dominance and control.

She had experienced similar dreams all week long, but this time she was sitting in front of the desk of Henry F. Potter, the man who had stolen Bedford Falls. The infamous actor Lionel Barrymore, had on a clean suit of clothes, with his white hair neatly trimmed and combed.

Inside the dream, Angela looked around her. This time everything was in color - not a natural, cheery color, but one that had been painted on in sloppy blotches - as if Micah and Cathy had colored the picture and been unable to stay inside the lines. She wore a bright blue suit, and when she touched the sleeve, the color came off onto her hands. And over in one corner was a computer - a large one.

"How do you like my new clothes, the haircut, the office, the whole ball of wax?"

Angela looked over at Mr. Potter.

"What's your point, Mr. Potter!"

Henry F. Potter looked at her sternly.

"My point! Well, I want to hire you. I want you to manage my business affairs!"

He leaned back in his wheelchair. Angela looked down at her left hand and was surprised to see she was now holding a lit cigar, and then she looked around as she spoke, as if she were being controlled by the dream.

"You're not talking to me, Angela Benning? There's not somebody else in this room is there?"

Mr. Potter's voice boomed out.

"I'm talking to you, Angela Benning, whose ship has just come in . . . provided she has enough sense to climb aboard."

Angela thought for a moment, and then took a puff on the cigar. She coughed and wheezed, suddenly remembering she disdained cigar smoke and held it out away from her as if it were a burning asp.

"But what about the newspaper? What about Hank?"

She hesitated a moment.

"What about the kids?"

Mr. Potter became annoyed.

"Oh, forget about the newspaper! I'm offering you a three year's contract at 250,000 dollars a year! Now will you take it or won't you?"

Angela hesitated a moment, and then a smile began to spread across her face.

"I'll take it Mr. Potter!"

Henry Potter's face looked surprised, and he turned his head to look at the third man in the room, his attendant who had been standing beside them. The man was unusually tall, and wore a white, linen suit. He had a shining radiance about him that seemed out of place, even in the surrealness of the dream. The man in the wheelchair looked back down.

"What do you mean, 'I'll take it Mr. Potter!' You certainly will not! Don't you realize how important this decision is? Don't you know how miserable you'll be? You love Hank and the kids!"

Angela looked confused, and she squirmed back and forth in the big overstuffed chair.

"Now give me a break, Mr. Potter, I've only had this dream once in my whole life, and you expect me to get it perfect the first time!"

Mr. Potter leaned forward in his wheelchair.

"Will you listen to me for just once in your life! You've only got one chance, Angela, just one last chance, that's all. This is all you've got left. You mess this up and . . ."

The old man stopped in mid sentence.

"Hey, now wait a minute. That's an idea!"

He looked across the desk at Angela and smiled.

"I'm going to show you what you'll be like someday if you miss this chance, Angela. And more importantly, I'm going to show you the wonderful things you'll miss if you make the wrong choice!"

Angela's cigar had gone out, and she dropped it onto the floor beside her. Mr. Potter motioned to the big computer in the corner.

"Look into that computer, Angela."

Angela leaned her good ear forward.

"What's that you say, Mr. Potter?"

"Oh just shut up and look at the computer!"

Angela looked over into the CRT screen, and it magically came to life. It started out as monochrome, and then turned color. Fireworks shot out of the screen and burst into the office over her head. A few seconds later, the pyrotechnics ended and the screen settled back to monochrome green, then grey, then back to full color.

A blurred image came to life, then it started to focus itself, slowly at first and then faster and faster as it took shape. Angela saw a woman behind a desk, with a computer in front of her, and she was typing away oblivious to the rest of the world, opening spreadsheets, making charts and graphs, analyzing financials.

Slowly, the translucent image of a man and four children appeared behind her. The man called out to her.

"Angela, come on! We have a picnic planned. Let's go!"

Then, the voice of a small child chimed in.

"Come on Mommy! Freida is bringing donuts and everything!"

The woman at the computer didn't reply. She was still typing away. The man reached his arms out to her, but before he could touch her, he slowly faded and disappeared along with the children behind him.

The woman kept on typing. Then she stopped, and turned to face Mr. Potter's office. Angela saw the dull, monochrome green eyes, her eyes, and then they started to glow, brighter and brighter, as if someone were boosting the power. The woman turned back to the screen and began to type again, this time faster, and faster, and faster. Her hands flew across the keys, barely touching them, as if the two were one, and then the screen began to glow brighter, like the woman's eyes, and soon the whole room was lit up in the eerie iridescence of the green thing.

Angela saw the muscles in the woman's arms begin to convulse as she started to shake in the chair, slightly at first, and then uncontrollably. Angela knew that the woman in the chair was her, that she was trying to get away from the desk, but the draw of the computer had grown too strong for her. It had too much power.

As Angela looked on helplessly, wires flew out of the keyboard and dug into the woman's hands. Again and again wires shot out in increasing numbers, growing and wrapping themselves around the woman's body, constricting on her like a snake until finally, Angela could no longer see herself through the twisted circuitry - just the glowing of her monochrome eyes.

Finally, the woman went still, as if the life had been strangled and sucked from her body.

Angela slumped down in the overstuffed chair and began to cry. Henry Potter creaked forward and shoved a paper across the desk.

"Just sign on the dotted line, my friend. Just sign and that computer can be yours."

The old man smiled.

"Actually, it can be more than yours. It can be you!"

The man in the wheelchair began to laugh, slowly at first, deeply, and then the laugh crescendoed, echoed around the walls and then back down at Angela, until it took on the high-pitched tone of a voice simulator.

Finally, the laughter faded, and Angela was left with four short words that echoed around and around inside his head.

"This is your life!"

Then Mr. Potter was gone. The office was gone. Angela opened her green eyes and looked up into Hank's slumbering face. She saw him and smiled. She looked down at the children, took note of the steady rise and fall of their tiny chests. Then, reassured that it had just been a bad dream, she closed her eyes and slowly fell back to sleep.

Chapter 29

"Oh holy night, the stars are brightly shining. This is the night of our dear Savior's birth."

Lance Stuart hummed along with the music on the radio as his fingers flew over the keyboard, keeping perfect time with the song. It wasn't something he did on purpose; it just kind of happened, and he hadn't even been aware of it until his wife, Irene, had pointed it out to him one day, many, many years ago.

The music suddenly stopped and so did his typing on the computer. He hated computers, and his wife would probably be surprised to see him spending half his days working on one. In fact, he had railed against them and vehemently resisted the capitulation into the electronic world, but, after all, he was a man of intellect, a teacher, and there was just way too much information out there that could only be accessed through the computer screen. Besides, it also enabled him to socialize without leaving the house and to keep in touch with the many friends he'd made over the decades of his life. He'd also made new friends as well, and had been surprised at how close you could draw to someone you'd never seen before.

Lance did a save and then closed out of the file. He had been writing a lot lately, and it felt so good to be into it again. He was creating stories and developing characters, and he was certain that Irene would be proud of him if she were here. He missed his wife so much. He always had. His 15 years with her had been enough happiness for an entire life, and he would never remarry - there was no reason to. He was totally content with only her memory. Oddly enough, he never got lonely for the presence of others except on holidays. He hated holidays, because those were the times when he missed her physical presence, missed her touch, the feel of her hand on his own, the way she used to walk up behind him when he was writing, and look over his shoulder and read. She had been his number one critic, the only person he'd ever felt compelled to make happy. There were times he'd edited his work just to please her, just to allow her to feel a part of his co-creating with God.

The radio interrupted his thoughts with a news broadcast, the terrorist alert level was being raised to red for over the holidays. Apparently that meant there was a specific, identifiable threat that pointed to an imminent attack. Lance thought for a moment. I guess that meant that just prior to nine-eleven, the whole country had been on red alert and not even known it. They'd slept right on through it, right up until the planes had crashed into the twin towers. He listened to the newscaster talk about nuclear threat and weapons of mass destruction. It was the same canned information he'd been listening to for three days, and he was surprised at how little the government ever confided in its own people. But Lance knew more than most. One of the benefits of being a famous, Pulitzer prize winning author was having friends in high places, and friends in high places always knew the straight scoop, and, on occasion, were willing to share, and that, in itself, put Lance in high places as well.

With all the information he'd been gathering over the past week, he was convinced that something big was about to happen, maybe even bigger than nine-eleven, but it was all speculation. Lance could justify ignoring the speculation, but over the years, he had learned to take the gut feeling deep down inside himself seriously, very seriously. Right now, his instincts were throbbing red alert and out of control. Something huge was on the horizon. Human nature dictated it so, and human nature was the way of all earthly things.

He was reminded of William Butler Yeats: "Things fall apart, the center does not hold." And things were falling apart right now, falling apart at the seams, and perhaps were already beyond repair. Life and all things related to humanity were so fragile. They had created an artificial world, artificial and temporary, and all things man-made were destined from the start to return to the ways of God. His own small vegetable garden taught him that; his lawn taught him that. Without his constant and tireless care, barring his human intervention, the weeds would grow up and choke out the tasty tomatoes and beautiful flowers of his life. They would return to the ways of God. It had always been so, and from the beginning of time, man had been locked in an eternal and hopeless struggle against nature and nature's ways – God's ways. And the world had become so small, just one tiny vegetable garden, but the weeds had taken over, and, no matter how fast the gardeners pulled, the weeds just kept popping back up. Their roots ran too deep, and they threatened to choke out anything that caused beauty and caring to dominate the world. It was the way of all things – the history of the world, of all humanity.

Now, decades after the publishing of his first novel, Lance Stuart felt partially responsible for the state of the world. He had withdrawn, surrendered, fled far from the fight, and now things had gotten out of control. He felt guilty, not that he could have stopped it and didn't, but because he hadn't even tried. He'd given in to despair and tried to hide from it, and he knew instinctively that the purpose of all art was to lend cosmos to chaos, beauty to the land, and hope to those in despair. Lance had always believed that art should do more than just imitate life; it should guide it and steer it; keep it on the true north compass heading of our creator. That was the purpose of the Bible, and all other literature was subordinate to it.

It answered the question, "How shall we then live?"

Lance had long believed that it is better to write the world, not the way it is, but the way it should be. And on that topic, Lance had been irresponsibly silent for far too long. He feared it was too late, but, he couldn't concern himself with that. It was his job to write, his calling, his duty, and he would never forsake his duty again. God had created him to write; therefore, he would write. I write, therefore I am.

Lance smiled softly to the room around him. Yes, it was good to write again - good to exist again.

Chapter 30

There was a bit of a green, monochrome glow emanating from the back room of the suspect's house, and Officer Fitzu was dying to know what caused it. He'd been on this secret stakeout off and on for 6 months now, and he felt like he was closing in on major criminal behavior. True, he had no hard evidence that a crime had been committed, was being committed, or ever would be committed by this man, but that had never stopped him from making an arrest before, and he wasn't about to let it stop him now. In his heart of hearts, he knew that Lance Stuart was a bad apple, a subversive, and probably plotting against the government even now as he watched from his black Ford Ranger pick-up truck 100 yards down the road. All he had to do was prove it.

Andy opened the door of his truck slowly and quietly, all the while cursing the dome light as he got out and softly shut the door behind him. Technically, he was trespassing, but Andy had learned over the years that an officer of the law possessed incredible discretionary powers. He could pull over anyone for any or no reason at all, and he sometimes did. All he needed was just cause, which, in Andy's mind could be just about anything – driving too slow, driving too fast, wandering within your own lane, inability to confirm a fastened seat belt – all were justifiable reasons in Andy's mind. He could pretty much do anything he wanted to with impunity, because the law couldn't touch him – he was the law.

Andy was wearing white pants, a white turtleneck sweater, white ski mask, and tan leather gloves to better blend in with the snow around him. His 9 millimeter was strapped to his side, and he carried a digital camera with a telephoto lens in his right hand. All he needed was a few pictures of Lance Stuart doing something dirty, and he would bring down a famous, Pulitzer prize winning subversive author. He'd read Lance's book, just to get into his mind, to know his enemy, but hadn't really seen what the big deal was. It was just a book, and he had no use for them unless they were giving him instructions on how to build something or replace the fuel pump in his truck. Those were the only real books in Andy's mind.

The snow reached up past his ankles, dragging against his feet as he trudged through the snow. He was almost up to the back yard now, and Andy was reminded of how disgusting it was that this man never mowed his lawn in the summer. In fact, he'd issued Lance several tickets for violating section 4(a) of the county's beautification ordinance, but every time, the powers at large had failed to support him on it. Lance had hired the biggest, most expensive law firm in the state and had filed suit against the county. Faced with the prospect of an expensive court battle, the county had quickly folded. They said it wasn't worth it, and a waste of the taxpayer's money. Weak-spined people like that sickened Andy. Of course it was worth it. It was the law! And if the law wasn't worth fighting for, then what was? Nothing, that's what. Short of the law, there was nothing, nothing but anarchy, confusion, and chaos. Andy loved the law. He had it all memorized and engraved on his heart forever.

He stopped and knelt down behind a bush, fumbling to get the lens cap off his camera. Lance was inside. He could see him now, doing something in front of his computer. Andy's heart began to race. Maybe he was a pedophile! Finally, the lens cap slipped free and he raised the camera to his right eye. It was difficult to see through the camera with the ski mask on, so he had to adjust the eyehole accordingly. There, now he could see the computer screen. They weren't dirty pictures though as he had hoped, just text that Andy couldn't read because of the glare off the desk lamp. Lance seemed to be typing, and he was singing something as well.

Andy moved from behind the bush and crept slowly to the window. What kind of person would be so bold as to leave his drapes open at night? It didn't matter, Lance's indiscretion was Andy's gain. Slowly, he peeked up over the window sill and peered at the computer screen. The singing had stopped now. He raised the camera to his eye, focused the lens and clicked the picture. Much to his surprise, the flash went off and blinded him, temporarily lighting up the back yard, and taking away the safety of the night.

Inside, he heard a chair scrape quickly across a wooden floor and then hurried footsteps. Instinctively, Andy turned and ran as fast as he could, but his eyes were still blinded by the flash and he didn't see the clothesline stretched out before him right about throat high. When the nylon rope hit his larynx, it held fast and flipped his feet up into the air. Andy came down hard on his back and neck. First he saw stars, blinking on and off in his mind, then they went away and he was able to open his eyes again. Something was running down his throat, so he reached up and felt the blood. It was difficult to breathe. He thought he heard a screen door slam shut and he quickly scrambled to all fours.

§ § §

At first, Lance thought the flash was lightning, but he quickly ruled it out. This was Christmas Eve. There would be no thunderstorms for months. He quickly slid his chair back and rushed from his office to the kitchen. He stopped at the basement door and opened it quietly. He whistled softly.

"Patrick Henry!"

The well-trained German Shepherd trotted up the steps and stopped at his master's feet. Lance reached down and quickly patted the dog's head, then he slowly opened the heavy steel door to the back porch and pushed open the outside screen door.

"Patrick Henry. Give me liberty!"

The dog shot out into the night like a bullet from his master's gun, barking and growling as he closed in on the intruder.

A few seconds later, when Lance Stuart stepped out onto the wooden deck, he carried a 12 gauge pump shotgun with him. He heard barks and snarls and then a few dead limbs break as if something were rolling around in the brush. Lance zipped up his coat before sitting down on the porch swing to wait. Probably another reporter after an exclusive expose on "What happened to Lance Stuart, one-time famous author, now secretive and hidden recluse".

It didn't matter to Lance. Patrick Henry was good at his job. Once Patrick Henry's barks and snarls had sufficiently faded into the night, Lance stepped down off the back porch and walked over to his office window. He turned on the powerful flashlight and immediately lit up the darkness around him. There were tracks leading up to his window, about a size 13 boot, looked like standard military issue. He followed the tracks to the clothesline, and then he chuckled when he saw the man's imprint in the snow where he had crashed onto his back. There were a few drops of blood contrasted against the white, and Lance wondered if it was from running into the clothesline, or if Patrick Henry had found his mark.

He knelt down to contemplate gathering up a DNA sample, and that's when he saw the camera lying there, outlined against the snow. Lance carefully picked it up by the strap and looked at it in the illumination of his flashlight. He was surprised to see that it was a cheap model. His first thought was that of Hank Simmons, but he quickly brushed it aside. This wasn't Hank. He had more character than this. Hank would just ask for an exclusive, and Lance would probably even give it to him, as he'd grown to like the guy since their last talk. Couldn't play chess for beans though.

Lance smiled in remembrance. No, this was probably a small publication, maybe even a college student trying to make a name with a big story.

He heard Patrick Henry coming back home through the brush, so he walked back up the porch and into the house again. Once inside, he removed his coat and leaned the shotgun up against the wall. He set the camera down on the kitchen counter, then he reached up into the cupboard for a dog biscuit for Patrick Henry. There was scratching at the screen door. Lance let him in and then reached down to pet him before giving him the reward.

"Good dog Patrick! Did you get the bad guy?"

Then he noticed the white ski mask lying on the floor between the dog's rear legs. He picked it up and looked at it carefully. Within the polyester fibers, he saw several strands of short, black hair – human hair – human DNA.

Lance smiled, stood up, and walked over to the cupboard above the coat rack beside the back door. He put the ski mask there, then placed the camera on top of it, along with the others. He had two 35 mm Nikons, one Olympus, even a couple of digital cameras with brand names that he didn't recognize. This was Patrick Henry's trophy case.

Lance reached over and locked and bolted the steel door. Tomorrow he would put in several of those motion sensor outdoor floodlights just to make things more interesting. But for now, he was tired. And then his mind wandered back to his writing. That was the way of it, about 10 hours of thought for every half hour he wrote, and he never had to edit; it always came out perfect. People had told him how unusual that was, but it was all he'd ever known and he would never dream of writing a different way.

The old man went to his bedroom, Patrick Henry close at his heels. Within 10 minutes, both were fast asleep.

Officer Andy Fitzu, however, was still on his way to the county hospital to have the gash marks in his backside sewn shut. He hadn't learned a thing.

Chapter 31

Agent Resnik walked slowly and quietly over to the woman on the bed, and, as he got closer in the dim light, he realized that she was not a woman at all, but a young girl of no more than 13. He heard the television come on in the living room, followed quickly by the voices and laughter of the terrorists. He knew he should just get out, that he was risking the mission, but he couldn't leave without checking. He couldn't just leave a child tied to the bed. After all, only God knew what terrible things they were doing to her.

The floorboard creaked and he hesitated. They could hear nothing in the other room with the television turned on so loud. As long as they stayed out there, he would be okay. But for how long? They could walk in and catch him at any moment.

He was standing over the girl now. Her mouth was taped shut, and old wounds on her face leaked puss and fluid, while fresh blood still trickled like tiny rivers from new cuts on her face. Richard reached down to check for a pulse, but the moment he touched her, she jerked upward and tried to scream through the tape. He quickly bent down beside her and whispered into her ear.

"Quiet please! I'm with the police. I'm going to get you out of here."

Her body became rigid and stopped moving. The battered girl looked up at him with terror-filled eyes, and a lone tear beaded up before flowing down her cheek and mingling with her own blood.

A myriad of emotions welled up inside Richard as he stared down at the pitiful sight. A seething rage began to course through his veins that was hardly containable. He lifted up his sweater on the right side of his waist and touched the grip of his pistol. The righteous part of him wanted so much to unholster it and kill them all. But another part of him, the rational part, demanded restraint. Even if he killed them all, the leader would remain free to carry out a plan that could exterminate a hundred thousand people.

But what about something less? Couldn't he just wait for them all to leave again and then walk her out the front door? In the meantime, he could hide in the closet just to make sure they didn't kill her. It would be a risk – a deadly gamble – and if he was caught, he would die, the girl would die, and possibly a hundred thousand other innocent men, women, and children.

And it would all be for the sake of one person. Reason coupled with his training told him that he should slip out the bedroom window and into the ally. She was a pawn. She should be sacrificed for the good of the mission, for the good of the country, for the good of the public and the national interest. In his head, he knew that the good of the many, greatly outweighed the good of the few.

He thought for a moment, and then sighed with resolute stillness. He would do what had to be done. He had no choice. He was an American.

§ § §

Momin moved swiftly. He was tall for a Bengali, a little over 6 feet. His straight, black hair blew in the cold wind. He knew they were watching him, and had been for some time. He rounded the corner and ducked quickly inside a doorway. Then he watched. Nothing. Good. He could move freely tonight. He waited another 5 minutes though just to be sure. Tonight was too special to risk any chance of exposure. In just one hour, he was going to meet with the Chechen. There, he would take possession of two suitcases. In return, his superiors in the Mid-East would transfer 15 million dollars into the Chechen's account.

It was the day he'd been planning for almost a year now, long before that pitiful little raid the Americans referred almost reverently to as "nine-eleven". Momin's day would be so great that mere words would be unable to describe it. Only tears, and blood, and death would begin to do it justice, and it would dominate the American destiny for generations to come.

Momin smiled and moved cautiously back out onto the sidewalk and into the bustle of human traffic. He walked a block just to be doubly sure and then hailed a cab. Then he drove to the far side of the small Chechen town and waited on a park bench next to the telephone booth just as he was instructed.

He pulled his hood up over his head and laughed inside at his comrades. They were planning another mission in Detroit. By nine-eleven standards it would be huge, but Momin's act of loyalty and devotion to Allah would bump their story off the front page a million times over. The name of the game was terror, and, true, their plan would certainly bring terror, death, and destruction. But it was just the appetizer, just the pre-game, a foreshadowing of greater things to come. Nonetheless, it would ensure their place in paradise.

His friends had procured two crop dusters, and they were going to load the pesticide tanks with gasoline, and fly them to the stadium. Then, during a playoff game, when 75,000 fans were packed in like sardines, the planes would fly over and dump its deadly load across the stadium, soaking everyone below with the flammable liquid. Chances are, the gasoline would ignite on its own, through a spark, or someone lighting a cigarette.

But even if it didn't, all they had to do was make one final pass and crash into the crowd. All the humanity would go up in smoke and blood and fire. Those who weren't quickly immolated, would die from smoke inhalation, or would be trampled to death in the rush for the exits. It was pure terror, and, best of all, it would be on international television.

He had to admit that it was genius, just as the Twin Towers had been. The Americans were stronger and more powerful, but they were also arrogant and uncreative. They had many weaknesses. Even their precious freedom worked against them, allowing their enemies to move freely wherever they wished, and it gave them access to information and materials they never should have been able to obtain.

And, because he was a Moslem, and dark skinned, no one dared touch him. He was seldom searched in airports. The Transportation Security Administration (TSA) was so politically correct that they were afraid of being accused of profiling. Momin thought it amazing that America was more concerned with what strangers thought of them, than of their own survival. He enjoyed watching old, white ladies being pulled out of line at the airport and being searched while they let him go by unmolested. They didn't even dare look at him, much less search him. Arrogant, weak, fools! They valued their precious freedom and their Declaration of Independence more than they did their own lives.

He quoted from it now under his breath with rancor and unconcealed disdain.

"We hold these truths, that all men are created equal!"

Momin spat on the ground and swore aloud in Bengali, forever proclaiming his disagreement.

"Equal? No! Shob manush shristitay shoman? Ashombhob!"

They were just infidels, deserving death and destruction. The West would never be equal to Allah. And they would never turn from their Christian false god; therefore, they must die! The Koran commanded it!

The Chechen arrived in a late model, SUV. Momin and the man spoke. Momin examined the suitcases and confirmed their contents. Then he made a phone call on his cell phone. The money transfer was made, and the Chechen confirmed it with a call of his own. The Chechen mobster drove away, leaving Momin holding two large, black metal suitcases.

They were heavy, so Momin hailed another cab and allowed the driver to load them into his trunk. They barely fit. He was well trained, and knew it was safe, at least for now.

Momin went straight to the warehouse and readied the cases for their transportation to America. Now, all Momin had to do was return to Detroit and wait for final orders. Perhaps, that would be the hardest part of all, the waiting, because he was impatient to kill, needed it, hungered for it, was consumed with a hatred and rage for America, the Great Satan, that fought to surface out of control on a daily basis.

However, the scope and magnitude of the final act would be worth the wait, so he bit his lip and boarded the plane for the return flight.

On Christmas day, he returned to the apartment where the others were pouring over last-minute plans and details. After a short discussion, Momin left them to their petty venture and went straight to his bedroom.

When he opened the bedroom door, the young girl was gone. The wind whipped in, making the curtains flutter at him tauntingly. The ropes were still tied to the bed and a cardboard sign lay on the dirty sheets where she had been tortured. The note was written in Bengali, and it said in big, bold letters:

HAPPY HANNAKUH!-GOD BLESS AMERICA!

§ § §

By sunrise on the day after Christmas, Special Agent Resnik had the apartment building surrounded and gave the order to move in. The heavily armed assault team moved in first, quietly they crept up the stairs and then quickly rammed through the old wooden door and on into the apartment unopposed. Within seconds, Richard came in behind them with pistol raised. They were surprised to find four resting terrorists: two reclining on couches and two more lying on the floor covered with blankets and their heads posed comfortably on pillows.

Richard ignored them all and rushed into the bedroom, anxious to find the cell leader. But the room was empty. In the middle of the bed, where once had lain the tortured girl, now rested a cardboard sign, propped up with a pillow. Inscribed in Hebrew, written with human blood, was the message:

"No god but Allah – All others die!"

A chill ran through Richard's veins. He heard a shout from the living room.

"Oh my God! They're all dead! Get in here!"

Richard rushed into the other room, and lowered his pistol when he saw all the blood. He examined the four lifeless bodies. Each of them had died in their sleep by having their throats cut. A brief search revealed a bloody box cutter underneath the pillow of one of the corpses.

Visibly shaken, Agent Resnik walked out to the hallway and leaned against the wall. He shook his head to clear it and wiped the cold sweat from his brow.

Who was this man? How had Momin known about him? The questions haunted him like a demon.

§ § §

Three days after Christmas, Agent Resnik walked out of his apartment and out into the cold, deserted parking lot. It had been verified that Momin had returned to America on Christmas Day. In fact, Richard had seen him walk into the apartment with his own eyes, then he had immediately arranged for the raid. But the rules and red tape of big government moved slowly, and by the time everything had been coordinated, Momin had slipped away from them. Now, he was nowhere to be found. Richard's worst nightmare had come true. The little girl was safe, but the bad guy was free, on the loose, free to maim and kill and kidnap again. Richard shivered, but not from the cold. This guy was creepy. He wasn't your textbook terrorist – more like a serial killer. He made a mental note to run it past their profiler as soon as he was back from Christmas vacation. Richard didn't take vacations.

He zipped up his heavy, winter coat and then pulled on his insulated leather gloves. Even after all these years in Michigan, he still hadn't acclimated to the harsh, cold winters. Michigan weather just didn't make sense to him: cold one day, hot the next, snow in May and thunderstorms on Christmas Day. It was like there were no rules for the weather here, and the Great Lakes didn't make it any easier. A snowstorm in Milwaukee could mix with warm air over Lake Michigan and be a thunderstorm by the time it reached Grand Rapids. That's where he was going now, to visit his parents on the west side of the state. It was only a 2 and a half hour drive, but he would be there in two. Then, he would be a Jew again, at least in their eyes. It sounded like a whacked out TV game show, "Jew for a Day".

It was still dark, but the snow on the ground reflected the neon light, making it seem brighter than it really was. It was funny, but he never dreamed that police officers would be afraid of the dark, especially federal agents, but he was. He always had been, and some things never changed, even after donning a badge. He reached down and put his hand reassuringly on the pistol beneath his coat. It was next to useless to him. He was wearing so many layers of clothing that he would never get it out, even if his life depended on it. Lousy Michigan weather! After this assignment, maybe he would transfer to the west coast.

Richard reached his car and fumbled with the keys before clumsily dropping them into the snow. He swore softly in Hebrew and then bent down to dig them out of the snow. Sometimes he amazed himself. He could handle any firearm made, rig high explosives, supervise a high-tech surveillance team, and curse like a drunken sailor in 6 different languages, but something as simple as pushing a button to unlock his car eluded him, especially when the temperature was three below zero. He reluctantly took off his right glove and dug through the icy cold powder.

"Do not move or you will die!"

The voice came from directly behind him, and it was spoken in perfect Russian. Richard's bloodstream filled with an overload of adrenaline. The voice spoke again, this time in German.

"Keep your hands where I can see them, and slowly turn around."

Richard struggled to slow his heart rate and breathing. Stay calm, relax, keep a clear head. Remember your training. In response to his own thoughts, the unseen man spoke to him in flawless French.

"Stay calm Mr. Resnik. There is no god but Allah, and Mohammed is his prophet."

Richard broke his silence.

"Momin!"

Momin smiled and took a step closer. Should he kill him now? He consulted the voice inside him and shook his head no. He would put him in the trunk and take him along. That would be more fun.

He fired the taser at Richard's body from 3 feet away, and Richard slumped over into the cold snow that he hated, convulsed a few times, and then lay silent. Then in perfect Hebrew, devoid of any accent, Momin proclaimed.

"Happy Hanukah, Mr. Resnik, you son of a pig!"

§ § §

Momin stood poised on a ridge to the north of downtown Grand Rapids, the second largest city in Michigan. He was close enough to see the tops of the tallest buildings, but still far enough away to be safe from the initial blast.

He wore an old, olive drab trench coat that needed cleaning, with a broad-brimmed hat that was pulled down low over his forehead, shading his eyes from the light of the winter sun. He walked back to the car and got back in behind the wheel. It was noon, time for the weather report. Momin turned on the radio and listened impatiently to an auto glass commercial until the news came on. Then he turned up the volume.

"Our top story today remains the massive manhunt for the remaining terrorist who recently eluded the FBI in Detroit, Michigan. He is believed to be a 30-year old native-born Bengali named Momin Islam who immigrated to the US five years ago. FBI sources say that Mr. Islam is believed to be the leader of a five-man terrorist cell group located in Ann Arbor. From documents discovered in the raid, it is believed that the cell group was planning to attack the superbowl at the end of the month. The details of the alleged attack are not yet known. However, superbowl officials have gone on record as saying, quote, 'The superbowl is an American icon, and it will go on as planned. Nothing can stop the American way of life.'"

"In other news, the Governor, Lt. Governor, Senators Stabenow and Levin, plus former President Gerald R. Ford, the State Senate Majority Leader, the speaker of the State House, and a host of other local dignitaries are in downtown Grand Rapids today to dedicate the newly renovated wing of the Gerald R. Ford Museum."

Momin smiled and leaned his head back against the rest and blocked it out. He was pleased to have so many dignitaries in town today, just the way he'd planned it. He had barely escaped the FBI last week, and now he had all he could do just to avoid capture. Police were everywhere and he had fled Southeast Michigan as quickly as possible. Detroit, with its large Moslem population, had never been his target anyways. It had always been Grand Rapids. They would never suspect that.

"B-93 weather today is partly sunny and 22 degrees, with a high later today of 29. Lows tonight will reach 11 degrees, with a wind chill factor of minus 15. No snow is in the forecast. Winds are out of the west from 5 to 10 miles per hour. Today's weather has been brought to you by Dickens Auto Glass, the glass professionals who care."

Momin smiled. The wind was perfect. He got out of the car and opened up the trunk lid. Agent Resnik's screams were muffled by the green duct tape over his mouth. The bound and gagged man squinted in the sunlight.

Momin laughed at him and spoke in near-perfect English.

"Good afternoon my little Jewish piglet. Can I get you a bagel?" Momin pretended to listen. "I'm sorry I can't hear you. Is that a yes or a no?" He shrugged his shoulders and sat down on the lip of the open trunk. "I'll take that as a no."

Momin looked out over the snow-covered empty field. There was a squirrel chattering away in a tree nearby and a lone hawk perched in another tree across the way, waiting for the squirrel to venture too far from safety. It was so peaceful.

He reached into the deep, side pocket of his trench coat and pulled out his cell phone. Then he looked back down at Agent Resnik and smiled again.

"Before I do this, Agent Resnik, I'd like to thank you for making all this possible. If you hadn't possessed the presence of mind to save that little girl, I never would have gotten away. In fact, I feel so appreciative, that I've decided to let you live long enough to watch this little event."

Momin reached down and patted Richard sarcastically across the face.

"I think you'll find this really quite interesting, especially since your parents and your sister now live in Grand Rapids. We're about 7 miles north of there right now. Did you know that?"

He gained satisfaction at the surprised look on Richard's face.

"What? How did I know that? It's really quite simple Richard. Do you mind if I call you Richard?" He paused. "Guess not. It's so simple. While you thought you were watching me, I was really watching you. The fact that you kept hanging around so much just made it more convenient for me. Do you have any idea what you can find out about someone on the internet? Your whole life's out there, Richard. There are no secrets in the 21st century. And as far as your relatives go . . . I hear Jewish families are close. Is that true? I guess we'll find out in a few minutes after I blow them all up."

A look of terror spread across Richard's face and Momin bent down closer to get a better look at it, seeming to feed off of it like some twisted parasite.

"That's right. Your father, the prominent neurosurgeon, Dr. Nehemiah Resnik, works downtown at the hospital overlooking the city. And, as luck would have it, that's exactly where I hid the 2-kiloton nuclear suitcase bomb. It's a lot like the one in the black case next to your head right now. Except the one next to you has a much higher yield. I've got bigger plans for that one, Richard, and you get to be a part of it. Isn't it exciting to be living historical events of epic proportions as they happen?"

He saw the look of terror replaced by remorse. Momin faked a sadness of his own.

"Don't worry little piglet. Daddy won't feel a thing. He was called into emergency surgery this morning. I know. I checked the schedule."

He stood up and raised the cell phone.

"Now, if you'll excuse me, I have to make a phone call."

Momin slowly pushed the buttons, hesitated, then swore in Arabic. He quickly smiled again.

"Dead zone. It comes and goes. Sometimes if I raise my left hand like this, and my right foot like this, then I get a better signal. Isn't modern technology wonderful?"

Momin chuckled as Richard looked out through helpless, tear-stained eyes, squirming back and forth in the trunk, hopelessly trying to loosen his bonds.

"Careful there Richard. I wouldn't want you to bump your head on that nuclear bomb." Then he looked up and off to one side as if thinking. "You know what's really satisfying about all this, Richard? You Americans are the most powerful nation to ever inhabit the earth. You've accomplished feats that no one else has ever been able to do. The other nations of the planet grovel at your feet. But, despite all that, you couldn't stop just one man, just one tiny, little Moslem boy from the poorest country on the face of the planet. It reminds me of that US Army commercial that inspires me so much. 'The power of one.' But, enough talk. They'll be plenty of time for me to rub it in later. I'm really starting to hate you in a much more profound and glorious way, Richard. Now watch this. Look over there. Straight towards the top of that tallest tree."

Richard tried to close his eyes while Momin punched in the buttons, but he couldn't force his gaze away.

"Just one more number. There! Hey! I think it's going to ring!"

Chapter 32

"This is Jonathon Stoddard of Fox News in New York, and we interrupt this regularly-scheduled broadcast to bring you a special bulletin."

Every patron in the Mudhen Grille looked up at the TV screen in interest. All conversation silenced. Lance Stuart and Spunky swiveled in their chairs, while Hank, Angela and Pastor McCullen, sitting two tables over from them, just had to look up to see the nervousness etched all over the newscaster's face to know that something epic had just occurred.

"A very large, man-made explosion of a magnitude unprecedented to North America has just occurred in the downtown area of Grand Rapids, Michigan, just several minutes ago. The origin and nature of the explosion are still, as of yet, unknown. In fact, the devastation and mayhem invoked by this explosion have made it impossible to receive any official information from local government sources whatsoever."

Josh McCullen pushed his chair back involuntarily and rose to his feet. The wrinkles across Lance Stuart's brow tightened and furled into a broad V-shape as he squinted his eyes and tightened the muscles in his forehead.

"We bring you now to Sandra Connors at our affiliate station in Grand Rapids, Michigan for an eyewitness account."

There was a moment of technical difficulty as Fox News switched from New York to Michigan. Hank put his hamburger back down on his plate as he waited impatiently for them to make the switch.

"Are we on, Jeff? Do we have New York? Jeff will you get this thing working!"

Sandra Connors was a blonde-haired woman about 35 years old. She was in the front seat of a news van, with the camera operator in the seat behind her shooting forward with the windshield as a back drop.

"Sandra, this is Jonathon Stoddard of Fox News in New York. We can hear you Sandra. You're live. Everything you say is live."

The picture jostled up and down as the news van headed down the road at a high rate of speed.

"They can hear us Sandy! We're on. Just go with it!"

Sandra Connors looked up anxiously. A combination of fear, anxiety, excitement, and remorse all seemed etched into her face simultaneously. She brushed the hair back out of her eyes, held the microphone in front of her mouth and began speaking.

"Jonathon, this is Sandra Connors, Fox17 news team from Grand Rapids, Michigan."

She hesitated as if not knowing what to say, as if she were totally unprepared for this broadcast. Then Jonathon Stoddard prodded her along.

"What can you tell us, Sandra? What's happening there?"

"Well, we were on a routine news story south of Grand Rapids in the small town of Plainwell, when we heard a very loud explosion to the north. Several moments later, we actually felt tremors in the earth. It must have been a very large explosion. We hopped right on to US 131 and headed north towards Grand Rapids. That was about 10 minutes ago and we're coming up on the Wayland exit right now, about 15 miles south of GR."

Jonathon Stoddard interrupted her.

"But can you see anything from where you are, Sandra? Tell us what you can see!"

Sandra rotated in her chair and looked straight ahead through the windshield so that the camera was pointed at the back of her head.

"Well, we're coming up on an overpass right now, so I can't see much in the direction of Grand Rapids at the moment. But right now it appears that everyone seems to be traveling south out of the city as fast as their cars can go. In fact, we're actually seeing 4-wheel drive trucks and SUVs driving through the snow in the median to get into the southbound traffic away from Grand Rapids. The northbound traffic has slowed to a crawl now, and . . . ."

She turned to the van driver who threw up his hands in desperation.

"Get to the right Dave! Get over on the shoulder and just drive right on past everyone. We have to see what's going on!"

The van took a violent turn to the right and Sandra was knocked out of her chair and onto the floor of the van. The picture continued to move up and down as the van moved off the road onto the right shoulder. Sandra regained her composure.

"Sandra, this is Jonathon. Can you still hear me?"

"Yes, Jonathon, we can hear you. It's just a little rough going at the moment. There have been a lot of accidents here on the highway. People don't seem to know how to handle this situation. On the one hand, some people want to drive a hundred miles an hour away from Grand Rapids, while still others have stopped their cars and now stand on the road gazing towards the city."

Angela reached over and put her hand on top of Hank's. She squeezed it, and looked at him with fearful eyes. She seemed to speak the unthinkable.

"Hank, how far away is Grand Rapids? Are we far enough away?"

"We're going under the overpass now, and I can start to see . . . Oh my God! Would you look at that! I can't believe it!"

Jonathon's excited voice broke in.

"Sandra we can't see what you're seeing. The windshield is too dirty. Get out of the van and send us back some pictures! We need you to tell us what's going on!"

Sandra seemed to suddenly remember she was a news reporter on the story of her career.

"Pull over Dave!"

Dave slammed on the brakes and sent Sandra careening into the dashboard and the windshield. The moment they stopped, another vehicle slammed into their rear sending her and the camera the opposite direction once again. The camera fell to the floor and the picture was motionless for a moment. In the background, Sandra screamed and swore to an audio backdrop of metal crashing on metal and the honking of car horns. Then the screen went black.

Angela looked on in confusion as the picture cut back to Jonathon Stoddard in New York City. He appeared to be taken off guard for a moment, but then quickly recovered.

"Ladies and gentlemen, it would appear that we have momentarily lost our connection with Sandra Connors of Fox17 news near the outskirts of Grand Rapids. But we'll try to regain that connection and give you real-time video from on the scene."

He moved his right hand to his ear as if listening to some unheard voice, and when he spoke again, it was faster, with more excitement and animation.

"Ladies and gentlemen, we have just received unofficial confirmation that a nuclear blast of unknown size and power has indeed occurred near the downtown area of Grand Rapids, Michigan. This news, however, is unofficial and comes to us from the government officials of Dorr, which is a small town to the south of Grand Rapids."

He stopped talking and listened again.

"It would appear that we have regained our feed with Sandra Connors from Fox17 news who is on location, about 10 miles south of Grand Rapids. Sandra, can you hear me?"

"Yes, Jonathon, we can hear you just fine now."

"Are you okay, Sandra?"

"Yes, Jonathon. We've moved closer to Grand Rapids now, just south of Byron Center, and we're standing on the side of US 131 along with hundreds of cars who have crashed into each other. Hundreds of people must be hurt, or maybe even killed. There's just no way to know at this early point in time."

Jonathon interrupted.

"Sandra we can hear you fine, but your video isn't coming through. Can you give us some pictures?"

There was a moment of silence, followed by muffled voices in the background. Jonathon swiveled in his chair to look behind him.

"Do we have her now?"

He nodded to the unseen person behind him.

"Ladies and gentleman, we go with you now on the scene to Byron Center, about 10 miles south of Grand Rapids, where a nuclear explosion was detonated about 20 minutes ago."

Sandra Connors once again came on the screen. Her hair was matted and unkempt, and her face was streaked in blood. When she spoke, her voice seemed less excited and more tired than it had just a few minutes ago.

"Jonathon, I'm going to assume we have both audio and video unless you tell me differently."

"We've got you Sandra. Please tell us what you see. Show us some pictures."

"Right. We can do that. Jonathon, we have confirmed from several refugees from Grand Rapids, that indeed at noon today a nuclear bomb was detonated in downtown Grand Rapids. One man we spoke to was in Byron Center when it happened which is just 7 miles south of ground zero. Thousands of people are fleeing the city in all directions."

She moved off to one side and pointed north.

"As you can see, a small, but distinct mushroom cloud has formed over the city."

Everyone in the Mudhen Grille seemed to gasp in unison when they saw the deadly black cloud. Everyone stood to their feet in unison and walked closer to the television, as if mesmerized and drawn by some unseen force. Hank was the first to speak.

"I don't believe it! I bought my car in Grand Rapids. I go there all the time."

Angela tugged anxiously at his shirt sleeve.

"Hank how far away is Grand Rapids?"

Lance Stuart replied to her.

"Don't worry Angela. We're safe enough. Safer than most in lower Michigan anyways."

Spunky responded to them both in an irritated voice.

"Shut up, both of you. I want to hear this!"

Sandra Connors was no longer saying anything, simply gazing out at the dirty, black, mushroom cloud, which was still rising up over the city and hovering there like a black malignant tumor. Finally, Jonathon Stoddard broke the trance.

"Sandra, are there any nuclear power plants or other nuclear facilities in the city which may have caused that explosion?"

Sandra looked back at the camera and, without saying a word, shook her head no.

"Are you sure, Sandra? What could have caused a blast like that?"

"I'm sure Jonathon. The nearest nuclear power plant is over 80 miles from here. There's only one thing that could have caused the blast. Only one thing."

She looked back again at the mushroom cloud, and lowered the microphone as she stared into the dirty, black pillar.

Lance, Spunky, Hank, Josh, and Angela were all huddled beside the television now in a tiny group. No one seemed to notice the stale alcohol and old perspiration smell emanating from Spunky. Lance was the first to speak.

"This changes things. This changes everything."

Pastor McCullen bowed his head and whispered.

"God help us. God help us all please."

Hank looked over at Angela. He couldn't say anything, so he just wrapped his arms around her and held on tight.

Chapter 33

After the nuclear blast, Momin had stood and watched the mushroom cloud for almost 15 minutes before finally getting back into his car and driving north on US 131. He immediately tuned his radio to the news and listened to every word, surfing back and forth from channel to channel, especially interested in stories of mayhem and terror surrounding the blast. People were dying everywhere, and not just from radiation. Terror and panic had set in all across the country, with nearly all the major US cities experiencing riots, looting, murder, and mass exodus of apocalyptic proportions.

The rule of law was breaking down, and it made Momin smile. Finally, America was getting a taste of how the other half lived. The rest of the world had long survived in anarchy, poverty, and chaos, and now, finally, they were finding out how the rest of the world lived on a daily basis. Momin was proud to be the instrument of America's reduction.

A newscast caught his attention and he turned up the volume, loud enough so that Agent Resnik could hear it in the trunk.

"The city of Grand Rapids is all but silent now. The people who remain, are either dead or soon will be. Those still able to function, have already been evacuated south to Kalamazoo for medical attention. The dead are estimated to exceed 50,000 and the death toll will continue to rise as the days and weeks go by."

Momin raised his fist in triumph.

"Yes! Praise be to Allah!"

"The state government of Michigan has broken down, and only law enforcement maintains a modicum of functionality. It is believed that the Governor, Lt. Governor, Former President Gerald R. Ford, two US Senators, and several members of the State House and State Senate, including the House Speaker and Senate Majority Leader were all killed in the attack. The President has declared martial law in Michigan and the US Military is being deployed to maintain order until a working state government can be re-established at some later time. The United States Department of Health has declared the city of Grand Rapids to be a contaminated zone, along with the surrounding communities of Byron Center, Moline, Dorr, Cutlerville, Walker, Ada, Lowell, Belding, Rockford, Kentwood, Cascade, Jenison, Grandville, and Wyoming. In addition to that, all areas in a direct path between the cities of Grand Rapids and Lansing are ordered to be evacuated. The US military has surrounded the city, and no one is allowed in the contaminated zone. The US Health Service urges anyone who was within 20 miles of the city at the time of the blast to seek out medical attention, should you begin to feel dizziness, nausea, or any other flu-like symptoms."

Momin was about 2 hours north of Grand Rapids now. He looked down at his gas gauge. Almost empty. His stomach growled in hunger, and he suddenly realized that he hadn't eaten in almost 8 hours. He took the next exit with a gas station and restaurant – a little town called Freidham Ridge.

§ § §

When Andy Fitzu saw the U.S. Government markings on the license plates, he knew that he had to pull the car over. After all, it wasn't everyday he got the opportunity to exert local control over the United States government. In fact, he was so excited that he didn't even take the time to run the plate through the LEIN system.

Andy had been in a giddy state all day since the bombing of Grand Rapids, and now he was waiting a mile off the freeway, anticipating the refugees pouring north, trying to escape the radioactive heap of rubble and ash. He had already pulled over three people in the past hour and issued citations to the tune of 85 dollars a crack. By nightfall, he'd have enough in the township coffers to ask for that new laser speed gun he'd been wanting for so long. It never even occurred to Andy that he should be grieving over all the thousands who had just been incinerated inside a radioactive hell. He just wanted his new laser speed gun.

The black sedan didn't pull over immediately, so Andy moved in closer and gave the siren a gentle nudge. The car in front of him turned off onto a side road and didn't stop until Andy let the siren blast steady for a full 10 seconds. Andy got out of the car quickly and stormed up to the sedan. The wind was blowing hard, and it had begun to snow. The wind chill was already 15 below zero and was expected to get down much lower after nightfall. But Andy ignored it. He was going to teach this guy a lesson.

"Yes, officer, what seems to be the problem?"

Andy saw the confident look on Momin's face and it infuriated him all the more. He didn't hesitate, but went straight to work.

"Driver's license, registration and proof of insurance please!"

Momin smiled.

"Yes, of course officer. No need to get angry. I'm Special Agent Resnik, with the Federal Bureau of Investigation."

Momin briefly raised the stolen wallet up over the car window, displayed the federal badge and then lowered it back down. Andy had never seen a federal badge before. He paused, not quite knowing what to do next. Martial law had been declared. Who had jurisdiction? He decided to play it out and see what happened.

"Really? We don't get many federal agents up here. Where are you going in such a hurry?"

Momin's tooth-filled smile flashed again.

"On my way up to supervise protection of the Mackinaw bridge. We got a tip last night that truck bombers might try to blow it up."

Andy thought about it a moment. It made sense, and he relaxed his guard a little. He'd never given a federal agent a citation before. Even though it would probably just be torn up, he would love to have that feather in his cap. Then he heard the banging over the wind, but couldn't quite tell where it was coming from. He looked back toward the rear of the car.

"What's in your trunk Agent Resnik?"

Momin's smile began to disappear. He hated this man.

"Nothing but my luggage and some special equipment we'll need up at the bridge. I'm in a big hurry officer. I just pulled off the highway to get some food and gas and head up north to the straits. How about we just stop fooling around here and you let me get on my way so I can keep the country safe from terrorism?"

Andy took a step back closer to the trunk. This time, even over the wind, he could hear the banging on the inside of the lid. Andy's right hand went instinctively to the grip of his 40 caliber Glock pistol. He released the thumb break, ready to draw if need be.

"Sir! Keep your hands where I can see them! Will you step out of the vehicle please. Slowly!"

Momin didn't move. The banging got louder. Andy drew his pistol.

"Get out of the car! I said get out of the vehicle!"

Momin's right hand tightened over the grip of his own pistol.

"Okay! Just calm down officer or somebody's going to get hurt. I can explain everything. There's no need to draw your firearm."

Andy took a step closer.

"Oh yes there is! It's ten below zero out here and you've got somebody locked in your trunk!"

Momin was furious, but he forced himself to remain calm under pressure. He slowed his heartbeat and his breathing rate.

"Yes, there's someone in my trunk, but it's just my partner. We had a bet going and he lost, so he has to ride in the trunk until we get to the gas station. It's an FBI thing."

A moment of doubt clouded over Andy's face. He stepped up even with the car door and lowered his pistol slightly. And when he did, Momin smiled again.

"That's right officer. This is all just a harmless mistake. Let me go back to the trunk and open it up so you can take a look inside."

Andy nodded suspiciously, and Momin slowly opened the car door and began to climb out.

"Just keep your hands where I can see . . . "

The first shot rang out and Andy never finished his sentence. There were six shots from Momin's gun, all entering Andy's chest. But Andy got off one lone shot before he died.

Momin got out of the car and stood over Officer Fitzu's body. The wind whipped into Momin's jet back hair and snow swirled all around him. There was a storm coming in, coming in fast.

He bent down to examine the wounds. He liked looking at them. Then he placed the barrel of the gun up against Andy's forehead and pulled the trigger, just to watch his head explode.

Only then did he realize that his arm was bleeding.

Chapter 34

"The estimated death toll stands so far at over 150,000, and this figure is expected to rise over the ensuing days, with many more tens of thousands who have been hospitalized due to radiation sickness and injuries related to the explosion."

"Holy Moses! That's a lot of dead people from one bomb!"

"Shhh! Shut up Spunky. I want to hear this!"

Many of the people in the room had friends or relatives who lived in or near Grand Rapids, and they were anxious for any news.

"In related news, martial law has been declared in the city of Los Angeles, bringing the total number of American cities to 12 which are now under military rule, due to this one event. Widespread looting, rioting, and violence have gone largely unchecked across much of the urban nation today as people flee our cities by the millions, pouring into the surrounding countryside, trying to find food and shelter for themselves and their families."

Lance Stuart looked uneasy. He reached down and felt the bulk of his 40 caliber pistol beneath his shirt for comfort and reassurance. Spunky looked over and nudged him before speaking.

"You think they'll come here Rock?"

Lance shook his head.

"Maybe a few, but not many. Most of Grand Rapids is dead, and

Detroit is too far away. We should be ready though – just in case."

The announcer continued on to the next topic, but it was just more of the same. At least for today, all news seemed to be related to the nuclear explosion.

"The National Weather Service has forecasted that winds will maintain their west-southwesterly direction, taking the radioactive cloud on a collision course with the state capitol of Lansing, Michigan, where another 150,000 people are being evacuated. Since the Governor, Lt. Governor, and much of the cabinet have been killed, the state legislature is meeting in emergency session in the city of Flint, further to the north and east."

Josh McCullen, who sat to the right of him, buried his face into his hands, and began massaging his temples.

"Some of those people will be coming this way. How can we get ready, Rock? What can we possibly do?"

Lance Stewart looked over at him, his gray and white hair glistening in the light of the Mudhen Grille.

"Go buy all the food and supplies you can. Once the refugees get here, they'll be eating everything in sight. It'll be like a plague of locusts. And buy extra ammo. Not all of them will be church goers."

Josh rose stolidly to his feet.

"Guess I'd better get on it then. Someone should call Hank and Angela as well. Let 'em know what to do."

Lance nodded his head.

"I'll take care of it, Josh. You just get home to Louise. From now on, everyone stays armed and ready for anything that might happen. Even city boys like Hank are going to have to step up to the plate."

Spunky took a good, long drink of his beer.

"I'll drink to that!"

Lance looked over at his friend.

"And no more drinking for a few days, Spunk. Your town and your friends need you. We need you sober. Time to step up and be the man my friend."

Spunky met Rock's eyes, as if gauging his seriousness and resolve. After a few seconds of thought, he nodded his head and pushed the beer away from him on the counter.

"Anything else?"

Lance smiled and slapped his friend on the back.

"How about some aerial recon? Take your plane down the US 131 corridor just to see what manner of hell is coming toward us."

Spunky nodded.

"Awful cold day to be flyin' sober. But, it don't matter. I gotta get high somehow. I'm gonna get back to the house and plow out my runway, then I'll call you from the air."

Josh hesitated before walking away.

"I could use some help, Rock. I need to spread the word about our emergency prayer meeting. It's at the church in one hour."

Rock rose to his feet as well.

"I'll stop by Hank and Angela's place, then help you spread the word."

Then a twinkle came to his eyes.

"Gosh! I feel just like Paul Revere!"

Josh and Rock laughed as well as they could under the circumstances as they walked away from the table. Spunky remained seated, raised his hand and snapped his fingers in the air.

"Hey Ruthie! Come 'ere baby! Bring me some coffee! Better make it strong and black, 'cuz I'm gonna save the world today!"

Ruthie looked over and shook her head in disgust, while muttering under her breath.

"Save the world? You can't even make your own coffee!"

Chapter 35

The smell of brains, blood, and death was overwhelming to Richard, but he mastered his body and resisted the urge to vomit. Because, if he did, the duct tape over his mouth would cause him to choke and die on the contents of his own stomach. Richard had never smelled death this strongly, this personally, so intimately that he was forced to experience it both physically and spiritually.

Richard had heard the shots, then watched as Momin had opened the trunk and thrown a dead police officer on top of him. What was left of the man's brain had spilled out and landed in Richard's face. It was a horrifying smell, and Richard had to force himself to focus elsewhere or he would lose it.

It was the same story with his parents and sister. They were dead, but he had no time to grieve, and no luxury to cry. All that would have to be done later, assuming he survived, which seemed highly doubtful given his dire situation.

For the past several hours he had been reflecting on the loss of his loved ones, the death of perhaps a hundred thousand people, and the overwhelming guilt that he felt at not stopping this mad man. It had been his responsibility, and he had failed miserably, even with the entire resources of the United States government. He had failed.

But something inside him reminded him of the little girl he had saved. Her smile still filled his mind, and the sight of her being reunited with her parents was being played over and over inside his mind. Yes, many had been lost, but one small girl he had saved. He focused on that, and found some small solace of hope. The God of his childhood came to mind now and he allowed himself a few moments to focus on that, but moments turned to minutes, then minutes into hours, and Richard had been thinking about God for most of the time he'd been in the trunk. What would his father be thinking? What would his father tell him?

"The creator is there for you, Richard Zechariah Resnik. He will help you in your time of need, as he helped our fathers Abraham, Isaac, and Jacob, he will also help you. But first you must ask."

Richard almost thought he could audibly hear his father's voice as he lay shivering in the freezing cold of the trunk. He knew for sure that he would likely die today. Momin would not leave him alive, that he knew. The only reason he'd survived this long was because of his Jewish heritage. Momin had something special in store for him, something particularly heinous and barbarous, something in keeping with his hatred for Jews. And then it occurred to him. He was still alive just because he was a Jew. Even now, after all these thousands of years, the God of creation, the Father of the Jews was protecting him, looking after him, and, perhaps, showing him the way out of this situation. And then the thought occurred to him: If God is real; if He does exist; if He does love this human race; if all those things were true; then He would undoubtedly be involved in everything that was happening today. If God loved His creation, then He would not sit idly by while some mad man did all he could to destroy it. God would intervene to save His children and His creation. Richard struggled to remember his childhood training, and the man Balaam popped into his head. Balaam had been a secular priest, a man who accepted payment to put curses and blessings on people. King Balak of Moab had offered him riches beyond compare if he would just curse Moses and the Israelites, but God had sent an angel to block Balaam's path. A donkey had spoken to him, and then Balaam had seen the mighty angel of God, standing in front of him with a sword, waiting to cut him to shreds should he choose to curse the chosen people of God. And then his training came flooding back to him. All through time God has chosen the weak and the meek, as well as the strong to carry out his purposes. Sometimes He had even chosen the secular to achieve His divine purpose. God would use anyone He chose, provided they were willing. Moses had a speech impediment, but was chosen to lead the people of Israel to the promised land, and he reluctantly obeyed. Jacob was the weaker of two brothers, but prospered and became the father of many nations. Yes, God did work in mysterious ways. Suddenly, Richard wondered if God was working now, through him. Was it possible. He heard his father's voice again.

"God will not call you and then abandon you. Never will I leave thee. Never will I forsake thee."

Richard believed those words now for the first time in his life. He'd heard it said that the end of man was the beginning of God. He was at his own end, and it was time for God to take over. He closed his eyes and prayed.

"Dear Jehovah, my provider, provide a way for me to escape and stop this man of evil."

And then the oddest thing happened. He felt a strange, relaxing, peaceful balm spread over his whole body. It warmed him despite the wind and cold raging outside him, filling him with hope, and strength and determination.

One thought came to his mind: God allows nothing to happen outside His will. God leaves nothing to chance. There is no such thing as chance. If that were true, then everything that had happened to him so far, was the act of God. In the light of this new perspective, Richard once again took stock of his assets and liabilities.

The liabilities were easy: He was locked in a trunk, bound and gagged; he had a nuclear bomb for a head rest, and there was a dead body lying beside him. The assets were a little more difficult. And then it hit him. If nothing occurred without God's approval, and he left nothing to chance, then everything that happened to him was part of God's larger plan. He thought about it. If all that were true, and God loved His creation, then . . . his liabilities were also his assets.

Richard took a closer look at his assets. The dead body beside him was a police officer. Police officers carried flashlights. Once he had light, he could find even more tools to work with.

Richard smiled as the new hope sprouted and grew inside his heart. A few seconds later, he found what he was looking for. He clicked the button.

"Let there be light!"

Chapter 36

"And we beseech thee, O mighty and righteous God, to pour the wealth of your mercy, though it be undeserved, onto the pour, lowly sinners of Lansing, Michigan. We implore thee, all powerful God, all knowing God, ever present and uncontainable God, we pray the magnanimousity of your love and grace."

Josh had never liked the prayers of Margaret Howard, but there wasn't much he could do about it. She was 87 years old and had been in the church since its founding back in the Great Depression. Josh tried to keep from judging her prayers, but he just didn't think anyone could pray in King James and still be sincere. Margaret always reminded him of the words of Jesus in Matthew where He said: "And when you pray, do not be like the hypocrites, for they love to pray standing in the synagogues and on the street corners, to be seen by men. I tell you the truth, they have received their reward in full."

Josh forced himself to recant his thoughts. He had no right to judge the woman like this. Maybe she truly was sincere and humble in her sanctimonious prayers? Only God knew – God and Margaret Howard. And then it occurred to him, "Was magnanimousity a real word?" Josh quickly and efficiently rebuked himself once more. "Shut up Josh! It's none of your business what this woman says to God." And then once more, "Magnanimousity, I have to look that one up in the dictionary when

I get home." Thank God no one could hear his thoughts.

"And it is in your name that we humbly present our prayers and petitions. Amen."

An entire chorus of "amens" reverberated around the church auditorium. Hank fidgeted nervously in the pew. It was his turn to pray. He hated it – not praying – but praying in public. He had grown to like talking to God the past few months, but it just struck him as something to be done in private. Hank had never been fond of public intimacy.

"Dear God, thanks much for everything. You're doing a great job up there, so keep up the good work. Please make that radioactive cloud miss Lansing. I think enough people have died already. Don't you?"

Josh smiled with his eyes closed. He always found Hank's prayers to be refreshing after a lifetime of listening to the prayers of the Scribes and the Pharisees. Hank was having a private conversation with God, but he was having it publicly, like a child to a father.

"We don't want those people to die, God. And we have no idea why all of this is happening. Life is so confusing sometimes that it drives me crazy. Please God. Give us hope. Help us to find the good in things, even when people are suffering and dying all around us. Please protect our faith. Amen."

Another chorus of amens went up from the small group of 10 people in the church auditorium. The wind could be heard, even from inside; it was driving the snow all around, creating drifts and piles the likes of which Freidham Ridge had never seen. Lance Stuart was next in line to pray. He didn't like praying in public either, but he had just come to show his support for Josh McCullen.

"Okay God. Here's the straight scoop. The lunatics have taken over the asylum again, and we need your help taking out the trash. You know what to do. Just send them all to Freidham Ridge, and we'll take care of the rest. There's more I want to talk about, but it can wait until I get home."

Lance paused.

"And please tell my wife that I love her. Amen."

Josh thought he heard a disapproving grunt from Margaret Howard, but the familiar chorus of amens went up again and echoed around the near-empty auditorium, although this time they were not quite so enthusiastic and sure of themselves. Now it was up to Josh to close out the prayer session.

"Dear God, sometimes your ways are not my ways. And it's probably good that you're in charge and not me. Because I would probably act too much and too often and really mess things up. So I beg your patience and your indulgence tonight as in all of my life. All of us have prayed to you in our own way, and I ask that you accept our prayers in the same spirit with which they were offered. I don't know how else to say it other than this: Please save all those people - any means necessary. We love you God. And we thank you for all you do and for who you are. Amen."

At the same moment that Josh said amen, the outside door to the church slammed open and blew in snow and wind all around them. Hank looked back at the door, as did everyone else in the room. Angela squeezed his hand when she saw the bloody man stagger through the door and fall face first down to the floor of the church.

Margaret Howard's ancient eyes looked over condescendingly, shocked that anyone would disrupt the house of God in such an outrageous manner.

Chapter 37

"Please help me God. Please help me get out of this."

Richard could still remember the last time he'd prayed. It had been on his sixteenth birthday, when he'd gone out drinking with some of his friends to celebrate and had wrecked his father's car. The prayer hadn't worked then either.

Richard's fingers were nearly frozen now, and he was having trouble feeling anything at all. That was probably good, since he had cut himself many times over the past hour, trying to saw through the nylon zip tie that held his hands firmly together. He had been trying to cut through them by rubbing the tie back and forth on the sharp bone fragments of Andy Fitzu's skull, but it was very slow going, especially without the flashlight, which had gone dim about a half hour ago. Every time Richard scraped his wrist against the remnants of Andy's head and missed the tie, the sharp bone dug into the soft flesh of his wrist and cut him some more.

He didn't know for sure how long he'd been in the trunk, but he guessed about twelve hours. The car was stopped, and had been for some time now. Richard surmised that Momin had run the car into a snow bank. At least that's how the sudden jolt and stop had felt to him. Before the dead body had been thrown in on him, he'd kept warm by moving his arms and legs up and down as quickly and as far as his bonds would allow. But now, he could barely move at all with the stiff body pressing down on him. Andy Fitzu was a very heavy man. Richard, on the other hand, was only 5'8" with a medium build. At first the dead body had given off warmth, which Richard hadn't been able to fully appreciate with the man's blood and brains falling down into his eyes, but Andy's body had since gone stiff, leaving Richard cold again.

The city of Grand Rapids was a radioactive cinder, a heap of rubble, and his parents were buried somewhere beneath it, probably vaporized in the first second of the blast. But Andy knew that they had been ready for death, in fact, always had been. His father had lived life close to his God, in full submission and obedience to all of God's laws and ways. His father was, or had been, a good Jew. Richard didn't know where he was now. He didn't even want to think about it anymore. If he didn't free himself, then he would soon freeze to death, or worse yet, Momin would return to finish the job personally. Richard knew that Momin would never leave the nuclear suitcase bomb. He would be coming back for the metal suitcase sooner or later. Either way, Richard was going to die.

Richard moved his head off the suitcase. The sharp metal corner of it kept digging into his head, and he thought his scalp was bleeding a little. Richard suddenly stopped moving and thought for a moment. The sharp edges of the metal suitcase – they were an asset. Richard pushed up on the dead body, giving him enough room to roll over and face the suitcase, then he let the body come back down on him. But this time his hands were right next to the metal case. Richard moved his wrists up to the corner of the case and pressed the nylon zip tie firmly against the sharp metal and began to move his wrists up and down as best he could in the cramped confines.

He made a mental note to himself. "If I ever get out of this mess, the first thing I'm going to do is buy a car with a bigger trunk."

Then Richard felt the nylon tie break, and his hands were free!

Chapter 38

The ten parishioners huddled around the man's body. Zeke Tyler had been a medic in the Korean War, so he bent down and stripped off the man's coat and shirt to get at the source of all the blood. He saw the entry point and the exit hole, and recognized it as a bullet wound right away. Zeke thought it odd, that even after 50 years of farming as a civilian, right now he felt like he was in the army again, and all his training came back to him as if he'd never been discharged.

"It's a bullet wound. Missed the bone, but he's lost a lot of blood. He needs a doctor, not a medic."

Josh stooped down beside Zeke.

"We don't have a doctor here. You know that, Zeke. And I doubt very much we could get through to Bentley right now at least until that storm lets up. The roads are half drifted shut already."

Zeke hesitated a moment, then Lance knelt down beside him and put his hand on old Zeke's back.

"Just do your best, Zeke. It was good enough in Korea, and It'll be good enough now."

Zeke turned his head and met Lance's gaze. Lance nodded reassuringly. They both looked down at the body, and then something seemed to click inside Zeke and he began barking out orders to everyone around him. They all obeyed him, scurrying off quickly to get what he needed.

He reached down to feel the pulse in the man's throat. It was weak, but it was definitely still there.

"Come on, let's go! Get me that soap and water! Get me those blankets!"

Sergeant Tyler was back on duty.

§ § §

Spunky hadn't seen a storm like this in all his years in Freidham Ridge. It had come up suddenly, like all the Great Lakes storms, but this one had a ferocity about it that made it seem alive, almost like it was out for revenge.

He had just finished plowing out his runway, but there was no way he could even get in the air much less fly reconnaissance until this storm let up. It didn't matter. His mission was to scout out the refugees coming up from the south, and there sure wouldn't be anyone coming in tonight. It would wait until morning. Visibility was almost zero.

Spunky slammed on the brakes when he saw the man jump out in front of his truck. The big, four-wheel drive truck came to a stop in the snow, barely missing the man. Spunky saw him fall down and not get up. He hesitated a moment, wondering who this guy was, knowing instinctively that he wasn't a local. The bulk of his .45 caliber pistol, strapped to his side infused him with courage. Spunky preferred alcohol over firearms, but, like Rock said, this is a national emergency, time to step up to the plate.

So Spunky opened the truck door and walked through the blowing snow over to the man's side. When he bent down closer, he saw that the man wore no coat, and that he was covered in blood from head to toe.

Then he saw the large, metal suitcase lying in the snow beside him.

Spunky was a big man, so he picked up the suitcase with his left arm and the man with his right. He threw the case in the bed of his pick-up and stuffed the man into the extended cab beside him.

Once back inside the warmth of the truck, he just sat there, wanting a drink, but knowing that he shouldn't. There had been only two people on this earth that were ever able to curb his drinking: the first had been his first wife Joyce, God rest her soul, and the second had been Rock.

He looked over at the unconscious man, already starting to thaw out and drip all over his leather seats. Spunky liked the smell of leather; it was one of his few luxuries in life. Then he looked way down the road and to the left. Through the blowing snow, he could barely see that the lights in the church were still on. Spunky shifted into first gear and lurched forward through the snow and on into the night.

§ § §

Zeke had survived the battle of Chosin reservoir in Korea, so he knew frostbite when he saw it, but even after thoroughly washing the man Spunky had brought in, he still had no idea where all the blood had come from. He was drenched in it, but Zeke suspected that it wasn't his own, and that it also wasn't the blood of the first man with the bullet wound in his arm. This new patient was wearing the blood of someone else entirely, and there was enough of it to safely assume that person was dead.

Hank and Angela had left for home a few minutes before to get their children in bed and to relieve Freida. So had Margaret Howard and most of the others. But the ones who remained, Lance Stuart, Josh and Louise McCullen, Spunky Cannon and Zeke Tyler, sat now in the pastor's office, trying to make sense out of all that was happening. Josh was the first to speak.

"Does anybody in here have any idea what's going on with these two?"

Spunky shrugged his shoulders.

"Beats the hell outta me."

Louise McCullen was quick to rebuke him. This time she'd made no promises to the contrary, and this had been a very emotional day.

"Please stop swearing Mr. Cannon. This is the Lord's house."

Spunky immediately respected her for confronting him, but he would never admit it to anyone.

"Ain't it enough that I quit drinking? Now you want me to quit swearing too? Why don't you just take away my air!"

Zeke Tyler interrupted them both.

"I think there's a dead person around here somewhere."

Lance looked up.

"Why do you think that?"

"Trust me on this one. I've seen enough mortal wounds to know that whoever used to pump that blood has been dead for a few hours."

Louise moved her hand up to her mouth in fear.

"So the question is: who is dead and where are they. Could it be someone we know? Someone from the church?"

Lance shook his head.

"I doubt it. No way to know for sure though. I strongly suspect they were related somehow to the two we have in the other room. There's just way too much coincidence here."

Josh, who was seated behind his desk, had spread out all the things in front of him that they had taken from the first man. He picked up the pistol, and, out of habit as an NRA firearms instructor, he unloaded the magazine and the chamber before placing it back down on the desk. Then Spunky broke the silence.

"So how much money is in that guy's wallet?"

Everyone else in the room gave him an annoyed stare, even his friend

Lance. Josh picked up the wallet and let it fall open. The shiny badge glinted off the fluorescent light overhead.

"This isn't a wallet! The guy with the bullet hole is an FBI Agent!"

Josh looked up and met the troubled gaze of everyone else in the room. No one spoke, not even a smart remark from Spunky. No one knew what to say.

Finally, Lance Stewart's voice broke the silence.

"Spunky, go find Andy Fitzu."

Chapter 39

Deep inside his dream, Momin was surrounded by seventy virgins, all dressed in burkas with their faces covered by veils, and they danced around him as he reclined and watched with anticipation. He could choose any of them he wanted, any day he wanted, for as many times as he liked. Momin had entered into paradise.

This was a recurring dream that Momin had been experiencing for seven years now, and each time it was the same. He watched all of them dance and disrobe in front of him, then, as they stood in front of him on display, he would choose one and have intercourse with her.

But this time, something felt different, and then he noticed that he was naked from the waist up, and that his upper left arm was wrapped in a white bandage. Blood seeped through, lending red contrast to the white, but none of that discouraged his deep abiding hunger for the virgins.

The nearest virgin stopped dancing and sat down on the bed beside him. This was not right. She was still fully clothed. The virgin reached down and caressed his bare chest. Moving down to his waist, she unsnapped his jeans and pulled them down off his legs, leaving him naked but for his bright red, polyester, bikini briefs. Momin looked down and watched as his endowment from Allah began to grow and surge and strain against the confinement of his briefs.

Momin seemed to be watching from a distance as the young virgin climbed on top of his prostrate body and straddled his waist. The familiar biochemical process began to course through his veins, and Momin tried to reach up and grab the virgin, but his arms felt like lead, and he couldn't move.

The virgin bent down close to his face, and propping herself up with her right arm, she slowly lifted the veil away from her face. Momin gasped in horror when he saw the rotting and half-eaten flesh of the leper, gazing blankly down on him through tortured, vacuous orbs, just barely hanging in their sockets. A piece of dead flesh fell down onto Momin's face and landed in his eye. He shook his head from side to side, trying to get it off, but it was stuck there like a determined leech.

Then, as Momin watched helplessly from the confinement of his bed, the rotting face of the leprous virgin began to magically transform. Her black crusted hair fell away, dropping onto Momin's bare chest; her eyes shrunk and turned red; and then the gaping hole that had once been her nose began to lengthen and grow, protruding out with two holes in the end, like a giant pink button.

Momin opened his mouth and screamed as loud as he could. In response, the virgin pig began to lick his face, and then to bite his skin, drawing blood. The pig began a feeding frenzy, biting again and again, eating the flesh off Momin's face. The blood splashed onto the bedding and then onto the floor. The other sixty-nine virgins stopped dancing all around him. They removed their burkas and lifted their veils. They were beautiful and young, but they simply smiled in satisfaction and watched as Momin was eaten alive, his painful screams filling the room and bouncing down off the ceiling, coming back on him in retribution for his many past sins.

And after the pig had eaten her fill, she plopped herself down onto Momin's chest . . . and smiled.

§ § §

"What's the matter Momin? Aren't you sleeping well tonight?"

Beads of sweat covered Momin's face. He turned his head and looked up at the man who was speaking.

"How do you know my name?"

The man in the wheelchair looked down, his bright blue eyes sparkled and Momin shuddered. Those eyes – they were too young, too strong, too powerful for such a frail, old body. Momin cowered beneath the old man's gaze.

"What's the matter Momin, cat got your tongue?"

The old man stopped smiling.

"Or should I say . . . pig?"

Momin tried to speak, but he could not. It was as if his tongue were made of sand, and whenever he tried to move it, it poured down off his teeth and out his mouth, down his cheeks and onto the clean white cotton bed sheets that covered him.

"No, no Momin. No talking for you today. You are here simply to listen. I will talk and you will listen."

The old man leaned forward in his wheelchair.

"Do you know who I am, Momin?"

Momin couldn't speak, so he shook his head from side to side.

"My name is not important, though it is very precious to me. I am old. Older than Mohammed, older than Moses, older than Abraham, even older than Adam. I am older than birth itself. Because, you see Momin, I was not born, I was created. And I do that which I was created to do."

The fear in Momin's eyes heightened, and the old man took on a more human tone as he chuckled to himself.

"No Momin. I am not the instrument of your destruction. I am a servant of the most high. He says go, and I go. He says stay and I stay." The old man paused for a moment and then chuckled again. "Think of me as a very loyal and obedient Golden Retriever . . . with sharp and competent teeth."

The old man watched Momin's fear heighten even more. He was used to invoking fear in humans, though he never gained satisfaction from it. Momin watched on helplessly as the old man's face became serious, like a storm.

"In times past, I've said things like, 'Behold, I bring you good tidings of great joy, which shall be to all people.'"

The old man's voice paused.

"But I can't say that today. I can only say what I was sent to say. It seems that despite all you've done, all the hundreds of thousands that you've tortured and killed, and the ones you yet intend to kill, my master still loves you. He loves you and wishes you to repent in sackcloth and ashes."

The old man reached his frail, wrinkled hands down to the black rubber tires of his wheelchair and moved himself closer to the bed until he bumped against it.

"This is your last chance Momin. After I leave, you'll have the free will to do whatever you wish. To wound, to kill, to maim."

The timbre of his voice changed, became more full, more solid, more resonant, more of everything that it had ever been.

"But you will also have the freedom to heal, to do good, to confess your sins and to turn from your wicked ways. The creator will forgive you. His son has seen to that, by the shedding of his own blood. You know what I'm talking about don't you."

Momin knew that it was not a question, but a statement of fact. And as he lay there helplessly, a tear began to form in the corner of his right eye. He fought to hold it back, but it formed nonetheless.

"In a few moments, I must leave you. My friend is outside holding back the hordes of evil that would possess your soul, but that will not last for long. So let me just leave you with these final words. The creator loves you. He wishes to take you home to Him. He wishes to wrap His arms around you as a father to a son. But the choice must be yours. If you choose Father God, the Creator, then all will be forgiven, and you will enter into your new life – heart pure – white as snow – free to choose and serve the creator who loves you."

The old man grasped the arms on either side of his wheelchair and pushed himself up. When he stood to his feet, Momin was surprised at the immense size and imposition of his figure. It was as if he'd magically grown and healed.

"But you must understand, Momin, that if you choose evil . . . I am empowered."

Momin shuddered and turned his head to one side.

"While I will not intervene personally, for my master will not allow it, I am authorized to use other means to protect and defend the lives of those the creator loves."

The imposing figure, bright, radiant like the sun, lessened itself as if the dimmer switch on a light bulb had been turned down. And when his voice returned, it was soft, but most assuredly, not less.

"Remember the eternal promise of the creator: 'If my people, who are called by my name, shall humble themselves, and pray, and seek my face, and turn from their wicked ways; then will I hear from heaven, and will forgive their sin, and will heal their land.'"

"It's because he loves you, Momin. He loves you!"

Momin felt a presence disappear, like a power switch had been turned off, and when he turned back around, the old man was gone.

Exhausted, Momin fell into a deep sleep – a sleep without dreams.

Chapter 40

"In all, the death toll has already exceeded 200,000, and is expected to climb throughout next week. To further complicate relief efforts, a huge storm has dumped 2 feet of fresh snow on most of western Michigan. Many of the fleeing refugees were caught in the storm and are now stranded on the road. The National Guard is doing all it can to rescue as many as possible before they die of exposure."

Lance, Zeke, and Josh had spent the night at the church watching over the two wounded strangers in 3-hour shifts. Now it was morning, and the storm had finally lifted. Sunshine filtered down through the stained glass windows as if to say, 'It's a new day – be of good cheer!'

Josh had moved a small television out into the worship auditorium, along with 5 cots and their associated bedding from the parsonage next door. They were all huddled around the small television now, watching the news, unaware that one of the strangers was finally waking up.

Momin opened his eyes and shuddered when he saw the large, wooden cross looming up over him just a few yards away. First he remembered his nightmare of the seventy virgins, then the cross reminded him of the man in the wheelchair.

"It's because he loves you. He loves you, Momin. He loves you!"

The old man's words echoed in Momin's mind like a blessing and a curse, confusing him, rendering him impotent and helpless. How could he be forgiven for all he'd done? And then another voice talked to him from deep inside, 'Why do you need forgiveness? You are doing the will of Allah. This is Jihad! Holy War! You are a warrior of Allah, and all the infidels must die!'

"The creator loves you. He wishes to take you home to Him. He wishes to wrap His arms around you as a father to a son."

Momin remembered back over 20 years to the bloody and battered body of his own father, pierced several times by the bullets of Israeli soldiers. He had been there and watched from a few feet away as his mother had held his dying father on her lap, tears cascading down onto her face as she cradled the man she loved.

Momin could still remember the strong arms of his father, but the remembrance brought him a multitude of pain, so he shuddered and backed cautiously away from the memory.

He turned his head and saw the Jew lying on the cot just a few feet away from him, and a rush of revulsion swelled up within him, and suddenly, he didn't want to be forgiven, didn't want to be held, or loved. He only wanted to kill!

"And now, here's Terri Newland with Storm Team 10 weather."

Josh McCullen was no meteorologist, but he already new the weather. It was cold; it was windy; and there was a multitude of snow. Spunky had been unable to find Andy Fitzu last night. In fact, no one in town had seen him since yesterday afternoon. Louise had called and reported him missing to the County Sheriff. They had tried to raise him on the radio, but with no response. He was interrupted by Zeke's raspy old voice.

"Hey Josh. Look! One of them's awake."

Josh and Lance both turned in their metal folding chairs and saw Momin watching them. Josh thought he sensed something strange in the man's eyes, but it soon went away, as if purposefully extinguished like the flame of a candle.

"Good morning sir. How are you feeling?"

Josh had tried to sound cheerful. He looked over at Lance and half smiled at the intensity of his friend's gaze. Lance was like that – a very serious man. Josh reached forward and turned off the television set. Now they would get some answers.

§ § §

"So after my car went in the ditch, I came here, meaning to send someone back for my prisoner, but I see that's no longer necessary."

Momin glanced down at Agent Resnik, still sleeping on the cot a few feet away. He should have killed him yesterday. Now he was just a risk and a complication.

"Has he spoken at all?"

Zeke answered.

"Not a word. He was unconscious when Spunky brought him in here shortly after you stumbled on in."

Momin appeared interested. He shrugged off the pain in his left arm, mastering control with the sheer force of his own will. He felt weak from loss of blood, but the sleep had rejuvenated him. He felt like Allah was giving him almost superhuman strength to empower him to continue his mission – bloody, radioactive, jihad.

"Spunky? Where is he now? I'll need to question him before I leave for Detroit."

Lance hadn't said a word. He was just watching, trying to figure out which way was north with this guy. Something didn't feel quite right, but he couldn't put his finger on it. He spoke now.

"He's out doing an aerial recon. Should be back pretty soon."

Momin's eyes perked up.

"He's a pilot?"

Lance nodded.

"Yeah, he's got several planes. He's a crop duster. Why?"

Momin tried not to sound too interested, but it was difficult for him. If he had a plane . . . then . . . he let the rest go unthought.

"Well it's just that you already told me all the roads are plugged up, and the phones are down. I need to get this prisoner back to my field headquarters in Detroit for questioning, and medical attention, of course. It's a matter of the utmost national security."

Lance relaxed his guard. The man's story did make sense.

"You sure you're ready to travel? How's your arm feel?"

Momin smiled.

"Feels great! I'm ready to save the world for democracy."

Josh laughed out loud and stood to his feet as he spoke.

"Tell you what, Agent Resnik. Why don't we get you over to the parsonage next door, and my wife Louise will cook you up some of the best fried eggs and ham in all of Iroquois county!"

Lance watched as Momin's smile faded away.

"Did you say ham?"

Josh nodded.

"Yeah. Ham. It's honey smoked too."

Momin seemed to recover slightly.

"Pastor McCullen, no offense, but I'm Jewish. I can't eat ham."

Josh lowered his head in apology.

"Sorry Mr. Resnik. I should have figured out that last name. We don't get many Jewish FBI agents up here. Will you settle for pancakes?"

Momin smiled. He was starved.

"Sounds great! Let's get on with it. And then I'd like to talk to this Spunky character about hitching a ride on down to Detroit. I really must get back. My superiors need to know that I've captured the terrorist. Plus I. . . ."

Then he stopped in mid sentence.

"Oh yes, one other important thing."

Josh got up from his chair as he spoke.

"What's that?"

"Did this man have a large, metal suitcase with him?"

Josh cocked his head to one side as if thinking.

"Not that I know of. Spunky brought him in. You'll have to ask him."

Momin nodded.

"All right then. Let's get some food."

Lance and Zeke watched with interest as Josh and Momin walked out of the church. The wind blew in a gust of snow, but the sun came in along with it, seeming out of place, an interesting mix of light and dark.

The door closed behind them, and Lance looked down at the captured terrorist, still sleeping on the cot beside him. He moved his hand up to his face and rubbed his fingers nervously across his stubbled chin.

"What's wrong, Rock?"

Lance shook his head slowly from side to side.

"Maybe nothing. Maybe something. I don't know. Just doesn't feel right. I've known FBI agents before."

Zeke tried to laugh it off.

"Yeah well, these are strange times, Rock. Turn the TV back on and let's catch some more news."

Lance turned on the TV and then looked over at Zeke one more time.

"Zeke, where did Josh put that guy's wallet and pistol?"

Zeke answered without looking up. He was already engrossed in the latest news on casualties.

"In his office I think."

Lance stood up and walked across the auditorium.

"Be right back, Zeke. I have to check on something."

Chapter 41

"So what's it's like to be a real, live G-man, Mr. Resnik?"

Louise had been asking Momin question after probing question and he had long lost patience with her, but he had to feign civility, at least until he got his hands on his suitcase and the plane.

"Well, it's much better than being a real, dead G-man, that's for sure Mrs. McCullen."

Louise pasted on a smile as she poured another ladle of pancake batter onto the hot, greasy skillet. She usually loved to cook, especially when there was someone around to talk to, but on this particular morning, she had to struggle to cover up her anxiety and nervousness.

"So what's it like to be a Jew, Mr. Resnik. You must be very proud to be one of God's chosen people."

Louise had the gift of discerning a person's spirit, and she was very uncomfortable with this man. Her husband didn't always agree with her, and once in a while they argued about that. He was too trusting, in her opinion. In I Corinthians 12:10, it talked about those who could discern the evil in another's spirit. She quoted it inside her head now and the words brought her comfort. 'To one there is given through the spirit, the message of wisdom, to another the message of knowledge by means of the same spirit, to another faith by the same spirit, to another gifts of healing by that one spirit, to another miraculous powers, to another prophecy, to another distinguishing between spirits. . . .' And right now, Louise was distinguishing evil and falsehood inside this man. Something about him just didn't feel right.

Momin didn't answer the question. He wanted to stand up, walk over and beat this nosey woman into sure death, but he had to restrain himself, at least for now. Besides, the bullet hole in his left arm had left him feeling weak and limited his options. He would just have to wait them out, be clever and cunning, then he could kill them, in any way he wanted.

"Mrs. McCullen, I need to use the restroom. Will you point me in the right direction, please?"

Louise raised her right arm and pointed toward the living room.

"The other side of the house, Mr. Resnik. Go through the living room, and it's attached to our bedroom. You can't miss it."

Momin cradled his arm as he left the room, and Louise couldn't help but notice that the dark cloud she was feeling seemed to leave right along with him. Josh walked back into the kitchen from his office.

"Well, the local lines are back up and I got through to Spunky. He'll be here in a few minutes. Better put on some extra pancakes. That guy eats like a . . . ."

He stopped in mid sentence when he saw the troubled look on his wife's face.

"What's wrong honey? You okay?"

Josh moved up behind her and put his arm around his wife. Louise turned her back on the stove and wiped her hands on her flower-printed apron.

"There's something wrong with this man, Joshua. I can feel it."

Josh cocked his head to one side.

"Are you sure? I can't feel anything."

"Of course you can't. You're a man! Besides, you don't have the gift of discernment."

Josh chuckled to himself. His wife was always sensing something bad about someone.

"Well, I guess we'd better get him fed and on that plane then. The sooner we get him out of here, the better."

She turned her back on her husband.

"Damn it Josh! Listen to me!"

All the blood drained from his face, and he suddenly felt cold chills sweep in waves across his body.

"Louise? Did you just swear?"

She turned back around and grabbed her husband's plaid, flannel shirt and held on tight, squeezing as hard as she could with her fingers.

"Joshua, please, believe me, just this one time. Be on your guard! This message is from God!"

Josh didn't have time to respond. The back door flew open and Lance Stuart burst through with his pistol at the ready.

"Josh! Where's he at?"

Josh drew in a sharp breath and his wife let her hands fall back down to her side.

"Lance, what in the name of God are you doing? Has everybody around here gone crazy? Put that pistol away! You're going to get some-one hurt!"

Lance Stewart looked over at Josh with terror in his eyes.

"Josh, that man is going to kill you!"

Chapter 42

Spunky hadn't gotten much sleep last night - not because he'd been up late plowing, or because so much had happened - he just needed a drink, and the fire burning in his veins had kept him awake. But he had given Rock his word, so he'd drank an entire pot of coffee to try and stem the tide of his addiction; but you can't hold back the waves, and right about now Spunky's blood felt like molten lava, slowly moving through his veins in a feeble effort to supply his body with oxygen. And to start out the day, he was going to fly an FBI Agent and a terrorist through a radioactive cloud, back to Detroit. Spunky furrowed his brow and frowned – not a good day to quit drinking.

He'd woken up this morning with a sour stomach, but he still needed more coffee. Spunky couldn't help but laugh out loud at the irony. He quit drinking for his health, and now he was sick. His frown returned. He knew he hadn't quit for his health, not really, he'd quit for Lance Stuart, the only man he respected. He didn't even give a rat's rear end what happened to the rest of the world, and, if the truth be known, he didn't really even care all that much about the 200,000 people who had just died.

Something in Spunky's heart seized up and turned cold. He didn't care? How had he gotten this way? He ran through a quick synopsis of his life: raised by loving parents, went to Harvard as a man of privilege, married the most wonderful woman in the world. He'd been happy. He'd had it all. That's when he had met Rock at the university. And then the woman he loved had come down with the cancer, and everything had changed.

Spunky turned the steering wheel on his truck, and pulled into the parking lot of the Mudhen. Time for coffee to go. And after that, he'd failed every test God had given him. Funny he hadn't seen it this clearly at the time. He'd become a classic alcoholic, drinking to escape the pain, and all those other women he'd married or slept with; it was just more of the same, another drug to take him from reality. The real molten fire and lava wasn't in Spunky's blood, but deep inside his soul. He saw that now, but he had been sleeping so soundly, that it had taken a nuclear explosion to wake him up.

The truck rolled to a stop, the sound of the frozen snow crunching beneath his big tires. Spunky sat there, slumped over the wheel in the deserted parking lot, thinking about the radioactive cloud moving across the country, wondering what other evil was yet to come, how many were yet to die, about his wife, gone these long years, and he let his forehead fall down onto the steering wheel and stop with a thud.

He sat there, tears streaming down the sides of both cheeks, wondering, is it even worth it?

He reached over and opened the glove compartment to get a spare magazine for his pistol, and when he reached inside it, his hand touched the glass bottle. His fingers closed around it and lifted it gingerly out, letting the light filter through the amber liquid, lending it life, and magic . . . and power.

Jack Daniels had always been his favorite.

Chapter 43

"Stay where you are and don't move! If you do, I'll shoot!"

Momin had just walked back into the kitchen from the bathroom. He looked surprised, but not befuddled, to find Lance Stuart pointing a .40 caliber Glock pistol at his chest. Instinctively, Josh curled his arm around his wife and moved her behind him for protection.

"Talk to me Rock! What's going on?"

Lance kept the pistol trained on Momin with his right hand and reached into his coat pocket with his left. He slowly tossed the FBI badge up onto the counter, then returned his pistol to a more stable two-handed grip.

"Look at the picture Josh."

Josh picked up the thin, black, leather wallet and looked first at the picture, then back up at Momin. He did it several times, then he cleared the loose ends of his flannel shirt away from his .45 caliber pistol and drew it quickly and firmly with one fluid motion. He raised it up and pointed it directly at Momin's center of exposed mass. The FBI badge fell helplessly to the linoleum floor.

Momin's dark eyes smiled.

§ § §

"Make sure that duct tape is good and tight Zeke. Only God knows how many more of us will die if that lunatic gets away."

Zeke finished securing Momin's hands and feet and slowly backed away from the 8-feet tall wooden cross made of barn beams. They had placed Momin squarely in the center of the podium, to the left of the preacher's pulpit and to the right of the prayer candle display where they could watch him and still not have to get close.

Momin looked up at the cross and sneered.

"You can't stop me! Allah has willed it! You will all die in blood and fire!"

Zeke yelled back at him, more out of fear than anger.

"Just shut up! You're not going to kill anyone else ever again. If I had my way you'd be dead already!"

Momin laughed out loud.

"Then I will pray that you never get your way. You can't kill me until my destiny is complete. Allah will protect me until my work is done."

Josh took a step forward.

"How can you say that? You're a murderer – a mass murderer – you killed almost 200,000 people!"

Momin stopped laughing and his face became serious.

"Jihad is not murder. It is honor. It is duty to God."

Josh put his pistol back in its holster.

"That's the sickest thing I've ever heard! You call killing innocent women and children honor? What is honorable about that?"

Momin glared back at them, then turned his head and spit on the base of the large wooden cross.

"There are no innocents outside of Islam. This is Jihad. All must convert or be put to the sword!"

Lance Stuart had been quiet, but he stepped forward now, replacing his pistol in its holster as he did.

"I know that you believe that garbage and are willing to die for it, but why? How did you get so misled?"

The darkness of Momin's eyes looked up at him from ten feet away and glistened in the fluorescent light. When he spoke, it was in Arabic, and he went on for several sentences, spewing the words out like venom.

"He's speaking Arabic. Would you like me to interpret for you?"

Zeke, Josh, and Lance, all turned around and looked at Richard Resnik, who had moved up to a sitting position on his cot. Josh walked over and sat beside him.

"You okay now agent Resnik?"

Richard smiled weakly and nodded.

"Yes. Just feeling very weak. And my fingers and toes are sore. They feel tender to the touch."

Zeke took a step closer.

"It's the frostbite. I saw a lot of it in Korea. A couple of your toes were black. You might lose one or two of them. But you'll be fine aside from that."

Richard looked up at the podium and met Momin's hateful gaze. He didn't flinch. This man had killed his family: his mother, his father, and 200,000 others.

"He was quoting from Osama Bin Laden who issued a fatwa against all Americans and Jews in 1998."

Zeke interrupted him.

"What's a fatwa? Never heard of it before."

"It's a religious ruling given by high-ranking Muslim leaders. This one was made public by the World Islamic Front in 1998 and supported by a great portion of the Muslim extremists."

Momin glared at him, his eyes full of hatred.

"Just shut up you stinking Jew! You are the first one I'm going to kill!"

Lance seemed to have adapted to Momin's fanatical spewings and just ignored him.

"What did the fatwa say?"

Richard stood weakly to his feet. Josh stood beside him, placing his hand on his back for support.

"Osama Bin Laden said: 'But when the forbidden months are past, then fight and slay the pagans wherever ye find them, seize them, beleaguer them, and lie in wait for them in every stratagem; and peace be upon our prophet Muhammad Bin-Abdullah, who said: I have been sent with the sword between my hands to ensure that no one but Allah is worshipped, Allah who put my livelihood under the shadow of my spear and who inflicts humiliation and scorn on those who disobey my orders."

Josh interrupted him.

"Slay the pagans? But we're not pagans. We're God-fearing Christians! We believe in God and we want to serve Him. America is still predominantly a godly country. So why are they killing us?"

Richard smiled weakly and shook his head from side to side.

"You don't understand radical Islam. It was founded by one man, a man with self-serving interests, and he spread his power and influence by conquering others. Muhammad claimed to be God's prophet, therefore, anything he said was considered equal to that of God. Did you know that Muhammad had 23 wives and concubines? Once he wanted to marry the wife of his step-son, something that was forbidden by Islamic law, so he simply claimed to have received a revelation from Allah that it was now lawful for him to take her as his wife. His step-son, who was a good Muslim, wanted to please the prophet, so he immediately divorced his wife so Muhammad could bed her. On another time, Muhammad, the great prophet of Allah, married a 6-year old girl, then consummated that marriage when she was only 9 years old. America must come to understand Islam for what it really is. Allah is not the god of Judaism and Christianity. He is not the god of love and tolerance."

Zeke turned away from Momin and faced Richard before the cot.

"I still don't understand why they want to kill us all. Even if all of that is true, it doesn't make any sense to me."

"It's because they define pagan as anyone who doesn't practice Islam. And, according to certain passages in the Koran, all pagans have to be converted or killed."

Richard looked down at the floor and thought for a moment. He wanted them to understand what kind of person they had captured. He needed them to help him retrieve the other nuclear suitcase bomb and then take it back to the bureau.

"Later in the fatwa, Osama Bin Laden said: 'We – with Allah's help – call on every Muslim who believes in Allah and wishes to be rewarded to comply with Allah's order to kill the Americans and plunder their money wherever and whenever they can find it. We also call on Muslim ulema, leaders, youths, and soldiers to launch the raid on Satan's U.S. troops and the devil's supporters allying with them, and to displace those who are behind them so that they may learn a lesson.'"

Zeke, Josh, and Lance all stood motionless, saying nothing, surprised to learn that according to Islam, they were servants and soldiers of Satan. Momin saw the looks on their faces and laughed out loud maniacally.

"And now you know the truth! You are infidels, pagans, arrogant soldiers of the great Satan! And since you are soldiers, then you are enemies, and you must die. America and the weakness of Christianity has stood in Islam's way far too long. And now, you will be crushed under the iron boot of Islam. It is time for America to die!"

Zeke turned and yelled at the top of his voice.

"Just shut up! We don't want to hear your garbage anymore! America is free, and I fought to protect that freedom. I watched hundreds of my friends die trying to stop tyrants like you from enslaving other people."

"Hush Zeke!" Josh silenced him with a stern rebuke and a stare. "Don't lower yourself. He's not worth it. He's going to prison now, and he'll rot there for the rest of his life."

Momin smiled a tooth-filled grin.

"Go ahead and kill me if you want! Seventy virgins await me, and Allah will welcome me personally at the gates of heaven."

Lance turned back around and glared at Momin.

"It's a good thing for you that we're in the house of God, because right now you are really getting on my nerves."

Josh walked up to the cross and looked down at Momin.

"Jesus commanded us to love you, so I can't go ahead and kill you, even though right now my fallen flesh wants . . . ."

Josh let the sentence die unended. He walked over to Momin, picked up the duct tape and wrapped it around his head several times, securely covering his mouth. When he was done, he stood up and nodded his head in satisfaction.

"There! You're easier to love when you're not talking."

Chapter 44

Hank sat beside Josh and Lance in the Mudhen, stirring his coffee and listening to the other three men talk about what had happened over the past 24 hours. So far, Special Agent Resnik had done most of the talking, bringing them all up to speed on what had happened over the past few days, but Hank interrupted with a question when a sudden thought occurred to him.

"Was Momin working alone or as part of a group? Is it possible that there are more of them right here in Freidham Ridge?"

Richard shifted in his chair before answering.

"He was part of a 5-man cell, but the other four are dead."

Hank nodded and took a sip of his coffee.

"Did you kill them?"

"No. Momin killed them. Slit all their throats while they were sleeping."

Josh set his coffee cup down on the Formica table top and a few drops sloshed over the side and ran down the length of his heavy glass mug.

"He killed his own men? Why?"

Lance leaned forward in anticipation. The very thought of pure evil amazed his writer's mindset.

"I'm not exactly sure. I think he saw them as a liability. They were planning an attack on the Superbowl."

Hank blurted out.

"So it's true! We heard that on the news just a few days ago."

Richard smiled weakly.

"You'd be surprised at half the things you don't hear on the news. They had gained access to a crop-duster, and were going to spray the stadium with gasoline and then ignite the crowd. They probably would have killed 50,000 people or more, all on national TV."

Hank looked around the restaurant. It was mid-afternoon, and a few locals were starting to filter in. He was surprised to see George Kenzie nonchalantly walk in carrying a rifle as if this were the first day of deer season. Richard glanced over, and his hand went instinctively to his sidearm. Lance reached over and put a restraining hand on his shoulder.

"It's okay. He's one of the good guys. Most people carry around here. Usually concealed though. I think people are really nervous right now. A lot has happened. Things have changed."

Josh blew the rising steam off his coffee and took a tiny sip.

"Half the country has gone nuts. Civil government is breaking down. I would hate to be in a big city right now. The beast is loose, and I think things are going to get worse before they get better."

All the men nodded together in agreement, and there was silence for a moment as they contemplated the breakdown of civilization.

"I wanted to kill that man, blow his head off right in church!"

Lance looked over thoughtfully. He liked that Josh was so open and honest, even about his own flaws.

"We all did, Josh. I think it's natural to want to step on a rattlesnake. Don't be so hard on yourself. That guy is pure evil. I could feel it emanate from him. I just didn't know what it was."

Josh looked over with red in the whites of his eyes.

"I know. It's just that I'm supposed to love that man, like Jesus does. But I don't. I hate him, and I want him to die! What does that say about me?"

Richard interrupted him in a stern voice.

"It says that you're human just like the rest of us."

He thought for a moment, and then continued on.

"When I was in Momin's apartment, I went into his bedroom, and he had a little girl tied naked to the bed. Momin had raped her everyday for almost two weeks. I got her out of there, but that tipped him off and he got away. I wanted to kill him too, all of them."

Everyone around the table was quiet now. They said nothing. Finally, Richard broke the silence.

"Where is that pilot friend of yours? I've got to get out of here and back to Detroit. I'm stuck here in this stupid little town and I can't even make a phone call."

Lance looked over casually.

"You can make a phone call with my cell."

Richard's eyes looked hopeful.

"I thought this was a giant dead zone?"

Lance nodded.

"It is, but all you have to do is drive 20 miles east closer to I-75 and you can get through just fine. The roads are drifted shut, and there won't be any snowplows through for several days. You'd have to take a snow-mobile though."

Richard set his mug down firmly on the table.

"Do any of you have a snowmobile?"

All the men laughed, even Hank. Josh was the first to speak.

"This is Northern Michigan. We've all got snowmobiles!"

Then Josh took control, and they all set out to plan.

"Lance, why don't you take my 2 machines and get Richard over to make his cell call. Hank, you get on out to Spunky's place and see what happened to him. Zeke and I will take turns babysitting the terrorist until everyone else gets back."

Everyone slid their chairs back in unison, except for Hank, who remained quietly seated. Josh stopped and looked down at him.

"What's wrong Hank?"

He didn't answer for a moment.

"What about Fitzu? I know he was a jerk, but we can't just leave him out there like that. Someone should go get him."

Josh smiled and nodded.

"You're right. I'll take care of it. And one other thing. I think we ought to pray before we all separate."

No one said a word. Finally, Agent Resnik broke the silence.

"Dear God. Please help us to conquer this evil and purge it from the land. Give us strength and wisdom. Let your will be done."

And all God's people said, "Amen."

§ § §

Momin was pretending to be asleep, but he kept one eye partly open, watching Zeke, and waiting for him to leave or to fall asleep, either way would work for him. According to his plan, he would need only a few minutes to make his escape, then he could find his other suitcase and the pilot who could take him out of here.

These people weren't like the other Americans he'd known. They put up a fight, but that was okay, Momin would just have to outsmart them. So far, Allah had arranged everything he needed, except for the duct tape around his wrists, but, even that, Momin considered to be Allah's will. Nothing happened without the approval of Allah, and all of this was Momin's destiny. Even the snow storm had been sent here to help him destroy these pagans. He just wasn't sure how it all fit in yet, but Momin had faith and confidence that all unknown things would be revealed in

Allah's time.

He thought for a moment about the men who had captured him, especially the pastor. That man's compassion would be his undoing. Momin would see to that. Imagine that, actually trying to love your enemies. Christians were so weak inside, no fortitude, no resolve; they couldn't do what needed to be done to rule. He had heard that the prophet Jesus had always referred to them as sheep, and now he knew why. Sheep for the slaughter; that's all they were, and Momin would gladly be the instrument of their destruction. While they sat idly by contemplating the morality of stopping him, he would kill them all in their sleep. Momin smiled inside at the thought of it.

He saw Zeke's chin drop down onto his chest, then he heard the steady, level sound of a man breathing his last breaths. Momin would see to that personally.

As quietly as possible, he slid his bound hands beneath his buttocks and worked them slowly and soundlessly down the back of his legs to his feet. Once his hands were out in front of him, he quietly worked his way over to the table with the burning prayer candle and stood beside it, with his hands and feet still bound.

Momin went deep inside himself, steeling his will in anticipation of the pain. Resolutely, he held his wrists over the candle, watching it as the flames took hold and licked their way up the plastic tape, giving off black smoke and orange flames. Soon the tiny conflagration peaked, purifying him, readying him for his own death and resurrection, and he had to tilt his head back to keep from burning his face. Momin smiled, knowing that Allah would find the aroma of his burning flesh to be a suitable and necessary sacrifice.

Once free, Momin walked over and stood beside Zeke's motionless form. His sleeping captor never awoke.

Chapter 45

"Are we going to die, Angela?"

The question, broke Angela's heart, even though she knew that it was a legitimate and obvious question to ask under the circumstances. She reassured the 10-year old boy as best she knew how, but she told the truth.

"Phillip, everyone dies. It's just a matter of when and how."

Phillip was wearing his flannel Winnie the Pooh pajamas, knowing that if his classmates saw him wearing Pooh, that they would tease him, but tonight he didn't care. He just wanted the comfort and remembrance of a simpler time, a time when nuclear incineration wasn't so much on the agenda, a time when his biggest worry was: what toy should I play with next? The younger kids were all in bed, but he didn't feel tired, so he had exercised his rights as the firstborn male to stay up an extra 15 minutes.

"You know what I mean, Angela. Don't treat me like I'm still little. Are we going to die? Is that poison cloud coming here?"

Angela wanted to laugh and cry simultaneously. Hank had warned her that kids would sometimes ask difficult questions, and this was one of those occasions. She bought herself a moment in time by leaning over on the couch and kissing the top of his forehead. She thought to herself, 'What would Hank say?' He always seemed to have the answers where his kids were concerned, but Hank was at the office, trying desperately to get the next issue out on time. She thought it odd, that even though the whole world seemed to be blowing up, Hank was desperate to document it all, to get it out on paper for all the world and posterity to see.

She looked down at Phillip's questioning eyes. They were pretty, brown, and vulnerable.

"You have pretty eyes, Phillip. Did you know that?"

The little boy frowned.

"Don't change the subject. I want to know what's going to happen to us. Are we going to die or not?"

Angela shook her head slowly from side to side.

"No, Phillip. Not today. I was listening to the news, and it seems that God sent a snowstorm to blow the radioactive cloud far away. The cloud is breaking up and will soon be dispersed."

Phillip's eyes softened as a look of relief came over his face.

"Good thinking. Guess that's why He's God and we're not."

Angela smiled and reached over to rumple his hair, but Phillip reached up his right hand to stop her.

"Don't mess my hair up, Angela. I just got it looking good."

He reached his left hand up to his head and pushed back an out of place lock of hair.

"So we're okay? For now, I mean."

"Yes Phillip. We're okay for now."

He leaned over and rested his head on her shoulder. It caught Angela off guard, and she didn't move at first. Then he reached over, grabbed her arm and swung it around so that she was hugging him.

"Did you know that my mom lived in Grand Rapids?"

Angela caught her breath. She didn't know, and she wondered now why Hank hadn't mentioned it to her.

"Oh, honey, no. I'm sorry."

Phillip tried to brush it off nonchalantly.

"It don't matter. She never came to visit anymore anyways. I still loved her though."

Angela squeezed him tighter as she spoke.

"She might be okay, Phillip. It was a small nuclear bomb. If she was outside the city when it happened, she'll be just fine."

Phillip shook his head in disagreement.

"I don't think so. Mom lived downtown, and she always got drunk every night. She was probably still in bed when it happened."

Tears welled up in Angela's eyes, but she fought them back.

"Maybe not, Phillip. Don't you believe in miracles?"

"I never saw one happen before. Have you?"

Angela thought for a moment, and then she sat up straight with the stark realization that she had seen a miracle.

"Yes, Phillip. I have seen a miracle!"

Phillip raised his head up off her shoulder and looked into her eyes as if probing to see if she was telling the truth.

"Really?"

Angela nodded.

"Did you know that I was in the Twin Towers on nine-eleven?"

Phillip's eyes got bigger as he spoke with more life.

"No! How did you get out?"

A thoughtful look came over her as she remembered back.

"I think it was a miracle, Phillip. I think God saved me. I remember feeling the airplane crash into the building just a few floors below me. I remember the fire and smoke and all the screams and the smells. I remember the heat. I was on the floor, and I distinctly remember passing out, knowing that I was about to die."

Phillip sat up straighter.

"So what happened then?"

Angela shook her head back and forth.

"I have no idea Phillip. All I know is that when I came to, I was in the ambulance on my way to the hospital. I was cut off from the rescue workers by the flames. No one could have saved me. I should be dead right now, but someone saved me, and I believe it was God."

She paused a moment.

"Did you know that before nine-eleven, I was an atheist?"

Phillip looked a little perplexed.

"I've heard of that before, but I can't remember what it means."

"An atheist is someone who believes that God does not exist."

"You're kidding me! How could you not believe in God? He's all around us!"

Angela thought for a moment and nodded her head.

"I can see that now, Phillip. But I was alone, and loneliness can confuse people sometimes. It makes them think stupid thoughts and do stupid things."

Her voice trailed off into nothingness.

"I guess I did a lot of stupid things."

A protective look came over Phillip's face, and Angela was surprised to see it, but also very happy about it.

"Everybody does stupid things sometimes Angela. You know that."

He thought for a moment.

"Jimmy Selzer stuck his finger in a light socket to see what would happen, and now his hair is all frizzy. Once I put my tongue on a frozen pipe and it got stuck there. That was pretty stupid."

Angela laughed and Phillip smiled.

"And everybody eats eggs. That's not very smart."

Angela's brow furrowed.

"What's so stupid about eating eggs?"

Phillip was still smiling playfully as he answered.

"Chickens shoot eggs out their butts, and then we eat 'em. Does that sound smart to you?"

The look on Angela's face softened, and her brow immediately unfurled. She laughed and reached over and started tickling him under the armpits.

"Why you little runt! Are you teasing me?"

Phillip laughed and squirmed back and forth trying to get away, and then he tried to tickle her back. Angela allowed him just enough success not to discourage him.

They laughed and talked for a few more minutes, and then, after putting him to bed, she lay alone on the couch, watching the colored lights on the Christmas tree blink off and on, off and on, off and on, and she found herself feeling a twinge of guilt at this strange, new happiness she'd found in Freidham Ridge. The rest of the world was imploding upon itself, and so many had suffered and died in the past few months, with many more inevitably to follow, that it didn't seem right that she should be resting on Hank's couch, basking in all the love that his family had to offer. It was better than her six-figure salary, her corner office, and all the power and prestige of her past. For the first time in her life she felt successful – she felt happy – she felt loved. Leaning back on the couch pillow, she slapped her left hand on her thigh and Toto hopped up beside her and snuggled inside the crook of her arm.

Angela pushed the guilt away and offered up a prayer to God. Phillip was right, God was all around her, even under the shadow of terrorist threat and nuclear incineration.

Toto watched her with unblinking eyes, then he felt her breathing level out and knew she was fast asleep. The little dog laughed, and then he burrowed in deep and fell asleep in her arms.

Chapter 46

Josh had never seen a man with his head blown away, and he was not prepared for what he found in the trunk of agent Resnik's car out on Miller Road. Even though Officer Fitzu was frozen solid, the smell of the blood and brains had overwhelmed him, all that, coupled with the cold, pallid look of death on what was left of Andy's face, had caused Josh to lean over and wretch in the ice-cold snow drift beside the car.

Finally, he had loaded Andy into the back of his truck like firewood, and had brought him back to the parsonage. The closest funeral home was in Bentley, so Josh had rolled Andy up in a several blankets and stored him in the corner of his garage for transportation after the storm let up and the roads were cleared. The garage would keep the animals away, but was also cold enough to keep him frozen.

Now, he walked in through the side door of the church, past due to relieve Zeke on guard duty. He closed the door behind him, took several steps and stopped. Something was different. Something was wrong. There were new smells in the church, odors here that should not be.

Josh unzipped his heavy coat, cleared it away from his waist with his right hand, and drew his firearm with one smooth motion. He walked forward cautiously, afraid of what he might find, but what he saw in the sanctuary made the sight of Andy's frozen body seem like a joy to behold.

There, hanging on the cross, with outstretched arms, tied to the wooden beams, was the headless body of his friend, Zeke Tyler. Blood poured down Zeke's chest, onto the base of the cross, where it soaked into the carpet.

Josh started to shake, but whispered a quick prayer and steadied himself. He raised his pistol defensively and swept it around the room, looking for danger. There was none. Momin was gone.

Josh walked slowly up to the cross and then noticed the prayer table off to the right of it. Centered on the clean, white doily, where once only the candle had been, now sat Zeke's head. And sticking up through a hole in the top of Zeke's skull, protruded the burning prayer candle. Josh moved closer, dropped to his knees and cried without shame.

Here, on this podium, where he had preached a thousand times before on love and compassion, Josh could only think of hatred and rage. Tears ran down his cheeks, and saliva dripped from his mouth as he spoke, out loud, to no one in the room.

"But if any harm follow, then thou shalt give life for life, eye for eye, tooth for tooth, hand for hand, foot for foot, burning for burning, wound for wound, stripe for stripe."

The wax on the candle beaded up near the burning wick, rolled over the edge and cascaded quickly down the length of it. It stopped and formed a pool on old Zeke's head, hardening on his scalp, mixing with blood and hair.

Josh stood up and walked resolutely to the door. When he opened it and stepped outside, he could no longer feel the cold.

§ § §

The snow was piling up fast in the road, but Hank's Blazer was in four-wheel drive, and making good progress through the drifts. He hated leaving his kids alone with Angela while so many bad and dangerous things were going on, but he had no choice. He had to check on Spunky and then get the paper out on time. Besides, the sooner Spunky took Momin and Agent Resnik out of here, the sooner his family would be safe again. As a precaution, he had asked Freida to come over and spend the day with them.

Hank shook his head from side to side in amazement. So much had changed, events, people, even the way he thought. Just a short while ago he had yelled at Freida for buying a gun, and now he was glad that she owned it. Six months ago he had never dreamed that he'd feel good about a 10 millimeter Glock, semi-automatic pistol with high-capacity magazines. But now . . . . He reached his right hand down to his waist and felt the bulk of the .38 caliber revolver that Lance had loaned him. It was a reassuring presence.

The snow was blowing worse now, so Hank slumped down over the wheel, trying to focus and see through the white. He reached up with his left hand and tried to wipe the frost off the inside of the windshield. He should have taken time to let the engine warm up. It was so cold outside, and the wind just infused it all with power and strength.

A few minutes later, he was relieved to see Spunky's house come into view. He wheeled the Blazer to the right and pulled into the drive. Good! Spunky's truck was there.

The frigid wind bit into him like a buzz saw, freezing his exposed face in a matter of seconds. Hank pulled up his hood and held it tight to his face with both gloved hands. He rang the door bell to the house, but there was no response. He beat on the steel door for several seconds, then he peered in through the window. No lights were on – no sign of life.

He walked out behind the house, making his way slowly through the drifts until he reached the pole barn where Spunky kept his planes. Without knocking, he walked on in and closed the door behind him, shutting out the wind and the cold.

It was dark inside, so he waited a few moments, allowing his eyes to adjust, and when they did, he saw Spunky's silent, unmoving body, leaned up against the tire of an old biplane. There was an empty bottle on the cold cement beside him, and a picture frame clutched close to Spunky's chest.

Hank found the light switch and saw the faint, steady movement of Spunky's chest – up and down, up and down, up and down – slowly, quietly, softly. The inebriated pilot looked more peaceful than Hank had ever seen him, so much so, that he felt guilty about waking him up. But there was great need. He remembered his children still back in town, without him, just a few blocks away from a man who had already killed thousands.

Hank reached down and gave Spunky's chest a gentle nudge. The rhythm of his breathing broke its stride, chopped short, then long, then short again. Finally Spunky's eyes fluttered and opened. He was alive again – alive to the world.

§ § §

Josh had always had trouble reconciling the God of the Old Testament and the God of the New Testament. But now he was starting to understand. This was no longer about revenge, or hatred, or killing; this was about survival. The terrorists wanted them all dead, and to turn the other cheek was tantamount to committing suicide.

The snow drifts were up past his knees, but he was slogging through them with a God-given determination that was focused on saving the lives of the innocent. If he allowed this man to live, then more people would die, more wives would be widowed, and more children would be orphaned. Josh thought back to his sermon the Sunday after nine-eleven. The words came back to him, blocking out the cold wind on his face and the wetness of the snow against his thighs, enabling him to plod on.

"The trick is this my friends. We must kill and love at the same time. We must hunt them down, kill them if they resist, but love them even as they lay dying. Be angry. Be indignant. Hate the sin, but love the sinner. We must pray for our enemies as well as our friends and the ones we love. Because if we pray for them, they may repent, seek God's face and turn from their wicked ways. And, if they repent, then we no longer have to kill them."

Josh laughed at himself and the naiveté of his words. Momin was not going to repent. Perhaps none of these people would; they were too far gone, too steeped in their own hatred, and, worst of all, they enjoyed killing. They had given themselves over so completely to evil, that it was impossible for them to turn back.

"Jesus loves those terrorists. He loved them when they slit the throats of unarmed passengers, and He even loved them when they flew those planes into balls of fire causing thousands of His children to die in flames and blood and agony. And He continues to love them still as they roast in eternal hell and damnation."

Well, Josh could admit it now. He didn't love them. In fact, it took every fiber of his being and self resolve, just to keep from hating them. But, at the same time, Josh understood that the only way to keep from hating someone was to love them. He knew intuitively that the laws of nature sometimes overlapped into the laws of the spirit, and, in this case, nature and spirit both abhorred a vacuum. The presence of love ensured the absence of hate, but the absence of love, would relinquish itself to hate. It was the way of all things.

Tracking Momin through these drifts was easy. He had picked up the trail at the church, and already followed him two blocks into town. He just had to find him before the tracks drifted completely shut. Puffs of steam came out of his lungs like a locomotive and were quickly swept away by the harsh wind. His muscles were sore, and his body was bone-cold weary and exhausted, but Josh staggered on, leaning harder into the wind, talking to God as he plodded along through the ice and snow.

"Okay God, here I am, doing your will, I think. How am I even supposed to know anymore. Momin thinks he's doing your will too, and he's already killed 200,000 innocent people. I know I'm supposed to love this man, but I don't know if I can."

Josh stopped for a moment and looked up into the face of the wind.

"Come on God! Give me a break! He just cut Zeke's head off and hung his body on the cross."

Then, as if in answer, Josh remembered a scripture verse, and it replayed itself in his head, shouting out to him over the howl of the wind and the slap of the snow.

"Father, forgive them, for they know not what they do."

Jesus had said that to the ones who were killing him, and Josh had no doubt that Jesus had been sincere.

"I'm not as good as you are God. I can't do that. It would take a lifetime to learn how to love people like Momin, and in the meantime, I have to either kill him or watch him kill others. You're asking too much!"

But over the howling wind, an answer came back to him: clear, concise, understandable and irrefutable.

"I am the good shepherd, The good shepherd lays down his life for the sheep. The hired hand is not the shepherd who owns the sheep. So when he sees the wolf coming, he abandons the sheep and runs away. Then the wolf attacks the flock and scatters it."

Suddenly, all his other cares melted away, all his questions on morality and philosophy, everything else blew away with the wind, and Josh was reduced to the essence of his soul – he was a shepherd – always had been.

He had to stop Momin, had to stop the wolf, protect the flock. He loved the flock.

§ § §

"I don't understand it! I thought you said 20 miles and we'd have cell service. We must have driven 20 miles by now."

The wind was blowing hard and Richard and Josh had to yell to be heard.

"I'm sorry Richard. I don't understand it either. Something must have changed."

Richard pulled his hood tightly over his face before answering.

"That's the understatement of the year! The twin towers are down and Grand Rapids is a smoldering ash heap. Why would we expect cell service to improve?"

Lance thought for a moment, trying to figure out the next best option. Richard interrupted his thoughts.

"It's driving me crazy not knowing what's going on back in Freidham Ridge. I should have stayed there to guard the prisoner. That was my first responsibility."

Lance smiled despite the wind.

"Don't worry about Freidham Ridge. We can take care of ourselves."

Richard remembered the man in the Mudhen carrying a rifle and was inclined to agree with him. These people were prepared.

"I think we should head on back by way of Podunk. They've got a phone there and we can check the long-distance service again. They may have it up by now. Can't hurt to check. Besides, they make some really nice coffee and cinnamon rolls."

Richard shrugged and climbed back on his snowmobile. The whole world was going to hell in a hand basket, and all Lance wanted was coffee and cinnamon rolls. People up here were strange.

Lance fired up his machine and sped away, leaving Richard to follow as best he could.

Chapter 47

Freida heard the knock on the door and wondered who it could be on a night like this.

"I'll get it Angela. Be back in a minute."

She left Angela in the kitchen sipping coffee. The kids were already in bed sleeping soundly. Maybe Hank forgot his keys again. As she walked past her purse on the couch, Freida hesitated, wondering if she was getting paranoid. She picked up her purse and slung it over her shoulder on her way to the door.

The door had no peephole, so she unlocked it, leaving the chain on and opened it a crack to see who it was. The door came crashing open, knocking her down to the floor. Her purse flew away and came to a rest under the coffee table.

When Angela came running into the room, she saw a man standing over Freida's body, holding a .357 magnum revolver. He was covered in blood from his face down to his waist. The wind blew in through the open door, and Angela wrapped her arms around herself and started to shake.

The man shut the door, locked it, and turned his bloody face back to Angela. He pointed the gun at her and smiled.

"You're not a virgin by any chance are you?"

Angela didn't answer. She was too terrified to speak. Momin laughed out loud.

"I didn't think so. There are no virgins in America, only pimps and whores!"

Finally, Angela managed to slow her breathing and her heart rate enough to speak.

"Quiet down. You'll wake the children."

Momin glanced over at the stairs and a gleam came into his eyes.

"Are any of them virgins?"

Angela's fear was transformed into rage as she lunged at the terrorist. Momin seemed surprised when she grabbed his gun and wrestled with it. She held on tightly to the barrel, but Momin soon recovered his wits and began punching her face with his free hand. A few seconds later, she lay there on the floor beside Freida, unmoving and unaware.

Momin laughed out loud and stood wearily to his feet. The wound in his shoulder had long ago lost any feeling of pain, and he believed that Allah had given him supernatural strength to fulfill his mission – to kill the Americans. This was jihad, a holy war.

"Drop the gun mister! Or I'll blow your head off!"

Momin turned around to see a little boy, sitting on the coffee table and holding a 10 millimeter Glock, which was pointed in his direction.

Momin smiled. Yes, this town was full of surprises; it was so unlike the rest of America he'd seen.

"What are you going to do? Shoot me?"

Momin laughed out loud.

"You can't shoot me. You're an American, and you're probably a Christian too. You believe in fair play, and justice, and love, and mercy. Besides, you're just a little boy."

Momin took a step closer.

"Stop!"

This time Phillip's voice was more commanding and Momin obeyed.

"Yes. I'm an American, but I'm just little and I haven't learned about justice yet."

Momin stopped laughing but continued his blood-toothed smile. He liked this boy. He would kill him quickly.

Momin raised his pistol, and a single shot rang out, deafening the silence of the room.

§ § §

When Hank left Spunky's place, he was half sober and still drinking coffee. A year ago, Hank would have been disgusted by a man who drank like that, but it was hard to judge him after Lance had told him all about his wife and her cancer. Spunky had been through some pretty hard times, and was justified in his remorse. Hank remembered his last trip to Bentley and the waitress at the bar who had sat down to talk to him. A familiar phrase reverberated through his mind. 'There but the grace of God go I.' He understood what that meant now. He had become a lot more humble these past few months.

The roads were worse now and Hank had all he could do just to keep his Blazer on the road. At times it was difficult to even see the road, much less navigate it.

As he neared the edge of town, he contemplated whether to stop at the church first or to head on home and check on his family. He slowed as he passed the church, saw Zeke and Josh's trucks and decided to drive on by. He would check on them later. Right now, he just wanted to spend time with his family.

Movement caught his eye as he rounded the last corner a block away from his house, and he saw a man running down the steps of his front porch. Hank sped up as best he could in the deep snow, but by time he got there, the man had disappeared behind his neighbor's house.

Hank pulled in to his drive and slammed the Blazer into park before jumping out and running up the steps as fast as he could in the snow. He fell down twice, but quickly got up and ran again.

When he burst through the open front door, he saw Freida and Angela lying on the living room floor, silent and motionless. His heart galloped at breakneck speed as he knelt down beside them. First he checked Angela's pulse and then Freida's. They were both still alive and he breathed a sigh of relief. Then he thought about his kids.

"Kids! Kids! Where are you? Are you okay?"

Hank started to run up the stairs to the bedrooms, but was stopped by a small, sobbing voice from behind the couch.

"Daddy!"

"Phillip! Are you okay?"

He rushed down the stairs and scooped his son up in his arms and held him.

"Phillip, what happened?"

His son's whimpers slowly subsided and then faded away completely. It was then, that Hank noticed the gun.

"I shot him, Dad. It's not my fault. I had to. He was a really bad man."

The pistol left Phillip's grip and slipped down onto the floor.

"It's okay son. I know. Don't worry about it. You had no choice. You saved the family. It's all going to be okay."

Hank sat on the floor behind the couch, quivering inside, holding his son, all the while, keeping a watchful eye on the front door in case Momin should return. Finally, he stood up, and helped Phillip to his feet as well.

"Okay son. Let's take care of Freida and Angela now."

Hank walked over to the front door and closed and locked it. Then he picked up the pistol and put it back in Freida's purse.

Angela started to groan softly, so he knelt down beside her and cradled her head in his arms.

"Phillip, go get a wet washcloth please."

Phillip left the room as Angela's eyes fluttered and then opened. She tried to get up, but Hank held her down.

"Relax, honey. It's okay. The man is gone now. Everyone is safe."

Angela let herself relax. Freida's eyes finally opened and she jerked upright and held the back of her head with a moan. Just then, there was a knock at the door. Hank moved quickly to his feet and drew his pistol clumsily from its holster.

"It's Josh McCullen. You guys okay in there?"

Hank breathed a sigh of relief and holstered his pistol. He felt exhausted.

Chapter 48

Spunky's head felt like a man was inside with a jack hammer. Too much whiskey on an empty stomach always did that too him. He drove on through the snow, the wipers on high, pushing away the snow as fast as it fell on his windshield.

It had been a surprise to see Hank Simmons at his place, and even more a surprise the way Hank had treated him. Hank hadn't said a word. He had just helped him to his feet, got him into the house, into the shower, and then fixed him a pot of coffee. They had both talked very little while he'd drank the coffee, other than to have Hank bring him up to speed on what was going on back in town.

Most odd, was that Spunky had felt ashamed of his drunken condition for the first time in over a decade. The town had needed him to stay sober and fly the plane, to get the bad guy out of here and back to the FBI, but he couldn't even do that. Spunky felt that old, familiar self-hatred rise up in his throat and stick there like a malignant lump. He swallowed hard, but it wouldn't go away. He felt the need for absolution.

Spunky was almost in town now and went over in his mind what he had to do. The storm was about to break, he could tell that just by 20 years experience as a pilot flying in all kinds of weather. Then he would have to plow off the runway one more time, then fly the FBI guy and Momin over to the Flint airport. Then he could come back here and restart his life exactly the place he'd left off. Spunky's teeth ground together in dissatisfaction, and deep down inside, he wondered if he could change.

Spunky let off on the gas pedal and slowed to a stop. There was a man lying in the middle of the road, and it looked like Zeke Tyler. The truck door opened, and Spunky piled out and ran over and knelt down beside the man who was lying in a pool of blood. The man rolled over on his own accord and pointed a .357 magnum in Spunky's face.

Spunky recognized Zeke's pistol, and his coat and hat, and deduced immediately what was going on. He smiled.

"So how's it goin' there Momin? How do you like America so far?"

Momin smiled as well, his once-white teeth now soaked with black, dried blood.

"I like some parts better than others. I prefer the city. Too many people out here with guns trying to shoot me."

Spunky saw the blood-soaked hole in his side and nodded his head.

"Yeah well, people in these parts just get grumpy when Islamic terrorists ride into town and start killing people. We're quirky that way."

Momin laughed and fresh blood trickled down his chin.

"Just take that gun out of its holster and drop it on the ground. Do it real slow."

Spunky looked for options and saw none. He complied.

"Great. Now be a good little redneck and drive me out to Spunky's place."

Spunky turned and walked back to the truck. Momin followed him, and soon both were on their way back to the airstrip. The lines in Spunky's brow tightened and furled. He thought to himself. "Not a good day to quit drinkin' – again."

§ § §

As soon as Hank was certain that his family was safe, he reluctantly left then to help Josh follow Momin's trail again. Josh took the lead, and this time it was easier, because drops of blood dotted the snow, and they could follow his trail at full speed.

Within five minutes, they came to a halt on the road beside Spunky's pistol lying in snow, sprinkled with blood. The weariness and disappointment was apparent in Josh's voice.

"These are Spunky's tire tracks. He's got those mud tracker tires on his truck."

Josh dropped to his knees in the snow, fell forward on his elbows and bowed down as if praying. Hank felt clumsy, and just stood there. Finally he spoke.

"You okay Josh?"

When Josh looked up, there were tears streaking his cheeks, and he answered in a wavering voice.

"I just don't understand the nature of this much evil. I don't understand this mindset. So much hatred, for so long."

Hank knelt in the snow beside him and placed his hand on Josh' shoulder.

"I don't either. They seem to enjoy killing people over there. Except now they're over here. And Americans seem to be easier to kill, because we don't think the way they do. I don't know if we'll catch on in time to survive."

Josh reached up and wiped away his tears.

"He cut off Zeke's head and hung his body on the cross."

Hank spoke through the rising knot in his stomach. He wanted to be angry, but too much tired got in the way.

"We're different than them Josh. We hunt for food – they hunt for sport."

Josh nodded but said nothing either. They both just knelt in the snow, looking down at the blood, contemplating all that had happened the past few months, and wondering what would happen next.

Suddenly, Josh began to pray, and the determination in his voice scared Hank. He had never heard him this way before. Something inside Josh, something core and central to his being had changed.

"Dear God. Please give us the strength and the courage to kill this man. And I apologize in advance for enjoying it. Amen."

Hank echoed him with an amen of his own, and then picked up Spunky's pistol and placed it inside his large coat pocket. As they both got up from the snow, they heard the distant whine of snowmobiles and watched the tiny black dots getting closer and closer.

In a few minutes, Hank, Lance, Richard, and Josh were speeding towards Spunky's house, doing their best, one last time.

§ § §

Spunky found it disquieting to go through his preflight checklist with a .357 magnum pointed at his chest, but, nonetheless, he took his time, going through each step slowly and methodically, knowing that the longer he took, the longer he had to think his way through this predicament. He leaned back in the pilot's seat of his little single-engine Cessna. It was his pride and joy, and flying had become Spunky's only respite from the pain of his past – that, and his legendary drinking of course.

"Hurry up! This is taking too long! I want out of this place!"

Spunky wanted to break this man's neck with his bare hands, but the pistol in his side gave him restraint, helping him to wait for a better time.

"What's your hurry? You haven't even told me where we're going yet."

"We're going south."

Spunky thought about Grand Rapids and furrowed his brow. They would have to fly over a radioactive ash heap.

"South? That's it? No destination?"

Momin smiled that evil grin that made him feel superior to everyone else.

"You don't need to know where we're going, at least not yet."

Spunky took a brief look at his captor. He was a mess. There was blood all over his face, dried blood in his clothes from the torso up, and the fact that some of the blood belonged to other people, made Spunky feel all the more uneasy. But Momin had taken a beating as well. There was a bullet wound in his arm and another in his side. Drops of sweat beaded up on the terrorist's forehead, and Spunky turned away again as Momin reached up and wiped it off with an effort from his wounded arm.

"Who shot you in the side?"

"A little man. A little man with focus and conviction."

Spunky glanced over again and thought he saw a look of admiration on Momin's face. This guy was crazy as a loon. Spunky started to taxi the plane out of his pole barn and out onto the runway. The snow had let up, but the wind was still blowing and drifting. With the weather like this, he'd be lucky to even make it off the runway alive. He thought for a moment about dying, and his pulse quickened. Funny, he never thought it would come like this, but then again, who would? At least he would get to fly one last time. He thought about Rock and the others back in Freidham Ridge.

"Do you mind telling me how many people you killed back there?"

Momin's jet, black hair was greasy and matted with blood. His lower lip quivered a little when he spoke.

"Less than I wanted to."

"And how many would that be?"

Momin leaned back against the side of the fuselage, keeping the gun out in front of him as he spoke.

"Just get the plane in the air! How many I've killed in the past is nothing compared to how many I'm going to kill today."

Momin glanced back at the big, metal case and smiled. Spunky grunted in disgust.

"Why? Why do you people like to kill so much?"

"Because Allah wills it. It is our destiny. We are his chosen people. We are his warriors."

Spunky wheeled the plane gently around onto the snow-covered runway. No respectable pilot would even try this takeoff, but for Spunky, respect was no longer an issue.

"That's not good enough. What's in it for you? People never do things without the proper motivation."

The barrel of Momin's gun, Zeke's gun, bobbed up and down when he laughed.

"You are an ignorant pagan. The only way to be guaranteed entry into paradise is by dying in jihad. Then, in the next world, I will be rich. I will be respected. Seventy virgins await me at the gates of heaven even as we speak."

Spunky stopped focusing on the plane and it gently came to a stop.

"You can't really believe that? There's not seventy virgins within 5,000 miles of here. At least not any that are full grown."

Momin smiled, showing the dried blood caked between his teeth.

"I prefer younger virgins."

Spunky shook his head back and forth in disgust.

"Why does that not surprise me?"

Then a thought occurred to him.

"But what happens after you bed all seventy of them? They won't be virgins anymore after that, and then you're stuck with the same women for the rest of eternity. And what if they get old? Worse yet, what if some of them are ugly?"

Without warning, Momin flew into a sudden rage and began to scream.

"Shut up! Just shut up you son of a pig, or I'll kill you right here!"

Spunky laughed inside. He knew that Momin wasn't going to kill him, at least not with that pistol. He was going to die in a sudden, infamous flash of nuclear light, unless, he could think of some way to stop him. The plane started moving again.

"It doesn't matter. We'll never survive this takeoff anyways. We'll probably crash a hundred yards off the end of the runway."

Momin calmed down again and looked confident and assured.

"No. Allah will guide the plane. He will see us through to the end."

Spunky laughed out loud for the first time in captivity. He thought it ironic that people like Josh McCullen and Hank Simmons could both exist in the same world as people like Momin and his ilk. And then it occurred to him – they can't exist in the same world. That's what this conflict was all about. Who would rule the world? Who would survive? Who would exist? Without even knowing it, he had been pulled into the timeless and epic struggle of good verses evil. Oddly enough, he never really thought of himself as good, but then again, he never thought of himself as evil either. Perhaps it was time to choose.

"Yeah, well, the end just might come a little sooner than you think."

He throttled up the engine and started taxiing down the runway, quickly gaining speed. Spunky had modified the plane specifically for short, rough runways. He was pretty sure he could get it in the air, after that, . . . some god somewhere was just going to have to help out.

Spunky contemplated praying, for a moment at least, then all he wanted was a drink.

Chapter 49

Richard stood on the empty, snow-covered runway, watching the little plane fly out of sight. The winds and the blowing snow had suddenly dissipated, just long enough to allow the tiny plane to get airborne, then, as if on cue, they returned with near gale force.

Lance walked up behind him and stopped.

"What is he going to do?"

Richard shook his head in frustration.

"He has a nuclear bomb and an airplane. What do you think he's going to do?"

Lance nodded in agreement at the unspoken fear.

"He'll kill as many people as he can, as soon as he can. That's his nature. His fatwa. This is jihad."

Richard turned to look him in the eye.

"That's right. Chicago is the second largest city in the country, and all he has to do is fly straight down the coast a few hundred miles."

Lance took a step forward, shaded his eyes from the wind and looked out after the disappearing speck.

"Isn't there any way we can stop him? There must be something we can do."

Richard thought for a moment, then shook his head back and forth in despair.

"Unless I can get another plane, or unless the phones come back on, then we're totally helpless. We can't stop him, and half a million people are about to die."

Lance nodded his head. It didn't look good. He kicked the snow with his boot and worked it back and forth, forming a little trench in the snow.

"I guess it's just Spunky now – Spunky and God. That's our only hope."

They were so focused on the end of the runway and the disappearing plane, that they hadn't heard Josh and Hank walk up behind them.

"I sure hope he's sober."

Lance turned and looked at Hank.

"He flies better when he's drunk. He's the only guy who can beat me at chess, drunk or sober. Besides, Spunky's not the kind of man to go down without a fight. He'll think of something, even if he has to die."

Josh McCullen nodded his head in agreement.

"That's right. Spunky's the best. He's a redneck – an American redneck."

Richard gave him a sarcastic look before he spoke.

"Well that's reassuring. The entire fate of civilization may rest squarely on the shoulders of an American, alcoholic redneck, who may or may not be sober. That's just great!"

Hank turned around and started to walk back toward the pole barn. He called back behind him.

"Well, I'm going to go back into the barn and listen to Spunky some more on the radio."

Richard, Josh, and Lance all turned and looked at him. The wind was blowing all around them, making it difficult to hear.

"What did you say?"

Hank stopped and turned a moment.

“I said I’m going back inside to listen to Spunky. He left the radio turned on inside his other plane. It’s warmer in there too.”

Richard took off sprinting past Hank to the pole barn. Hank looked after him and shrugged his shoulders.

“What’s he so excited about?”

Lance walked past him, leaving just himself and Josh standing in the wind.

“It’s not just a radio, Hank. It’s a transmitter.”

Josh stood there a moment more, then he slapped Hank on the back and guided him toward the pole barn.

“Let’s get in out of the cold, my friend. There’s still hope!”

§ § §

"Onward Christian soldiers marching off to war. With the cross of Jesus, going on before!”

Spunky sang the song as loud as he could, just to aggravate the Moslem. If he was going to die, and there was nothing he could do about it, then at least he was going to make the man pay for it as much as he could.

“I said shut up!”

Spunky laughed.

“Shut up or you’ll what? You’ll shoot me? I’m going to die anyways. And if you shoot me now, then you’ll crash over Lake Michigan and you and I will be the only ones to die.”

Spunky snickered to himself.

“Wouldn’t that be great? Mohammed meeting you at the gates of heaven saying, ‘Nice job, Momin. You had a 3-kiloton nuclear bomb and you only took out one infidel!’”

He smiled triumphantly over at Momin, who glowered back at him, his eyes brimming with hatred and malice. Then he went back to singing.

"And I'm proud to be an American, where at least I know I'm free. And I won't forget the men who died, and gave that right to me. So I proudly stand up . . . next to you and defend her still today. Cuz there ain't no doubt I love this land. God bless the USA!"

Spunky ended the song by holding the last note as long as he could.

"Man I could use a drink."

He reached underneath the seat and pulled out a brown paper sack. He uncapped the bottle and took a long drink. Momin looked over at him, a look of apprehension in his eyes.

"Should you be drinking and flying?"

Spunky snorted back at him and put the cap back on the bottle.

"Now that's really rich. You just murdered 200,000 people and you're going to lecture me on the morality of drinking and driving?"

"I don't want you to crash the plane before we get to Chicago. You should stay sober."

"Yeah, that would be great. I'd like to have a full cognizance while I'm helping you to kill every man, woman, and child in the greater Chicago area. Good thinking Momin."

He uncapped the bottle and took another drink just to make him mad. He offered the bottle to him, but Momin spit on it.

"Way to go, Slick!"

Spunky wiped it off and placed the bottle between his legs for easy access. The gun was pointed right at him.

"What altitude are we at?"

Spunky didn't answer. He just pointed at the altimeter and then tapped it with his finger for emphasis. Momin nodded.

"Stay above 2000 feet or the bomb will detonate."

"What in tarnation are you talking about?"

Momin smiled his cocky grin.

"I set the bomb to detonate at 2,000 feet. This plane will never land. It will be incinerated before the pieces reach the ground."

Spunky looked at him and shook his head from side to side.

"Now why did you go and do that for, huh? You've taken away my last shred of hope!"

Momin nodded.

"That's right. You don't need hope. Besides, an air blast at 2,000 feet will kill more people than if we simply crash into a building."

Spunky swallowed the lump in his throat. He had underestimated this guy. He thought hard now. He was a chess player. He needed a plan. What were his options, his assets, his liabilities? Then he spoke out loud, hoping that someone would be listening.

"The country is on red alert. There might be air cover flying over Chicago right now. We'll be high enough so that O'Hare will pick us up on radar."

Momin shook his head in disagreement.

"It doesn't matter. They'll question you, but by time they figure out something is wrong, it will be too late for them to stop us. The plan is perfect."

Spunky took the bottle from between his legs, uncapped it and took a swallow.

"Let me drink about this a minute."

He began to sing again, and Momin cringed in his seat.

"And I'm proud to be an American, where at least I know I'm free."

Chapter 50

Lance smiled as he heard Spunky singing the final note over the speaker. The four of them now sat huddled around the plane in Spunky's pole barn, listening intently to everything that was being said in the high-jacked plane.

"Does anyone know how to work this radio?"

Lance nodded.

"I think I can manage it. I've flown with Spunky quite a bit. We just have to switch to the emergency frequency, and that will put you in touch with the FAA. Eventually, I would think they could patch you through to the FBI."

Hank stayed in the background with Josh, just hovering, knowing that he wasn't much help at the moment. He wanted to go home to Angela and the kids, but he had already called them and they were fine. Besides, here he had a ringside seat to history as it was unfolding, and he couldn't tear himself away. It made him feel a bit like an ambulance chaser.

"Let me write down Spunky's frequency so we don't lose it. I want to be able to get to him and listen in on how he's doing."

Richard nodded.

"Good idea."

Then he looked around the room and smiled weakly.

"Thanks guys. I really appreciate everything you've done so far. Maybe we can still pull this off."

Josh smiled as best he could and nodded his head before speaking.

"I wish there was more we could do. I'm going to move to the back of the pole barn and pray for a while. That's probably the best use of my time right now."

Josh turned and walked back towards the far corner, and Hank followed him.

"I may as well pray with you, Josh. These two can talk to the U.S. Government, and you and I can go over their heads."

They moved off, and Lance kept fiddling with the dials and buttons on the radio. It was old, but it was sturdy and powerful. Finally, he handed the microphone to Richard.

"Try it now. I'm not sure who this is, but Spunky had the channel preset, so it must be somebody important."

Richard moved the microphone up to his mouth, took a deep breath, and began to speak.

"This is an emergency! Can anyone hear me."

There was silence. Outside, the snow and wind picked up intensity.

"Hello! This is an emergency! Can anyone hear me! I need to get in touch with the FBI as soon as possible. This is a national emergency!"

After a few seconds of silence and static, an official sounding voice came over the speaker.

"This is air traffic control at Traverse City International Airport. Please identify yourself."

A small chorus of cheers went up from the pole barn. Hank and Josh went back to praying even harder than before.

"My name is Richard Resnik, I'm a Special Agent with the Federal Bureau of Investigation, and I need you to patch me through to FBI Headquarters in Quantico, Virginia."

There was silence for several seconds, then the speaker came to life again.

"Stand by Mr. Resnik. I'm going to put you in touch with my supervisor."

Richard and Lance breathed a sigh of relief. They had cleared the first hurdle.

§ § §

"You son of a pig! Stop singing!"

Then Momin started swearing first in Bengali, then Arabic, then back to English again.

"Hey! Lighten up Momin. If I'm going to die today, then I'm going to die with a smile on my face and a song on my heart."

Momin cringed. He wanted so much to kill this man, but he had to wait until they were close enough to Chicago when his services were no longer needed. Spunky took a sip of whiskey.

"Well fine then. I'll stop singing, but only if you tell me a story."

The hatred and rage in Momin's eyes was more than apparent to Spunky, but he no longer cared. He was going to die anyways, so he might as well torture his killer as long as he could.

"I will not tell you a story! You are a pig and a son of a pig! You are a decadent swine and a pagan unbeliever! And you must die in blood and fire!"

Spunky laughed out loud, and then he shook his head in a half-drunken rebuke.

"Oh just calm down now buddy. Answer me this. Why are you so preoccupied with pigs all the time?"

Momin clenched his teeth. The plane hit some turbulence, and he bounced up and down in his seat.

"I am a Moslem, you fool! I am not allowed to eat or even touch a pig. They are unclean to me!"

Spunky thought about that a moment.

"Do you mean to tell me that you've never eaten so much as one little piece of hickory smoked bacon? I don't believe it."

Momin groaned and looked away for a moment. When he responded there was newfound anger in his voice.

"I have never even touched a pig. It is blasphemous to even think of it. If you weren't so ignorant, you would know such things."

"Well, I'm not ignorant. I went to Sunday School when I was little. I know all the stories about Jesus and all his disciples. I'm a very religious man. In fact, I do a lot of things very religiously."

Shaking his head in disgust, Momin spit on the floor.

"Just shut up and tell me where we are. How close are we to Chicago?"

Spunky laughed again.

"I thought I was ignorant? What are you asking me for? I'm just an ignorant pagan. You're so smart and enlightened, why don't you tell me where we are?"

Momin raised the pistol a little higher and spoke in a menacing tone.

"Where are we? Now!"

Spunky stopped laughing and his voice took on a serious tone.

"You won't kill me. At least not until we get to Chicago. Then my life's not worth a plugged nickel."

Momin smiled with satisfaction. He liked this man almost as much as he hated him.

"You are right. I will not kill you . . . yet."

He lowered the pistol until it was pointing at Spunky's right leg.

"Death can come quick, or it can come slow. The choice is yours, Mr. Spunky."

Momin cocked back the hammer of the revolver, and the sweat started to bead up on Spunky's forehead. Reluctantly, he gave in.

"We're due west of Grand Rapids, off the coast of Lake Michigan."

"What is our altitude?"

"Four thousand feet."

"Our speed?"

"One hundred fifty knots."

"Our heading?"

"Almost due south."

Momin smiled and eased the pistol hammer slowly back into place.

"Much better. Let's just see how quick and uneventful we can make the remainder of this flight. No more singing. Understood?"

Spunky ground his teeth together and nodded up and down. As a chess player, he found Momin more than a worthy opponent. But . . . just perhaps . . . he could still pull this one off. He would feel better knowing that someone back at the pole barn was picking up his transmissions.

§ § §

"Yes, sir. That's correct sir. I will sir."

The long-distance telephone service had come back up several minutes ago, and Richard nodded up and down into the telephone as if the Director of the FBI could really hear him.

"I'll wait for the helicopter sir, then I'll see to it immediately."

He nodded his head one more time and then slowly hung up the phone. He turned around towards Lance.

"There's still hope Lance."

Lance nodded his head.

"I understand. Hope for Chicago, but not for Spunky?"

Richard looked down at the floor, then back up again. His voice was nervous and unsure of itself.

"I'm sorry, Lance. I know you two are friends. I wish there was a different way."

Lance looked around Spunky's living room. He had been here many times before. He let out a big sigh, and then turned and started to walk out. As an afterthought, he hesitated and turned back around when he spoke.

"How much time does he have?"

Richard walked up and put his arm on his left shoulder.

"They're scrambling the fighters now. They'll move in from the east out of Detroit and try to cut them off before they get south of Kalamazoo. If they miss them, there are planes coming over from Madison that will intercept them over Lake Michigan, just north of the border. But we'd just as soon they didn't get that close to the city with that bomb."

Lance nodded and his shoulders sagged heavily. They both walked out of the house and back out to the pole barn where Josh and Hank were listening again to the radio transmission.

Spunky was running out of time.

§ § §

Spunky guessed they were about 60 miles north of Chicago by now, and he felt his life slowly coming to an end, ebbing away like a weak tide. Momin hadn't spoken in several minutes. He was just sitting over there, staring at him, glaring hatefully, not saying a word.

The sky had been overcast all the way, but suddenly, Spunky's plane broke through the clouds and into bright sunlight. Spunky saw the fighter jets above him almost immediately, and guessed them to be F-16s. He had suspected this, in fact, had hoped for it, and he knew that as soon as they identified him, he would be shot down.

"So what now, Momin. We're about 60 miles out. Any last prayers?"

Spunky watched as a peaceful look came over Momin's face. This chess game was a stalemate. They were both going to die, both would lose, and neither would win. Spunky hated a stalemate.

"I only pray at certain times of the day. Next time I pray, I'll be in paradise."

Spunky nodded.

"I suppose that's true. I won't be that lucky. My wife is in heaven, but God wouldn't let me near that place with a ten-foot pole. But that's okay. I deserve hell. I can't argue that."

Momin looked surprised.

"Well, it's not too late for you to convert to Islam? Perhaps Allah would have mercy on you if you were to pledge allegiance to him and voluntarily fly into Chicago with your whole heart committed to jihad."

Spunky thought he saw a momentary spark of humanity flicker in Momin's eyes, but it quickly went away when Spunky responded.

"I'd sooner roast in hell than submit to you and your maniacal god!"

Spunky lifted his voice and began to sing once more. Momin's eyes turned to flame, threatening to consume the entire cockpit of the small plane.

"Oh say can you see, by the dawn's early light. What so proudly we hailed, at the twilight's last gleaming. . . . "

Momin brought the gun up and yelled as loud as he could.

"Shut up! Stop singing or I'll shoot!"

Spunky winked at him and sang even louder.

"Whose broad stripes and bright stars, through the perilous fight, ..."

A shot rang out and Spunky leaned hard over the yoke, sending the plane into a steep dive. Momin was thrown upward into the ceiling, cutting himself on the back of the head. He recovered and then leaned over to push Spunky's body off the yoke. As he did, Spunky reached out and grabbed the pistol in Momin's hand.

As the plane continued to dive, the two of them struggled for control of the gun. Wrapped in a deadly embrace, the pistol fired again, and both men grew suddenly still.

Chapter 51

Lance, Josh, Richard, and Hank all huddled closely around the radio speaker. Hank flinched when he heard the gunshot, then, nothing but silence. A few seconds later, they heard heavy breathing, a groan and a soft thud.

Then a new voice broke the silence.

"Cessna N2363, southbound at 5,000 feet. You are instructed to turn to a heading of 090 and land at Holland airfield for national security reasons."

Silence.

"I say again, Cessna N2363, southbound at 5,000 feet. You are instructed to turn to a heading of 090 and land at Holland airfield for national security reasons!"

Lance wrapped his arms around his torso and began to rock impatiently.

"Come on Spunky! Say something!"

Then the Flight Leader spoke to the other three planes in his command.

"His dive is leveled off at 3,000 feet. Demon Three stay in cover, two, go combat trail. I'm going to set up for the shot."

"Roger that Demon One."

Two of the F-16 Falcons broke formation and came in from behind and slightly below the little plane.

"Give them one more chance to comply, then we have to shoot them down. Word is if we let anything get through, we'll be ringing the old man's door bell by sundown. This must be important."

The lead fighter closed the distance.

"All weapons armed up. Stand by for the shot."

There was a moment of silence, then one last plea.

"Cessna N2363. This is your last chance. Comply immediately or be shot down."

A deafening silence emanated from the tiny plane. The four men stood around the radio, Hank shifted nervously from one foot to the other, while Lance let his head drop down onto his chest. The fighter pilot spoke one last time; it was almost over.

"Here goes."

Demon One's finger stood poised over the firing button, but something was holding him back. He knew his orders, and he had never questioned or disobeyed an order in his 14 years in the service. But this was a civilian plane, and something . . . something felt different. He looked on his right wing and his mouth dropped open.

"Demon Two, take a look at my right wing. See anything?"

The response was almost immediate.

"Negative."

Demon One shook his head and looked over at the wing again, but the image of the man in the wheelchair was gone. Perhaps he had been flying too many hours these past months since nine-eleven. He put his finger back on the button. And then he heard a voice, small at first, and then a little louder.

"Demon Two, please tell me that you hear that. I'm starting to think I'm going crazy!"

"I hear it sir. It sounds like Lee Greenwood, but it can't be."

Spunky's voice was soft but growing louder by the moment.

"And I'm proud to be an American, 'cuz at least I know I'm free." He paused to take a breath, the bullet hole in his lung made it difficult to sing.

"But I won't forget the men who died and gave that right to me. So I proudly stand up! Oh man that hurts like the dickens!"

"Demon One, that doesn't sound like a terrorist."

Back at the pole barn, the four men cheered and danced.

"Cessna N2363 – who are you?"

There was a moment's pause.

"Well, sir, I'm an American redneck patriot, just trying to serve my country as best I can."

Spunky began to wheeze and placed his hand over his chest.

"Okay American Redneck. What is your situation?"

"Do ya want the good news first, or the bad news?"

The Flight Leader responded.

"We could use some good news today. My commanding General and the President of the United States are both standing by."

There was silence, then a gentle wheeze as Spunky built up strength to speak.

"Tell the President . . . Checkmate!"

"Excuse me?"

"Tell Mr. President . . . Momin is dead. I have a dead body and a nuclear bomb in my cockpit."

"That's the good news? How could it get worse, American Redneck?"

Spunky's voice wavered as his strength ebbed and flowed.

"Well, the bomb is preset to go off at 2,000 feet above sea level. If I try to land . . . ." Spunky's strength failed him.

When Spunky looked out of the cockpit again, he saw one F-16 off his Left wing, and another off his right.

"American Redneck, I'm off your left wing. Can you see me?"

“Roger that. I see ya.”

“What’s your real name Redneck?”

“My friends call me Spunky.”

“Okay Spunky. It’s a pleasure to serve with you. My name is Don, but you can call me Yooper. Roger the dead terrorist in the passenger seat. You sound hurt. Can you still fly?”

Spunky looked off his left wing and nodded his head.

“I thought I recognized that accent. You from da U.P eh?”

“Roger that, Spunky. You know where Iron Mountain is?”

Spunky wheezed again and gasped for air.

“Listen, I got a bullet in one lung, but I think I can fly long enough to turn this thing around and fly it up north where no one will get hurt when this thing goes off.”

The Major hesitated and thought for a moment.

“Spunky. Did you say 2,000 feet above sea level?”

“Roger that, Yooper, 2000 feet and we’re having barbecued redneck for dinner tonight.”

Spunky waited for a reply.

“You still there, Yooper?”

“Affirmative, Spunky. I’m still here, but not for long. You’re going way too slow for me. If I maintain this speed, I’ll stall out for sure. I’m calling some friends in the Battle Creek Air National Guard. We’ll get you the right tool for the job.”

Spunky rested his head on his chest. He looked over at Momin’s dead body and couldn’t help but wonder if he was enjoying hell. The yooper’s voice came back on.

“Don’t send the barbecue invitations yet. I have an idea.”

“I’m all ears, Don.”

“Now here’s what I want you to do, Spunky. Trim your airspeed back as much as you can, then turn around and set a course for heading . . . .”

Chapter 52

The four men had stopped dancing and were now standing again as close to the speaker as they could get.

"What did he say? I couldn't hear that!"

"Quiet down, Lance. I'm trying to hear!"

The static got louder, and the voices faded away.

"Damn! What's wrong with that thing?"

Hank looked over at Pastor Josh McCullen and frowned.

"Pastor. Did you just swear?"

He looked down sheepishly.

"Oh, sorry. I'm not perfect, just forgiven. Did you hear what he said?"

Richard started for the pole barn door, and Lance followed him.

"You guys stay here and listen to the radio. I'll go back in and call Quantico and see what I can learn."

Lance and Richard opened the door and the snow and wind gusted in and then was blotted out again.

Josh and Hank looked down at the radio, listening to the silence of the snowy static.

"We'd better pray some more, Josh. Over there in the corner again I guess."

Josh nodded his head and walked over beside a greasy, old 55-gallon drum, covered with a combination of flaking blue paint and rust. Josh and Hank knelt down on the oil-covered, cement floor. Josh spoke first.

"Dear God, we acknowledge you as our Lord, as our master, and as our king. Please God. Please be with Spunky. Bring him home."

And Hank said softly. "Amen."

§ § §

It hurt to breathe, so Spunky took only shallow breaths, being careful to exhale and inhale very slowly. The F-16 fighters had left and had been replaced with an A-10 Warthog which was bigger, and much slower. It sat off Spunky's left wing tip, watching over him like the noisiest angel on earth.

"Mo, I'm about out of gas, so you better bug on out of here before I start losing altitude. I don't want to take you with me."

From off the little Cessna's left wing, the A-10 pilot smiled.

"Not a chance Redneck. I signed on for the duration. And if you do this right, I'll be able to go home next week to my wife and three kids. You married, Spunky?"

There was a long silence.

"You okay over there Redneck?"

Finally, Spunky's voice came back.

"Yeah, I'm okay. Got no wife and kids though. It's been a long time now. Nothing sad about it. Nothing to talk about."

The A-10 pilot nodded to himself. He sensed a longer story was more true, but out of respect, he wouldn't pry. There were a lot of people monitoring their conversation, and it was being recorded.

"Well, that's okay. You still have that to look forward to then. The important thing to remember here is that there's no pressure. If you blow up, then I blow up. And then my wife and kids will be without a husband and a father."

Spunky wanted to laugh, but he didn't have the strength.

"What's that you're drinking over there, Spunky?"

Spunky lowered the glass bottle back down before speaking.

"Fruit juice – very old and very tasty fruit juice."

The Major hesitated before speaking.

"Is that a good idea Spunky. You're about to make a crash landing on top of a mountain. If you survive, the FAA could revoke your pilot's license."

Spunky laughed spontaneously and it sent him into a coughing fit. When he recovered, he answered the question.

"That's funny, Mo. They don't give pilot's licenses to alcoholics."

The other pilot raised his eyebrows and smiled.

"Well, Spunky, just between you and me and everybody else who's listening, you got my vote for flyer of the year award. You're one ace of a pilot in my book."

There was no response.

"Okay Spunky, we're coming up on that plateau now, and you'll probably only get one shot at this, so stay alert. I'll stay right off your wing. Rescue helicopters are standing by, so as soon as you land, they'll be down to help you to a hospital. Have you ever been in an emergency landing before, Spunky?"

"Every day of my life, Mo. Every cotton-pickin' day!"

For the first time, the A-10 pilot laughed out loud.

"Okay Spunky, you got the ball. You have a 10-knot SW wind, gusting to 15 knots. Get as slow as you can and flare the nose before you hit. There should be at least 6 feet of snow on that plateau, so get ready to stop pretty fast. I'm going to back off now, but I'll be close by in case you need me."

Spunky glanced over and watched as Mo threw him a snappy, military salute. Spunky raised his glass bottle and finished the contents.

"One more thing, Spunky. Make sure that suitcase bomb is off the floor and secured to the seat. Keep it secure and up as high as you can inside the plane. We're going to need all the altitude we can get on this one."

Spunky paused a moment before preparing to enter his glide path.

"So exactly how high is this mountain, Mo? You never told me."

The Major paused a moment.

"We don't know for sure exactly, Spunky, but I won't lie to you. It's somewhere close to 2,000 feet. If it's less than that, we'll all find out in a few minutes."

Spunky glanced over at Momin's body, disappointed that he wasn't alive to die again in the crash. Then he clutched the yoke with both hands and gently eased it forward. As the plane slowly lost altitude, he gave his instrument panel one last look. Altitude, 2200 feet, fuel, sucking up fumes, wind speed, he eased back on the throttle just as the engine coughed and died out.

His plane went down into a shallow, steady, glide. He'd been right all along. This was a lousy day to quit drinking.

"Hold it steady, Spunky. You're too steep!"

The plane crashed into the snow, it's nose dug in, flipping it end over end, then it came to a rest. Spunky's forehead hit something hard, and everything went black.

The altimeter read 2,000 feet exactly . . . with 6 feet of snow beneath him.

Chapter 53

Angela had never been this far south before, indeed, she'd never had a reason to go here. It was ungodly hot, and she took out her handkerchief and wiped her brow. Hank and the kids were beside her, waiting in the reception line at the President's ranch in Crawford, Texas. She'd met Senators and the Mayor of New York once on business, but never before had she seen anything like this.

"See those guys with the ear plugs? Those are secret agents who watch the President to make sure he doesn't do anything wrong."

Micah nodded his head in awe.

"What do they do if he makes a mistake?"

Phillip shrugged his shoulders.

"I think they shoot him in the foot or something just to teach him a lesson. I think it's against the law to kill him straight out."

The secret serviceman looked down at the two little boys and tried not to smile. It was a great effort on his part.

The President moved closer, dressed in blue jeans and flannel, shaking hands and smiling as he went. Angela reached over and squeezed Hank's hand firmly. He was talking to Lance Stuart now.

"A Pulitzer prize winner eh? I apologize, Lance, but I haven't had time to read your new book yet. But I want to thank you for your service to our country."

Lance nodded and squeezed the President's hand appropriately. He had met presidents before, but never at a backyard barbecue. He looked around him, saw all the faces from Freidham Ridge and thought it only proper and fitting that they were grilling steak.

"That's okay Mr. President. The pleasure is all mine."

"Well, Lance, you just remember to send me a copy of your next book, because this is one story that I intend to read."

Lance nodded and the President moved to Josh and his wife.

"And you must be Pastor McCullen and his wife, Louise."

Louise gushed and her face turned red with excitement. Josh simply stared in amazement. He looked so much taller on TV.

"Thank you for your service, not only to our country, but also to the kingdom of God. We appreciate your sacrifice. Both of you."

Josh shook his hand, but was too nervous to say anything more than, "Thank you Mr. President."

The President slid on down the line as if he'd been doing it his whole life.

"And you're the two newlyweds, Hank and Angela Simmons?"

Angela held out her hand and the President grasped it firmly and appreciatively. She was speechless as well.

"Thanks for inviting us Mr. President. We're glad to be here."

The President's blue eyes looked at Hank squarely as he spoke.

"The pleasure is mine, Mr. Simmons."

Then he laughed out loud.

"And you can quote me on that, Hank."

Suddenly, 6-year old Susan stepped forward and thrust out her right hand. The President looked down and smiled from ear to ear.

"Well who do we have here?"

He reached down and picked her up and held her in the crook of his right arm.

"My name is Susan Simmons. My phone number is 459-9860, and I live at 320 Sycamore Street in Freidham Ridge. That's in Michigan. It's a whole nuther country."

The President laughed out loud and Susan bounced up and down in his arms until he stopped.

"Well, I bet it is! Now Susan I live at 1600 Pennsylvania Ave in Washington DC, at least for now, and I can tell you for sure, that sometimes it feels like a whole nuther country as well, especially during election year. Why I can't wait to get back home full time to Crawford. It was a pleasure meeting you Susan."

He set her back down and reached out to shake Phillip's hand. Phillip reached over as manly as he could and squeezed the President's hand.

"Wow! That's quite a grip you got there son. You must milk cows every morning with a grip like that!"

Phillip shook his head.

"Nope, I just watch cartoons."

The President laughed and moved on down. He reached his hand out to Micah, who grabbed on to it defiantly.

"We're not avorced anymore. We got us a brand new Mom!"

The President shook Micah's hand and smiled.

"Yes, that's what I heard. Congratulations. But you make sure you do what she tells you to now. Okay?"

Micah nodded, and the President reached over and reached his hand out to Cathy, who was standing behind Angela, grasping her left leg firmly with both hands and trying to hide.

"What's the matter, sweetheart, all this commotion scare you?"

Cathy nodded her head, but stayed behind her mother. The President smiled softly and winked at her before moving on down the line.

He stopped when he came to the last guest, and Hank could see that tears were welling up in the President's eyes. The man reached out his hand, but the President moved around it and hugged Spunky as best he could, being careful not to hurt the bullet wound still healing in his chest.

"Thank you, Mr. President."

The President smiled broadly and took a small step back. He nodded his head in approval.

"No, Spunky, it is I who should thank you. You succeeded where I failed. As President, I'm responsible for keeping America safe, and I let one get through. I want to thank you from the bottom of my heart. All of America is indebted to you, and I have a special gift that I think you'll like."

One of his aids stepped forward and handed the President a piece of parchment and a pair of shiny, gold wings.

"On behalf of the Federal Aviation Administration, I would like to present this pilot's license to you. It's good for 5 years, or, until you take a drink, whichever comes first."

The President laughed again and Spunky followed suit.

"Hey listen Spunky, all joking aside, if there's ever anything I can do for you, just call one of my aids, and I'll do whatever I can to help you out."

Spunky nodded and held still while the President pinned on his new wings. Finally, he spoke.

"Mr. President?"

The President held up his hand and everyone around him grew silent.

"Yes, Spunky."

"There is one thing I would like that I think you could arrange."

Spunky leaned forward and whispered in the President's ear. The President immediately began laughing and called over to one of his aids.

"Frank, get hold of the Chairman of the Joint Chiefs and have him call

Spunky here and give him whatever he wants. It's my treat."

The President shook Spunky's hand one more time and then stepped back up onto a stage where a band was waiting to play.

"Now everybody gather on around here and listen up a minute. I want everyone to hear this."

Everyone, about 50 people in all, gathered around the stage, everyone except the Secret Service who were watching with deferential paranoia, every move that was made.

"Listen folks, I didn't prepare a speech, because I just wanted this to be a fun time, free of politics and stress and everything else that's been going on lately. So, suffice it to say, that I love you all, in my own special way, and I thank all of you for the sacrifice, the commitment, and the blood and toil you've exhibited on behalf of your country. You honor us and do us proud."

Applause broke out, but the President waved it off with both hands.

"Go ahead and have a good time. There's steaks on the grill, ice-cold lemonade and tea, potato salad, you name it we got it. All courtesy of the United States of America. Eat all you want 'cuz you paid for it with your taxes."

He stepped down off the stage.

"Now if you'll excuse me, I have to run up and get the first lady and bring her on down here to meet everyone. And while I'm gone, we flew in a special treat for Spunky. Ladies and gentleman, I'm honored to introduce, Mr. Lee Greenwood! He's going to sing for y'all."

Immediately, the band queued up the introduction and Lee Greenwood took the stage. The crowd clapped and began to hoot and holler. But when he took the microphone and began to sing, a gentle hush went over the crowd as if he were singing a sacred hymn.

"If tomorrow all the things were gone, I'd worked for all my life, and I had to start again, with just my children and my wife. I'd thank my lucky stars to be living here today, cuz the flag still stands for freedom, and you can't take that away."

He sang with great reverence, and every man, woman and child listened in silence and awe, but when it was time for the chorus, the whole crowd joined in and sang at the top of their voices.

"And I'm proud to be an American, where at least I know I'm free. And I won't forget the men who died, and gave that right to me. So I proudly stand up . . . next to you and defend her still today. Cuz there ain't no doubt I love this land. God bless the USA!"

Tears welled up in Angela's eyes. She looked over and watched Hank as he sang, then down at the two small children grasping her legs firmly. Something caught her eye, and she looked off to her left and a little behind the crowd.

She squinted her eyes to adjust to the brightness of the Texas sun. She couldn't be sure, but she thought she saw an old man seated in a wheelchair. His bright, blue eyes seemed much too young for their sockets and the wrinkled, dry skin surrounding them. They were smiling, softly smiling, compassionately and intelligently smiling.

His attendant who was standing beside him, was unusually tall, and wore a white, linen suit. He had a shining radiance about him that seemed out of place. But no one else seemed to notice. They just kept on singing. Angela smiled and sang as well.

Finally, she understood. Fatherhood. God really did bless the U.S.A.

Epilogue

The fighter jet stood poised on the runway, with every circuit, electron and molecule, charged and ready to launch itself out with a great and mighty thrust.

Spunky was in the back seat and Major Don Nesbitt was in the front.

"Okay Spunky, go ahead and call the tower for final clearance."

Spunky smiled from ear to ear. He had never flown a jet before. A crowd of officers and enlisted men had gathered off the runway to watch Spunky, the man who had saved Chicago. Some waved and others saluted.

"Tower, this is American Redneck. You got yer ears on? Come on back now."

Major Nesbitt laughed quietly in the front seat.

"American Redneck, this is tower. You are cleared for takeoff."

Major Nesbitt taxied the F-16 trainer to the runway, and lined up on the center line. He gave it full afterburner, and Spunky was pressed hard back into his seat, adrenaline coursing through his veins during the acceleration. In a matter of seconds, they were off the ground and rapidly gaining altitude.

Spunky looked down, and knew that his crop duster would never thrill him the way it used to. He'd have to buy a jet.

"Ya know what Don?"

"What's that Spunky?"

Spunky looked down at the rapidly shrinking houses and highways below.

"I think that today . . . is a very good day to quit drinking."

The Major smiled and began a very steep climb, moving up and up and up. Finally, they leveled off.

"Okay Spunk, you ready to fly this bird?"

Spunky smiled.

"You got it Major. Let's see how fast this baby can go!"

Skip Coryell now lives with his wife and children in Michigan. He works full time as a professional writer,. He is an avid hunter and sportsman who loves the outdoors. Skip is also a Marine Corps veteran, a graduate of Cornerstone University, and the Chief Pistol Instructor for Ted Nugent United Sportsmen of Michigan. Skip is the former Michigan State Director for Ted Nugent's organization. He has also served on the Board of Directors for Michigan Sportsmen against Hunger as well as Iowa Carry Inc. He is a Certified NRA Pistol Instructor and Range Safety Officer, teaching the Personal Protection in the Home Course for those wishing to obtain their Concealed Pistol Permits (www.mwtac.com). He also teaches Advanced Concealed Carry Classes for the more seasoned shooter. Skip is the President of White Feather Press and the co-owner of Midwest Tactical Training.

For more details on Skip Coryell, or to contact him personally, go to his website at www.skipcoryell.com
(email: skip@whitefeatherpress.com).

Acknowledgments and Thanks

I wish to thank the following people for their support and devotion to this novel. Their technical expertise ensured authenticity and greatly improved this novel.

- Lt. Colonel David Morris – Battle Creek Air National Guard
- Alan Sheets – Nuclear Survivability Engineer
- Phil Walsh – Islamic Cultural Consultant
- Dr. Hadley Kigar and Carol Sheets – Literary Consultants
- Sara Coryell – My wife and my best friend.

Dedication

This work is dedicated to all parents who love and protect their children, and, most of all, to God, our heavenly father, the creator of all, who loves us, nurtures us, and sent his son to die for us, so that we might live.

Special appreciation goes out to all the military mothers and fathers serving in harm's way in the war on terror, and, to those family members keeping the home fires burning.

Heartfelt prayers go out to all children with a parent who is fighting to protect our great country.

To you, we cry out with joy, "Abba – Father!"

You will see them again. God bless you.

Other Books by Skip Coryell

Bond of Unseen Blood
Church and State
Blood in the Streets
Laughter and Tears
RKBA: Defending the Right to Keep and Bear Arms
Stalking Natalie

Available anywhere books are sold.

Signed copies are available only at
www.skipcoryell.com

www.ingramcontent.com/pod-product-compliance
Lightning Source LLC
LaVergne TN
LVHW091021080826
845145LV00002B/317

* 9 7 8 0 9 7 6 6 0 8 3 2 5 *